SELLING
NOSTALGIA

A NEUROTIC NOVEL

MATHEW
KLICKSTEIN

PERMUTED
PRESS

A PERMUTED PRESS BOOK
ISBN: 978-1-68261-869-1
ISBN (eBook): 978-1-68261-870-7

Selling Nostalgia:
A Neurotic Novel
© 2019 by Mathew Klickstein

Cover art by Cody Corcoran

PERMUTED
PRESS

Permuted Press, LLC
New York • Nashville
permutedpress.com

Published in the United States of America

for
Gnossos Pappadopoulis
Nathan Zuckerman
Riggan Thomson
BoJack Horseman

"When you're young you think the world of adult services is reliable, proficient, and cost-effective. Then you grow up to a life of fatboys and four-eyes, bullies and bookworms, fudgers and smudgers."

—*Martin Amis,* Money

"Idol worship is no more. There are no longer any gods and goddesses on the screen; just human beings of varying degrees of interest."

—Photoplay Magazine, *November 1928*

"No one's life is a sitcom."

—*Brandon Tartikoff,* The Last Great Ride

"Beware of the corporate invasion of private memory."

—*Douglas Coupland,* Microserfs

CHAPTER 1

"So, do you know who Gil Gladly is?" asked Milton Siegel, not expecting much of an answer.

He didn't receive one.

The attractive young black chick mixing and serving drinks on the other side of the airport lounge bar had her back turned. She reached beyond her lavender-tipped fingernails up toward a bottle of crystal clear vodka above her head. Her matching lavender braids cascaded down her back.

It wasn't that she was ignoring his question, Milt reasoned. She'd probably not heard him, lost in her own world of business, the way he had been these past few weeks getting prepared for the month ahead.

Jesus, he thought. *The past few weeks? The past few months. Two* years, *maybe!*

He thought of all the work he'd put into this fucking thing.

Milt had earlier exchanged some polite chit-chat with the bartender. She had smiled with her thin, fire-engine red lipstick-ed lips and her wide hazel eyes behind her matching red large-rimmed glasses. Along with her thin black tie, pinstriped white button-up shirt, and tight black apron hugging her svelte midsection, she could almost pass for an NYC hipster intellectual moonlighting in the service industry.

Although she wasn't exactly his typical flavor, Milt had found himself flirting immediately after she'd asked him, "What are we thinking about the menu?"

"The paper's a little thin," Milt had said, folding up the corner slightly.

She smiled with a subtle snort.

"No," she said, subtly eyeing three other customers who were sitting down at the end of the bar. "You want anything?"

"Wild Turkey if you have it," Milt said. "Maker's, if not." Too many places these days rarely had Turkey anymore, but they always had Maker's Mark for some reason Milt couldn't figure out.

"Single or a double?"

"You know what? I...better have a double," Milt said. "Just in case."

"Just in case," she repeated dutifully, with the upward lift of the right side of her mouth, which made for a magnificent smirk. The bartender turned to grab Milt's second choice from the gleaming bottles of spirits that lined the wall behind her.

Further conversation had followed between the two, as had a few more double Maker's on the rocks.

All the while, Milt sat on his bar stool turning his head toward the smudged and dusty floor-to-ceiling windows to his right, through which planes landed and took off from an elaborate network of runways, where terminal tubes stretched out in all directions, and where neon orange-vested laborers could be seen driving carts and hauling luggage in the mid-morning white light of heaven.

The bartender had inevitably asked what Milt did for a living.

As usual, he had—more than three doubles in by now—spurted out something protectively vague along the lines of, "Whatever pays the bills."

I'm a writer and a filmmaker, Milt always felt meant one of two equally pathetic possibilities. One: Having the audacity to directly state such a thing translated to, *I work at a coffee shop.* A teacher, maybe. Perhaps living at home with his parents. He certainly was not a *professional* writer and/or filmmaker.

Two (worse): If you were—like Milt, for good or ill—an *actual* writer and sometimes filmmaker, someone who made his or her living as a writer, someone the IRS considered a writer, then what came next was the awkward Q&A period. You had to tell the person what you'd written, what outlet you'd written for, what TV show or movie you'd worked on.

Which meant now it sounded as though you were bragging, you arrogant prick. Yeah, you don't work in retail or live at your mom's well into your thirties, but you are a douchebag.

To make matters still worse, Milt was not flying off to LA for a writing project. He was going there to premiere his latest documentary as the first part of a preview tour around the country.

He did have one trick up his sleeve. A way to state what he did for the time being, where he was going, and what he was doing without coming off as too much of an aforementioned prick-douchebag.

Milt could talk about his documentary subject. He could ask the lovely bartender if she happened to know who Gil Gladly was, and from that he could build something more substantial.

Because on the flip-side of all of this silly paranoia and neuroticism born of his genetic Jewishness, what Milt was doing *was* pretty cool. He was going on a tour with a documentary about someone most people had heard of before.

Or a lot of people, at least.

Some people?

Not the bartender.

When Milt, wobbly and emboldened by his six or ten Maker's Marks, had again asked the bartender, "Hey, do you know who Gil Gladly is?" she finally came back down the bar toward him and from the other side of the slate-gray Formica bar asked, "Sorry, who?"

"Gil Gladly. Did you ever watch *KidTalk* when you were growing up?"

"No, sorry." She spun around, her lavender braids whipping from left to right across her small shoulders, and plucked a generic looking bottle of gin from the sparkly mother lode wall.

Turning back to him, she inquired, as she mixed whatever cocktail had been ordered, "Was it on Disney Channel or Nickelodeon?"

"Neither. Balloon," Milt said. "*KidTalk* was pretty much the show that made that whole channel happen back in the late eighties. Gil Gladly was the host for like ten years. He's done a few other things since then, but mostly behind the cameras. He produces and consults a lot."

"Oh, cool," she said, loudly shaking an urn-shaped tin, inside of which were ostensibly the fixings for a martini. "I don't really watch TV. Mostly just look at stuff on YouTube. Sometimes Netflix, I guess. It's kind of dumb, but on weekends or when I get home from work at night, I love sitting on the couch and vegging out on my laptop. Sometimes I can just play on my phone for hours. I know it's stupid, but it's a way for me to relax."

Maybe her parents couldn't afford Balloon when she was younger. Perhaps that was why she never saw *KidTalk*. But more likely—yes, this had to be it—she was too young to have ever had the chance.

Christ, age forty for him was getting closer all the time. Two of the last girls he had fucked before he met Laney had only been three or four when Kurt Cobain killed himself. *That* had been weird to realize.

"*KidTalk* was basically an eighties version of Art Linkletter's *Kids Say the Darndest Things*," Milt continued, not bothering to acknowledge the inanity of his trying to get a millennial to understand the format of an old show she'd never heard of before by referencing an even older show she *definitely* never heard of before.

"Huh," the bartender said. "I thought Bill Cosby did that show."

"Well, yeah," Milt said, looking down at his drink abashedly. "But these days we try to, um...keep the comparison between *Art Linkletter* and Gil Gladly. *You* know."

"Yeah, I remember Gil Gladly."

Milt turned his head to the bedraggled old guy who had apparently at some point sat a few stools down to Milt's right, blocking a bit of the hornet's nest of planes landing and taking off.

The bartender handed the fellow customer his martini. He nodded his white-haired head beneath his faded sunflower yellow trucker hat, sipped his drink, and pulled out a ten from his greasy denim shirt breast pocket, placing it on the Formica counter before setting his drink back down.

"Mmm, now that's something I don't normally do," he said without turning to Milt. "Normally I go for a Bud. But sometimes, brother, you need yourself a good, stiff gin martini. Know what I mean?"

The bartender forced her crooked smirk as though he had been talking to her. She slipped off to go help two middle-aged patrons now entering from the blurry crush of passengers clogging the corridor outside the lounge to Milt's left.

Milt turned slightly on his stool toward the man on his right and got a better look at how tan and leathery he was, how broken-down and wrinkled. Not so much chubby as stocky.

"You watched *KidTalk*?" Milt asked.

"Nah, but my kids used to watch Balloon all the time when they were younger. All grown up now. I remember that Gil Gladly fella was on the TV a bunch when the kids would get home from school. They musta been playing that shit ten hours a day. Seems to me that guy was *always* on."

"They had to repeat a lot of their shows, because back then Balloon didn't really have any money. It was early cable."

"Yeah, I know about that," the old man said, sipping his martini, a simple act which made him more and more of an incongruous image. His fingernails were outrageously caked with oil or god-knew-what, Milt noticed. "I used to read the *TV Guide* a lot back then. Good material for the john."

Milt attempted a grin, nodding laconically.

"I overheard you saying you're traveling with some movie about him? Talking about it to that pretty girl you've been hitting on?" the man continued.

As blitzed as he was, Milt was nevertheless relieved the bartender was on the other end of the bar and likely couldn't hear the conversation he'd unwittingly become part of. It was a sobering statement, though only for a moment. Then the booze went right back to pickling his brain, and Milt felt that familiar arctic crispness wash over him in a rush. He smiled beatifically and enjoyed being drunk.

"Yeah, well, you gotta use what you have," Milt said, raising his glass, filled mostly with melted ice, up to the man who was still not turning his way.

"Hey, that's him there, right?" the man said, pointing to the muted TV Milt hadn't been aware of until now. The screen was nestled into the rightmost side of the bejeweled wall of liquor bottles.

The man was right.

The bartender came back right on time, because there he was, Gil Gladly on whatever morning news show was playing soundlessly off the TV.

"Is that him?" the bartender asked, hearing that last part and becoming visibily interested in Gil Gladly on TV.

"Yeah, he's been doing a lot of press for our film tour," Milt said, trying to vaunt without being that arrogant douchebag.

"Jesus Christ," the man with the martini said. "How old is he now?"

"Sixty-five," Milt answered.

The old man took a sip of his drink, shaking his head. "Am I crazy or does he look like Danny Bonaduce? The *old* Danny Bonaduce. The way Danny Bonaduce looks *now*. They could be twins, with the reddish, graying thin hair, the bloodshot eyes, and the ginger skin. All bulky with those big ol' arms. Jesus, *just* like Danny Bonaduce."

"Who's Danny Bonaduce?" asked the bartender.

Milt and the old man answered at the same time, "*Partridge Family*."

They both looked at each other and smirked.

"You're into the old stuff, huh?" the man asked.

"Yeah," Milt said. "A lot of Nick-at-Nite when I was a kid. Read George Burns' autobiography when I was in sixth grade. I was probably the only thirteen-year-old boy in 1994 who had an autographed photo of Phyllis Diller on my wall."

The old man, Milt, and the bartender turned back to the TV to take in Gil yammering away on mute to the cabal of hosts in their sumptuous gray suits, silver ties, daisy-colored dresses....

"Huh," Milt said. "I never really noticed that before. But you're right. He *does* look like Danny Bonaduce. They both have that same gleam in their eyes too."

"That's *right!*" the old man said, snapping his fingers. "Two peas in a pod, my boy."

Noticing the man was now staring strangely at him, Milt asked, "What?"

"I was just realizing, *you* kind of look like someone too."

"Hopefully myself."

"No, no," the man said to Milt, waving over the bartender for another drink. "You look like...you know, that kid...from all those goofy movies...the Jewish guy. With the beard and glasses? The curly hair?"

"A Jewish comedian with curly hair and glasses? Could you be a *little* more specific?"

"The guy from that funny movie where he gets that angry uptight bitch pregnant. What's-his-name."

"Seth Rogen," said the bartender.

"Yes!" The man clapped. "You look like that Seth Rogen kid. Jewish kid. Very funny."

"He's definitely popular," Milt said, trying not to reveal his disdain for the comparison that had been made at least once a month since 2007.

"Hey, but you're doing pretty good there too, guy, huh?" the old man was quick to say. "Making your own movie about Gil Gladly. Not bad. Not bad."

"It *is* pretty cool," the bartender said, watching Gil on the TV screen. "And now you're traveling around with it?" She turned around to Milt and at long last appeared to actually give a shit.

"Yeah, you know, we're—"

"Hey, doesn't he have something weird going on there? He's got, like, a real bad stutter, right? In real life when he's not on the TV?" interrupted the old man, who suddenly dropped his martini on the floor, shattering the glass loudly. In the confusion, the man cartoonishly spilled off from his stool, toppling over onto the one next to him. "Aw, *fuck*, my elbow!"

Rushing around the countertop to the man, the bartender's braids trailed behind her, and Milt had a joyful opportunity to see how petite and beautiful she really was.

It was time for Milt to make his grand escape before he made any more of a fool of himself, like this guy who was now on the ground, clutching his elbow.

Milt's flight was about to board.

And yes, Gil Gladly did have a stutter in real life. When agitated.

CHAPTER 2

"**D**-d-d-did you s-s-s-s-see the interv-v-v-v-iew?" Gil Gladly's radio-friendly voice boomed from the other end of Milt's cell phone speaker pressed to his ear.

Milt, unsurprisingly tipsy, scrambled as best he could through the onslaught of what continued to be a blurring crowd of passengers pushing and shoving, careening off his right shoulder upon which one of his two beige backpack straps ran up and down.

"Ooof, sorry," Milt said to whomever it was who'd just bumped into him in the katzenjammer airport melee on his way to his terminal.

"*What the h-h-h-hell was th-th-th-that?*" Gil barked.

"Nothing, Gil," Milt said, straightening his shoulders in mid-rush toward Terminal 24.

Get it together, Milt.

Knowing it was a mere sitcom trope but giving it a try anyway, Milt shook his head vigorously in a feeble attempt at sobering himself up. It didn't work; this wasn't a sitcom.

"Jus'omeone bomping in'o me," Milt mumbled back to Gil.

"*Assholes,*" Gil growled. "*They're all assholes. Ev-ev-everyone in those places. I hate airports. Assholes everywhere you look. L-l-l-l-like a pr-pr-pr-proctologist's office.*"

Those years at the Ha Ha Hub back in Gil's New Jersey of the 1970s had really boosted his repertoire of such Borscht Belt *bon mots*. Milt didn't exactly tire of Gil's endless string of dad jokes, but this was neither the time nor place for one. Milt's mind was elsewhere, and still marinating in alcohol.

There was something to be admired, if only on a historical level, about Gil's comedic stylings, mimicking the masters of the old school—Henny Youngman, Groucho, and people of their ilk—"Take my wife, *please*...."

Then there'd be those times when Milt would be walking with Gil, orbited by a gaggle of adoring fans, and the former television host would bust out an anachronistic relic like, "He wasn't gay...but he *was* a near miss." Milt would flinch, but immediately get over his fear in the realization that none of the besotted, star-dazed fans were actually paying attention to what the subject of their adoration was saying, and thus there was no real danger of any of these people, say, tweeting out whatever inappropriate thing Gil had just said.

Pressing onward through the airport mob madness, Milt was bumped into again on the right side in the inebriated swirl of chaos all around him on the way to Terminal...23. (No, wait. Terminal 25. Terminal *25* was where he was supposed to go.)

"J-j-j-esus, again?" Gil's voice fired out from the phone.

"Definitely glad to be getting away from all these assholes here, that's for sure," Milt said, vying as he often would to stay on his pseudo-mentor's level. "That's why I'm *so* glad to be flying to LA."

This got a laugh from Gil, tinctured by a short wave of static.

It always made Milt proud of himself when he could get Gil Gladly to laugh at something he said. Milt was no geeky fanboy; he was a filmmaker, or writer, or journalist, or whatever it was he felt most comfortable qualifying himself as, depending on the circumstance.

But as with many celebrities—big or small, past their prime, or heading up the hallowed peak at that very moment in pop culture history—with whom he had interacted in his fifteen years or so since graduating from film school back in LA where he was about to head, Milt did get a special charge from knowing he was working with, friends with, and could make (*thee*) Gil Gladly laugh at something stupid he had said.

Not that making fun of people who live in LA was that hard. Terminal 25. Finally.

Milt bent slightly backward to slip off his backpack, making sure it didn't drop that hard onto the seat next to him since his office (read: laptop) was in there. He collapsed into another chair and exhaled heavily, too drunk to care about taking up two seats in an overcrowded airport terminal.

Milt couldn't imagine how Gil coped with traveling as much as he did, particularly considering the man's semi-celebrityhood and all. All those extra annoyances in situations like this.

Then again, the guy probably didn't get spotted or called out as much as he had back in the eighties and nineties. Besides, Gil was one of the few celebrities Milt knew who actually *liked* being hassled by fans running up to him for an autograph, brief chat, selfie, or occasional awkward hug.

Gil knew that without his fans he'd still be in Jersey, emceeing wet t-shirt contests and hosting open mics for irritating comics and terrible singer-songwriters. Gil did love his fans. You had to give him that.

When Gil asked again, *"S-s-s-o d-d-d-id you s-s-s-see the interview?"* he received no immediate response because Milt was too busy lusting after a young swain so stunning he wished he could give her a certificate.

"Man," Milt gushed, respiring slowly.

"Wh-wh-what? Was it that b-b-bad? It was b-b-b-ad, wasn't it?" Gil asked, truly anxious. It was easy to tell, even beyond his telltale stutter.

Even though Milt wasn't really paying attention, what with his being *completely* drunk by now and just as intoxicated with the vision of that girl standing over there looking like an out-of-time damsel who, if pixie wings were to suddenly sprout from her twee back, it wouldn't have surprised Milt in the least.

"No, it was fine, Gil," Milt was able to get out. His eyes were locked on the girl in her gray peasant dress that might as well have been a loose, dishabille nightgown. It was semi-covered by a waist-length black button-up sweater, languidly revealing her right alabaster shoulder blade.

Her light auburn hair was tied loosely into a long, thick braid that fell lazily down her flat chest, upon which a silver filigree necklace dangled. Two earrings sparkled from her tiny earlobes, matching a stud jutting out from the middle of her bottom pink lip. The slightest impression of black eyeliner sealed the deal for Milt.

"Yeah, Susan always does her homework and knows how to talk to people on her show," Gil said. *"She's a pro. But that new moron they have on there—I can't even remember his name*

right now—he had no idea what the fuck was going on. The entire segment!"

Milt was snapped back into the conversation with Gil Gladly on his phone, noticing at once that the man had stopped stuttering.

Sometimes that was a clear sign that Gil was *really* upset. It was as though he couldn't even be bothered by his own stutter in these instances. Or maybe he was just talking faster than he was thinking, which was so often the case with Gil Gladly, who, like Larry King, Winston Churchill, and the Micromachine Guy before him, talked for a living.

"It was good, Gil, really," Milt said comfortingly. "Actually, I was watching it in one of the airport lounges, and there was this old dude next to me who said his kids used to watch you on Balloon all the time when they were younger."

"Oh, y-y-y-eah?" Gil asked with the kind of gleeful inno-cence that Milt found so hopelessly endearing. After thirty years in the limelight (as dim as it would be from time to time, espe-cially over the past decade), Gil still loved hearing that people, yes, knew who he was.

Milt decided to leave out the whole dude-being-a-broken-down-crusty-fingered-degenerate-who-slipped-off-his-bar-stool aspect of the story.

Milt felt his phone vibrate briefly, signaling a text message, but he assumed it was Silverstein. He didn't have time for that right now, particularly while massaging Gil's capricious self-confidence and trying to relocate the pixie girl he'd been scoping out through the ever-growing, rumbling crowd of fellow passengers, mostly overweight and slovenly, some who had given up altogether and simply wore pajamas.

"What'd they say about your heart, Gil?" Milt asked, knowing bringing the conversation back to Something Real would help wrap things up.

"Wh-wh-what? Oh, yeah." (Faster now.) "Uhhh, I've either got six months or will live to be one-hundred and five. Depends on which doctor you talk to."

Milt was really paying attention now. He took the bait. "Wait, what?"

"Don't worry about it," Gil spat out. "I gotta run."

"Who you doing next?" Milt asked, finding the girl and watching her scratch her ear with the sparkly, roseate diamond lodged in her perfect earlobe.

"They're gonna give me five minutes at the end of Bret's show," Gil said. "Can you b-b-b-b-b-bel-l-l-lieve th-th-th-that? Five fucking minutes! Th-th-th-that's it. I made that guy's career, and h-h-h-h-he g-g-g-g-gives me five minutes to talk about the movie t-t-t-tell-l-l-ling the s-s-s-s-story of m-m-m-m-m-my l-l-life! Nice friends in Hollywood, huh? It's wh-wh-wh-why I've always h-h-h-hated LA."

Milt's eyebrows furrowed and he caught a blessed glimpse of the girl's bare ankle when she lifted up her dress to scratch that now too. (Dry weather?) "I mean...at least Bret's having you on at all," Milt tried, his heart not really in it. "Didn't you say before you couldn't get a hold of him now that his head was bigger than his ass?"

"Ehhh, I g-g-g-guess he ch-ch-changed his mind," Gil said. "S-s-s-see in y-y-y-y-you in LA."

Milt breathed in deeply. The airport aroma was that of greasy french fries and gritty exhaust.

He checked the text message that had come in. It *had* been Silverstein, and the fucker was still sending screenshots of emails he'd received from his (and Milt's former) editor at the paper Milt had "resigned" from earlier in the year.

Silverstein wouldn't stop sending these damned texts and leaving long, rambling, explosive voicemails, often while outlandishly drunk, on Milt's phone. Milt knew it wasn't worth texting back to say something along the lines of, *"Kiddo, I love you and am proud of you for standing your ground at that hell-hole. But I quit more than six months ago and your staying there is your own fault. If you want out, leave like everyone else has been doing. Stop being a battered housewife, and get out of there!"*

It wouldn't be worth the time, especially since Milt had already sent almost the exact same text five other times over the past month alone.

Besides, another text message had popped up, this time from Jessica Chen.

Oy.

Jessica Chen had been one of the child "stars" of another Balloon show that Milt had been too old to watch by the time it aired. Her show, *KidTrek*, was essentially a *Star Trek* rip-off featuring a space crew manned by children. The telltale larger budget, glitzy special effects, and more conventional style of the show made for a noticeable break between the kind of weirder, irreverent, scrappily low-budget programming that had been airing on Balloon in the early days and what was to come.

Actually, for the past two decades, there had been a contentious debate about the so-called "classic years" of the Balloon network—marked by the fancy-free, absurdist, sometimes sophomorically disgusting shows of the 1980s—versus series like Jessica Chen's, which were glossier and appeared to be the brand of programming that belonged under the pristinely polished Disney aegis.

It was around the time of Jessica Chen's *KidTrek*, in fact, that Balloon started giving Disney a run for its money in the "children's market," rebranding itself as a contender that would eventually become the billion-dollar global juggernaut it became in the early 2000s.

Balloon went through exactly the same process that other cultural touchstones from around the period underwent—Nickelodeon, punk rock, hip-hop, *Saturday Night Live*, MTV. What had started as a small, independently-minded, somewhat DIY affair erupted into the mainstream to become a massive, corporatized, worldwide moneymaker.

Milt had never even talked to Jessica Chen before when he'd been doing all his research for the articles he'd written about Balloon's scrappy eighties and early nineties programming. But ever since people got word of his documentary about Gil Gladly, Milt had been hearing regularly from former actors, actresses, and producers involved in other Balloon shows asking him if they could get tickets to the screenings happening all month around the country.

Jessica Chen had been the most ambitious (a nice way to put it) in her barrage of texts and emails, some of which included her headshots, CV, and EPK, along with clips of her from various fanboy YouTube web series.

Milt wouldn't have bothered responding to her *"Can't wait to finally meet you in LA at the screening!"* text. But Jessica Chen also happened to be one of the handful of Balloon alumni who were involved in their own documentaries about themselves along with the ever-flowing series of nostalgic pop culture docs allegedly coming out about both individual Balloon programs and the network itself.

Best to be magnanimous and play into the "all for one" millennial Hollywood hype that fueled the cross-promotion of these projects burbling forth from the precarious soap bubble of the fan community that had frothed up over the past five years now that those who had grown up on these shows, like Milt, were old enough to start concocting said documentaries... and podcasts, articles, books, and other content detailing the behind-the-scenes shenanigans of the early Balloon years.

Most of these upcoming documentaries promoted heavily on the entertainment blog circuit would rarely get past the Kickstarter phase. Many of the projects were produced by former or current publicists who were able to get their project heavily promoted through the contacts they had at all the big entertainment blogs even before their project had been fully funded or began shooting interview one. Milt, and a few other like-minded individuals who were actually paying attention to the dichotomy between the hype and reality of such endeavors, knew better.

So, it was to Jessica Chen's credit that her doc was *in production*—according to IMDb—and boasted interviews with eighties icons Julie Brown and Lea Thompson. Brown had guest-starred on a few episodes of *KidTrek* as a snarky, villainous alien queen, and Jessica Chen had been a recurring guest star on Thompson's mid-nineties sitcom, *Caroline in the City*. Although these weren't big names, per se, not in 2017, they were big enough to get Jessica Chen's doc into a few of the medium-tiered festivals and most likely a coveted spot on Netflix's tumescent lineup.

Milt needed to play nice. Without swallowing too much of his pride or integrity, he sent a meme of Robert DeNiro's heroic character from Terry Gilliam's *Brazil* emblazoned with the large white text of, *"Listen, kid, we're all in it together"* and thought that would be that until Jessica Chen's next text or email, which would likely arrive while he'd be in the air with his phone thankfully off.

He then texted his wife Laney, telling her he was about to take off and that he loved her. She texted back almost immediately to say he was a faggot..."but you're MY faggot." Which was about the best he could expect from a girl he lovingly described to friends as "a walking *South Park* episode."

Milt smiled, and in so doing, looked up to peer through the undulating crowd in which the pixie girl across the way was smiling back.

It was a bit of a jolt, to be honest. Was she smiling at *him*?

He was drunk, no doubt about it. He didn't know this girl. Obviously. He was married. Uh-*duh*. Why did he still stare at and think about other girls? Was this normal? Was this what all newly married people did? Would this irrational craving dissipate after a few years?

The announcement was made that boarding of Milt's low-priority section of the plane had commenced, and the somnolent pajama'd cattle were prodded toward the inside of the terminal, with Milt himself being shoved diffidently by the mass of movement.

He couldn't believe he was actually going back to Los Angeles, his least favorite place on the planet. But off he was drifting, slowly, toward the gate, handing his thin paper boarding pass to the attendant, stopping halfway into the terminal tube along with everyone else, mostly on their phones, texting their own wives, husbands, girlfriends, boyfriends, parents, and looking up the latest news or into their social media feeds, playing *Candy Crush*....

The booze was back on his mind. Better put: *At* his mind, twirling the world around him alongside all the people he was being corralled with toward the plane, hoping he'd somehow be sat next to the pixie girl.

He wished he'd get the email he'd been waiting on about his Unemployment. Why weren't they depositing his final claim? *Now* what was the problem? Before he could complain aloud about the General State of Things, he was on the plane, and checking his ticket, and seeing that he was to sit—passing the pixie girl sitting down to his right—to his left.

It was a middle seat. Fuck. Cross-country, from Boston to LA, nonstop. Fuck. With a selfishly obese man overloading the window seat and wearing the kind of oversized headphones that would normally make Milt laugh but now only scared him into realizing he'd be hearing explosive video game sounds and blaring electronic music for seven or eight hours of hellish torture. Oh, what had he done to deserve this fate? He was sorry! He was sorry for everything evil he had ever done, intentional or otherwise!

Please, God, or whomever else: No!

Milt deposited his beige canvas backpack into the miniscule legroom he'd never get to enjoy and lowered himself into his seat, leaning to his left away from the blob blasting electronic music to his right.

He turned his head to his left farther and saw, across the cramped space of their aisle, the pixie girl sitting there, oblivious. She was also in the middle seat. Her window seat was empty and would end up remaining so. Her aisle seat was then filled with someone who looked virtually identical to Milt, another Seth Rogen type, and the two immediately began talking.

The pixie girl laughed at whatever Milt's doppelgänger was saying.

Milt sighed heavily, moving his right arm away from the left arm of the gargantuan man to his right. A grizzled old biker with slicked back silver hair and matching goatee sat down in Milt's aisle seat. The biker wore a Harley-Davidson shirt that read, "We do bad things to bad people."

Yikes.

Milt ventured to ask the biker if he could have a little room on their shared armrest.

"You kiddin'?" the biker asked rhetorically.

Milt understood and scrunched himself further into the little bit of room he now had in his uncomfortable seat. He asked the passing, harried stewardess if he could have a blanket and a pillow.

"We don't have blankets or pillows on this flight," she confessed apologetically, assisting a once-gorgeous soccer mom with a paedomorphic ponytail and skin-tight black yoga pants to her seat along with her screeching child and yapping Pomeranian. Right behind Milt.

Fuck.

The robotic stewardess shifted imperceptibly from apologetic to delighted, handing the soccer mom her squawking bird in a cage she'd been carrying. The biker turned around and said in his gravelly voice, "I had a bird like that once." Then he ordered two Budweisers from the same stewardess who closed her eyes to smile wide like Janice the Muppet.

The soccer mom laughed politely, juggling her bitch dog, her bastard kid, and her vicious bird. "Good thing I got all three seats to myself!"

Milt sighed again, this time overheard by the biker who turned and groused at him, all but shoving Milt's elbow off their shared armrest. There would be no armrest on either side for Milton Siegel on this particular cross-country flight.

The announcement was made that all passengers needed to turn their phones to airplane mode, and Milt used the opportunity to text Laney again.

"We're off! Love you!"

He waited. No response. He turned off his phone.

He pressed his armrest button to lower his seat back, hoping he'd be able to sleep through the trip.

"Sir," Robo-Stewardess, now set to authoritarian mode, said, handing the biker his two beers, "you need to raise your seat up for take-off."

The fat man next to him turned up his music and Milt steadied himself for the flight to LA, and the premiere of his movie ahead.

CHAPTER 3

"**L**ook at this fat motherfucker right here!" Frankly's spiky-haired anime avatar shadow called out from beyond the darkness toward Milt, standing under a streetlamp's white moon glow.

"I was gonna say exactly the same fucking thing!" Milt called back to Frankly, emerging from the shadow and cobwebby tendrils of fog that cocooned them both around the corner from Milt's mom's two-bedroom apartment.

It was true, Frank Lee, Milt's old Hollywood roommate and friend from film school, had clearly put on a few pounds since last they'd seen one other.

Milt had the excuse of having gotten married to blame for his additional poundage.

"Frannkkklyyyyy," Milt said in mock bro-ish greeting, hugging the squat little gargoyle tight. Frankly reciprocated with an equally powerful I-still-work-out-a-little-and-also-it's-good-to-see-you hug.

Frankly was Korean, had a small growth that appeared to be another smaller ear underneath his actual left ear, was about four to six inches shorter than Milt depending on if one were to include Frankly's jet black spikes of tenaciously moussed hair, never knew his father, and had moved back home with his mom in blue-collar Costa Mesa after Milt had moved away forever, or so he'd hoped, from LA, leaving Frankly sans roomie almost a decade earlier.

Smart, ambitious, and infectiously likeable, Frankly made relatively decent money. Especially when it came to Milt's small circle of fellow UCLA film school graduates. Surprise, surprise.

The two old roommates were close. They'd spent many a late night playing endless games of cocaine-fueled speed chess while watching all manner of obscure art films courtesy of their slightly illegal all-region DVD player and equally endless supply of imported DVDs purchased from the Amoeba Records up the street from where they had been renting a tiny duplex in the slightly-but-not-especially shitty area of Hollywood. This was all back in the days when friends of theirs would refuse to visit at night for fear of the area being east of La Brea. These days, Milt and Frankly wouldn't even be able to afford to *park* in the hipster-gentrified region. Ah, the circle of life.

They had both been pretty fat then. It was a lot of late-night roach coach burritos/tacos and free booze from the Chinatown bar where Milt's young and adorable waif of a managing editor at the paper he was editor-of-chief of moonlighted at back when no one went over *there* past dark. The days when Amy Winehouse had just started getting blasted on the speakers in the bar, with Milt looking up to say, "Hey, this girl's onto something! She's goin' places!"

Frankly and Milt went through a lot together in those hungry days. As time went by, they'd eventually arrived at the point where they could comfortably have discussions about whether or not girls ever fooled around with Frankly's supernumerary ear during sex (yes, sometimes).

They could talk about how, why, when Milt confessed he was leaving LA "forever," Frankly decided to move back home. Why Frankly had to take care of his mom, who was suffering from Alzheimer's. Why Frankly had to take care of his younger brother, who had also moved back home after a few failed attempts at rehab. This was just part of Frankly's heritage as a first-generation Korean, he'd say, blunt as ever. Family first.

Milt was typically loud; Frankly was typically quiet. Milt asked a lot of questions that sometimes got him in trouble with the wrong unwitting interviewee, and Frankly would only speak when spoken to. Once, when they robo-tripped on Coricidin, Frankly hallucinated that he was in the desert, while Milt hallucinated he was in the ocean. All of this going on in their living room straight out of a 1980s TV sitcom, furnished with vintage items aplenty; an explosion of brown, yellow, and orange.

The boys were still, nearly a decade after they had moved apart, close enough that they were telepathic about where they were headed without a word spoken between them. They both knew what they were after and what they would get before night's end.

Milt smiled at Frankly, whose eyes were on the road, one relaxed hand on the wheel, celestial rictus smeared across his mug, and knowing what adventure did lay ahead that night.

Milt turned his head to the fingerprint smudged passenger window and thought about how he had arrived at this very moment.

Less than two months earlier, Milt was finishing his preparation for the LA premiere while working on his MacBook Air with the *Giving Tree* decal on the back. He sat in a booth in the back of a trendy coffee shop in Boston where he had been living for the year with Laney.

Milt had, rather impetuously, accepted an invitation to work for the *Star*, an alt-weekly in Boston that was supposedly one of the last in the country to still be turning a profit. A small profit, of course, but a profit nonetheless. Milt had wanted to give working as a staff reporter in the predictable structure of an office a try one more time.

He had reverse-*Green Acres*'d Laney after—high on acid and wearing a meretricious electric-lime dress and black leather fuck-me knee-high boots—she had more or less picked him up at a bar where they had both been living in Lincoln, Nebraska. Laney had ended up in Nebraska for school. Milt had ended up in Nebraska as a way to keep adventuring around the country, remotely and locally plying his trade as a writer-filmmaker, doing his best to stay as far away from the loud noises, funky smells, and maddening hordes of LA's and NYC's robo-zombie masses.

Oh, fuck, Milt realized.

He was sitting there at his Boston coffee shop, multiple windows open on his screen detailing the forthcoming LA premiere, a stack of scrawled-upon pages piled up next to his two empty paper coffee cups that comprised the autobiography of an underground but "important" rapper from the early nineties named MC Phliphlop he was also working on at the moment. He'd been bouncing back and forth between film premiere prep and his ghostwritten life story of someone he had only met a year earlier through the auspices of his agent, who had mercifully tossed him an assignment that had been languishing around the agency office.

Milt looked up from his work to see Gilbert Sidfeld, managing editor at the paper Milt had quit or been fired from, depending on who you asked. Gilbert Sidfeld would likely have informed you of the latter scenario. Gilbert Sidfeld, that irritating cur who resembled a hapless garden gnome, was standing across the café in line for coffee and holding a pink book.

Milt texted Silverstein.

"Shitsmelled just fucking walked into the coffee shop where I'm working right now."

"FUCK, DUDE! HE WAS SUPPOSED TO BE HERE TEN MINUTES AGO! ARE YOU SURE IT'S HIM?" Silverstein texted back.

Milt looked up from his stack of pages and laptop. He was sure. It was *absolutely* Shitsmelled with his goofy glasses, ginger wizard's beard, Boys' Gap khakis, and tucked-in white button-up shirt.

"Yeah, there he is, man-bun and all," Milt texted to affirm.

"Dude, I'm about to scoop the fucking Herald on this story I've been working on all weekend, I need Shitsmelled to approve it, and you're telling me that that shit-stain piece of FUCK is waiting on line for coffee with a goddamn fucking book in his hand like a little cuck? Yell at him to get his bony little ass over here or I swear to fuck I'm gonna throw my computer through his office window," read Silverstein's characteristically vulgar, frantic, and right-wing leaning text.

"Oh, and his book is pink," wrote Milt, laughing at his own text, knowing what it would do to the already-enraged Silverstein.

"WHHHAAAAATTTT???!!! FUCCCCCCKKK HIMMMMMM AND HIS FAGGOTY FUCKLE PINK BOOK!!!!"

Silverstein was twenty-five, a few years out of journalism school, and forever bragged that his dad was an old man when he had him. To Silverstein, this officially meant he was *not* a millennial. Yes, he was twenty-five, but that old man dad of his had raised him like he was always twenty years older.

Silverstein made Milt laugh and always spoke his mind. Milt could *trust* him, a rare commodity these days. Silverstein would also rail about rich kids almost as much Milt, even though Silverstein still lived at home. "Saving for a house of my own" was always the excuse Milt heard in such seemingly hypocritical cases.

Silverstein was Boston through and through, aside from being Jewish. And he was one of those provocateurs who proudly bought and showed off to his friends via text his MAGA hat, but would never dare wear the red target in public.

"I CAN'T FILE MY STORY UNTIL SHITSMELLED 'GOES OVER' IT! FUCK THAT PIECE OF CUCK SHIT! MY NOSE IS STRESS BLEEDING AGAIN BECAUSE OF THIS FUCKLE! IT'S ALL OVER MY DESK."

To be as clear as possible, Silverstein texted Milt a photo of his desk splattered with droplets of cranberry-red blood.

Milt had learned a lot of new words from Silverstein, "cuck" being a favorite of the latter's, who used it unsparingly. Especially in reference to Gilbert Sidfeld, who Silverstein called a cuck because of Sidfeld's feebleness and total inability to properly manage the paper.

Milt and Silverstein had also discovered that Sidfeld's fiancée, who ran a non-profit that worked with prison labor to clear the streets of roadkill, wrote most of his weekly editorials for him, uncredited. Apparently this was *extreme* "cuckness," according to Silverstein's definition.

What a trip it had been that there was an approximately six-month period there in which the two most important men in Milt's life were named Gil. Then again, Laney Jenkins wasn't the only girl named Laney Milt had ever had a serious relationship with either, and most of the other men in Milt's life were named Dave, including both his dad and former stepdad.

Milt's phone vibrated from an email notification. He clicked on the screen's Gmail icon and waited for his inbox to pop up, hoping like an adolescent girl waiting by the phone for a call from a boy she had a crush on that it was an email from CineR-anchero. The independent theater chain had been screwing up quite literally every possible aspect of the largest and most elaborate screening "experience" on the upcoming Gil Gladly documentary tour.

Nope. It was an event e-vite from Jessica Chen.

Milt didn't bother reading it, and answered the incoming call from what read out across his screen as GOOD GOLLY GIL GLADLY.

"S-s-s-so, is this g-g-g-guy Latham a complete and t-t-t-total f-f-f-fraud?" Gil screamed into the phone. *"Or is he j-j-j-just a c-c-c-complete and total f-f-f-fuck-up?"*

It was over almost exactly the same time span that Milt learned colorful new words and phrases from Silverstein that he also had the illuminating experience of getting really intimate with Gil Gladly over the phone, email, and their occasional meetups during the wrap-up phase of the doc. He became familiar with the peculiar paradox that Gil Gladly, a man known mostly for his *children's* show, swore like a stand-up comic from the seventies which, after all, was also what he was.

It had been somewhat difficult to edit all of Gil Gladly's profanity, not to mention what Milt would call if he were a blogger certain "tone deaf" jokes, from the documentary. That had been Wallace Connors' idea.

Wallace Connors had been a longtime friend of Milt's whom he knew through the nostalgia industry channels. Wallace had set up a modest series of publicly-held reunions for stars from yet another old Balloon show called *KidKidding*, which was essentially *Whose Line Is It Anyway?* with kids.

Milt had brought Wallace on as the editor of the project, despite the fact Milt was in Boston and Wallace worked from his office in Atlanta. The bonus, aside from Wallace being a long-time trusted friend of Milt's, was that Wallace's office also had all of the top-notch editing and audio postproduction equipment they'd need, along with a small staff Wallace was happy to put to work at night and on the weekends, with Milt calling, emailing, and Skyping in with his notes over those three blistering months of cut after cut after cut of the doc.

Wallace's family, originally Mormon, had been on a ministry mission in the Middle East back when Wallace was a boy. For whatever reason, his parents decided over time that Islam was the true way, and thus they converted, which was why Wallace Connors, pale as a ghost with premature shockingly white Steve Martin hair and an otherwise absolutely Teutonic appearance, was a devout Muslim who would not drink, do drugs, or swear.

Milt wanted authenticity in the doc. He wanted the fans to see Gil as his complex, contradictory, nuanced, real-human-being self. But Wallace had convinced Milt that leaving out Gil's volcanic potty-mouth would give the film a broader appeal. It would be more accessible to larger audiences and thus, *bing-bing-bing*, more marketable when it was time to sell the fucking thing.

Milt looked down, away from the line of folks waiting for coffee, from Shitsmelled and all the rest of them.

"I'm s-s-s-s-serious, man!" Gil continued on the other end of Milt's phone, stuttering maniacally.

This was Gil Gladly the *businessman*, the *executive producer of the documentary* now. The *boss. Not* to be confused with Gil Gladly, your ol' pal from TV's *KidTalk*.

Milton Siegel well knew the difference.

Milt was up on his feet, leaving his laptop and pages of copyedited manuscript at his table. Making sure not to be noticed by Shitsmelled, who was nearing the front of the line now with the bewildered look of a child lost from his parents in a grocery store, Milt clamped his phone to his ear and used his right elbow to shove his way through the glass door.

He made his way through the pastel-colored outdoor tables of the café where a few brave bundled-up souls were reading, laughing, talking, and having their morning coffee and breakfast sandwiches in the grayish, fantastically funereal 9 a.m.-ish morning.

"I emailed Latham yesterday, Gil, and told him that this has been getting out of hand," Milt said into the phone as he sliced through the windy, semi-wintry air, across the café patio and away from the other patrons. "I said if he couldn't get back to us by the end of this week, we are going to have to move on to another theater. This is getting fucking ridiculous. I feel really bad I recommended him, but I'm telling you, his theater would be perfect for our LA screening. His film society has a *huge* following, all the big press out there is always promoting his special events, and I had no idea he was such an asshole."

"Yeah, I just s-s-sent him the s-s-s-same exact email before I called you," Gil said, calming down.

"Well, I guess we'll just have to wait and see how Herr Latham deigns to respond."

"I just don't know what he expects me to do." Gil sounded wounded now. *"He's been totally condescending and patronizing, demanding I send him this clip and that clip and photos from my personal archives, and I don't have all that stuff, as you know. I threw out most of that shit after I closed my office last year, and I don't know how to work any of these stupid programs on my computer where the rest of my photos and clips are, and—"*

"Gil," Milt said, stopping the man before it was too late. "I know. I know. I'm sorry Latham's been putting you through all of this."

"I tell you what, if he doesn't get back to us, fuck LA. I hate those people anyway. I've never done well in LA. Ever since my stand-up days. Fuck LA. We don't need it. All the other screenings are set, right?"

"Yeah."

"What the fuck is going on with that huge-ass motherfucking thing in Chicago? What's it called again, CineRamaDama?"

"CineRanchero. It's their flagship theater and we gotta do it. It'll be the big one on our tour. I'm dealing with them. You don't worry about it. You have enough shit to deal with right now, okay? Watch your fucking heart too, man."

"Don't you w-w-w-worry ab-b-b-bout th-th-that. Y-y-y-ou're n-n-n-n-not m-m-m-m-my m-m-m-m-mother."

"I thought you didn't get along with your mother," Milt said with a friendly huff.

"Y-y-y-y-eah y-y-y-yeah, s-s-s-mart guy."

Milt had gotten Gil calm enough that was he was stuttering again, ratcheted down to perhaps anxiety level seven.

Milt turned his head, breathing in the crisp Boston morning air...and almost choked when he saw Shitsmelled coming through the glass door. Luckily, their eyes didn't meet and Milt whipped around before his ex-boss could find a place to sit and drink his coffee, enjoy his pink book, and abandon Silverstein back at the paper tearing out the last few hairs on his prematurely balding Jewish head.

Speaking of the devil, Milt's phone vibrated with a text from Silverstein: **"TELL THAT CUCK TO GET BACK HERE RIGHT NOW!"**

"S-s-s-so you're h-h-h-h-handling Chicago is w-w-w-w-what you're t-t-t-t-telling me, Milt?"

"Yeah, Gil, I'm handling it all. Don't worry. You know how the CineRanchero people have been this whole time. Christ, just two days ago I saw they couldn't even fucking spell the movie right on their ticket page for the flick that they *finally* put online."

"W-w-w-why aren't th-th-they t-t-t-tweeting anything out about our screening?" Gil shouted.

"I'm handling it, Gil," Milt said. *"I told you. You gotta trust* someone *in your life, and it might as well be me!"*

There was a pause. Had he crossed the line?

Milt turned around slowly to see Shitsmelled lost in his book, unconsciously playing with a few strings of hair flowing out of his man bun.

"Y-y-y-y-you're r-r-r-right, man," Gil said. *"Y-y-y-y-you've b-b-b-been k-k-k-k-killing it,"* Gil said, calming down to the point of cycling back to dropping the stutter altogether. He spoke clearly and slowly. *"Without you, none of this would have happened. I just wish I could pay you for everything, but, you know..."*

"Yeah, I know," Milt said, biting his bottom lip. "It's okay. I'm not...doing this for the money. I'm doing okay right now. Just as long as we sell this thing and get *something*. Netflix should take the doc, if nothing else. That'd be nice. And it's a calling card for all of us. Especially Ronnie."

"Who the f-f-f-fuck's Ronnie?"

"Ronnie Clark. Our DP, remember? You were nice enough to meet up with him for a lunch a few months ago after we finished shooting so he could pick your brain a little about all the Hollywood bullshit. I told you, you're like his hero, and he thinks this thing could really kick start his career."

"Right," Gil said. *"How's Donnie doing?"*

"He's okay, and his name is *Ronnie*. He's based out of Denver and he's been getting hit pretty hard by that 'snowstorm of the century' deal, but—"

"Right," Gil said, then mumbled, *"Hmm, the snowstorm. Denver. Mmm."*

Milt had gotten used to these mood swings, the ups and downs of Gil Gladly's mind.

"Actually, Gil, I think the snowstorm might have something to do with all the fuck-ups CineRanchero has been having. I know the storm's been hitting Chicago really hard and—"

"W-w-w-ell, that's no excuse for them to not get back to us w-w-whenever we're trying to get in t-t-t-t-touch with th-th-them!" Gil fired back. *"Just l-l-l-let me know the n-n-n-n-n-n-next time they contact you. Better be s-s-s-oon. This fucking tour is right around the fucking corner, and I haven't slept a w-w-w-w-w-wink in weeks!"*

"Yup," Milt said. "I'm on it. Say hi to Mandy, and talk to you later."

Gil hung up without saying goodbye, as per usual, and Milt went back inside, gliding past Shitsmelled, lost in his book and strings of hair. Milt's phone vibrated nonstop in his pocket. Fucking Silverstein! He should just quit the job if he hated it so much, like everyone else had been doing.

Milt sat back down at his laptop and stack of papers, and it dawned on him that the first screening *was* only right around the corner. The LA premiere would be at Latham Harrison's specialty art house theater where all the Hollywood hipsters and a few people with familiar names would hang out for screenings and cinema-themed community events.

He decided to check the theater's website and make sure the documentary's premiere was listed on the upcoming calendar. Even CineRanchero had done *that* much, despite having initially misspelled the title of the movie.

Milt Googled "Latheatre" on his computer, then sat back against the cold, white wall underneath a framed abstract painting of a blurry yellow taxicab driving through what was probably supposed to be Manhattan on a rainy day.

On the laptop's screen was Google search entry after Google search entry with essentially the same clickbaitable headline about Latheatre and Latham himself.

"Shit," Milt whispered, shaking his head. He got up and opened the glass door, slinkered past Shitsmelled, who didn't look up from his pink book, and marched over to the other side of the patio away from the other patrons.

He called GOOD GOLLY GIL GLADLY on his phone, and held the device tight to his ear.

"Yessir," Gil said as though they hadn't just talked two minutes earlier.

"I know why we're not hearing anything from Latham Harrison," Milt said.

"Okkaaaaaayyy..."

"Are you by a computer right now?"

"Yesssssss..."

"Google his theater," Milt said, waiting.

"What's that one called again?"

"Latheatre," Milt said. "L-a-t-h-e-a-t-r-e."

"British, huh?"

"No."

Four seconds of pregnant silence later, Gil came back with the inevitable, *"Holy fuck."*

"Yup, it's all over the place. *Variety, Hollywood Reporter,* Huff Po. I'm sure it'll only be a matter of minutes before it's on

BuzzFeed. It's everywhere. That's it. I have a feeling we're not going to be hearing from Latham again."

"How do you know this guy again?" Gil asked, audibly typing away on his laptop on the other end.

"When I was at UCLA, a bunch of us used to hang out at his bookstore over by the ArcLight and Amoeba," Milt said. "He was sort of like our own personal Comic Book Guy from *The Simpsons.*"

"Mmm hmmm...."

"With the help of some of his more high-profile regulars, he started his own theater maybe six or seven years ago. I'd always heard good things, though even back then he was kind of a jerk."

"So, exactly *like Comic Book Guy on* The Simpsons."

"Well, yeah, but his store was awesome and his theater has done a bunch of cool shit like what would've happened with the premiere of our documentary," Milt said.

"Okay, well, with all this sexual harassment stuff and his resigning as director of the theater, we obviously can't have anything to do with this organization right now. So, just cancel LA. Fuck LA. We don't need them."

Milt turned around again and looked out to the seated customers, who'd multiplied since he'd last come out only a few minutes earlier, and was almost certain Shitsmelled had looked up briefly, caught sight of him, and hid his face back into his book.

Milt exhaled deeply. "Gil, we can't cancel LA. There are too many important people who have already been invited and are definitely coming. There's a bunch of your fans out there, and I know from all the social media nonsense that they want to come too. *LA Weekly* already did a blurb about it. It'd look terrible if we don't go. Wallace was planning on going out there from Atlanta on his own dime because he has some business stuff out there to deal with around that time."

"Wallace is going? Shit," Gil said. *"I like that guy. Okay, I don't care about that other junk, but if you really think we need to do LA..."*

"I do," Milt confirmed. "I really do."

It wasn't just about the "important people" allegedly coming out, nor about the fans and the bullshit online rep of the film to come. Milt wanted to make sure LA still happened because he did not want to be told he couldn't do something. He didn't want to know that something was out of his control, that something wouldn't work out, particularly not a premiere he had been putting together for more than half a year, that had fallen apart only last minute because of that jerkoff Latham's sticky fingers around his employees.

Go to one of the infinite brothels in Tijuana for a night just two-and-a-half hours away! Why do it at WORK where everyone can SEE YOU and fuck up everyone's lives?! Guhhhhhhdddd...!

"We can't just cancel screenings because of stupid shit like this," Milt said, glowering at Shitsmelled sitting there in his little chair, reading his little pink book, fiddling with his little ginger man bun, and leaving Silverstein back at the office in the lurch.

Milt knew what he needed to do, he had to needle Gil Gladly's impulsive emotionality. Milt needed to crank it to eleven, *Spinal Tap* style. "We *have* to do LA just like we *have* to do Chicago. These things are already fucking set, even if we have to find a different theater to do it at in LA. Fuck Latham and fuck

CineRanchero and fuck everyone and everything except for you, me, our families, the film, and everyone who worked on it."

"You're crazy," Gil laughed. *"And I mean that in the best way."*

"Yeah, I learned from the best, fuckface." Milt beamed, secretly delighted that he could call *the* Gil Gladly a fuckface on the phone and actually make the guy laugh about it. Just in case, he quickly added, "I mean...*fook-fah-shay.* I always mispronounce that word."

"You miraculously made everything else happen, Milt," Gil said without a stutter. *"So, go make this happen too, fook-fah-shay."*

"You got it," Milt said. "See ya soon."

Gil hung up without a goodbye, and Milt went back into the coffee shop, purposely knocking Shitsmelled's chair with his elbow and not bothering to turn back to see if the fucker noticed.

The copyediting on his ghostwritten Phliphlop autobio would have to wait for now. Milton Siegel had *work* to do.

At thirty-six, Milt was the same age his father had been when he was born. He was in a new, possibly precarious marriage with a woman he had eloped with only four months earlier. He had been putting on too much weight after years of remaining relatively fit. He was living off of financial fumes but surviving for now.

And he had less than two months to set up an alternative to his full-fledged premiere in Los Angeles for the documentary he and his small team of filmmakers around the country had been killing themselves over for the past two years while dealing with all their real-life responsibilities and problems.

As it would turn out, Milt would actually be able to accomplish just that, in less than three hours. Fuck *yeah*.

CHAPTER 4

That was how Milton Siegel had ended up in SoCal, visiting his mom for a few days before getting ready to head up to LA with Frankly acting as his Kato (*Green Hornet*, not Kaelin) for the premiere of his Gil Gladly documentary. They would be showing the film at the prestigious Egyptian Theater in Hollywood, where Milt had worked throughout his college years. He still had some supportive friends working there who had said, "A documentary about Gil Gladly, with Gil Gladly *in person*? You can have the space for free! Will he sign our *KidTalk* VHS tapes?"

Milt agreed to let them keep the profits from the door, a deal he'd been getting reluctantly used to going along with when it came to locking down venues over the previous few months. Free meant *free*. All good, since he and his band of merry men could still have their premiere in LA. As long as the people who had bought tickets from Latheatre could transfer over to the Egyptian (they could; the Egyptian folks were very helpful with this), all would work out.

Milt had even been able to convince popular YouTube star Astra Singh to host the Q&A after the screening. Astra was too young to have been around when *KidTalk* first aired but, as with so many other geeky YouTubers, brought in much of her traffic through the eighties/nineties nostalgia industry channels and often talked about Gil Gladly as one of her childhood heroes.

The fact she still lived at home with her parents and thus didn't need to be paid was helpful too. Milt found it strange that it seemed so *many* YouTube stars still lived at home, well into their twenties and thirties. Stranger still, their reasoning usually had something to do with their suffering from some form of agoraphobia, introversion, or social awkwardness, as they'd put it in countless interviews, despite being so eager to be interviewed or end up on stage at conferences, comic-cons, and other panels or live performance opportunities.

The contradiction reminded Milt of how he'd felt when he first heard the term "ADD" as a fourth-grader. "It means I can't focus," said the pig-tailed platinum-blonde girl sitting next to him. When Milt asked how Blondie had trouble focusing when she was right then and there meticulously sketching an elaborate castle for a princess character she was always talking about in her short stories for class, the girl answered, "Well, I can focus on things I *want* to focus on."

Gil had cringed at the idea of having to explicitly promote a "YouTube Star," a phrase which he had multiple times in the past referred to as an oxymoron. But it was a way to bring in a few more ticketholders and get word out about the film itself. After multiple all-caps texts and frantic phone messages from Gil upon landing and turning on his cell, Milt had looked into it to discover they had indeed sold-out the Egyptian premiere to come.

The flight hadn't been easy, what with Milt having to cope with his fellow passengers—be they badass bikers, blimps, birds, or bourgeoisie—not to mention a raging thirst from his drunken bacchanal earlier in the airport bar.

Once down the escalator to the baggage claim, he texted his principle crew members and closest compatriots Wallace Connors and Ronnie Clark.

"Landed in LA, boyyyysssss." It was a riff on the rural doyenne of the place he had set up for them when they had spent a week in Gil's boyhood town just outside of Missoula, Montana. Every morning, it had been a mellifluous sing-songy "Morning, boyyyssss" with her perfect, stately southern-belle countenance.

That Montana was decidedly *not* in the south didn't seem to matter much. But the woman sure could whip up some fantastic waffles. Milt never really cared for the cakey breakfast food, but Mrs. Cuthbert resoundingly changed his mind. And there were a lot of crucifixes around the house Milt had rented and shared with Wallace, Ronnie, and her for the week of Gil Gladly's childhood interviews.

Ronnie immediately texted back, "Have fun, boyyysssss."

Wallace didn't respond until a few minutes later, while Milt was still wandering around trying to figure out which of the flashing numbers on the endless line of baggage claims was the one that matched his flight.

"Good luck. Keep us updated. Love you, man."

It was rare and incongruous to the personality of the semi-portly, seven-foot-two Wallace whenever he ended a conversation with, "I love you, man." But it was *because* of how upright he could otherwise often appear to be that when Wallace Connors said it, you knew he meant it. It wasn't Hollywood bullshit.

Which made sense, because Wallace had tried the scene for a few years back in his early twenties and had, as he himself claimed, run back to Atlanta with his tail between his legs. Thankfully. It led to his starting his own independent production company, focusing mainly on local promos, commercials, and the occasional wedding video. This allowed Wallace to buy a house at thirty and, around the same time as Milt, get married to a beautiful, equally religious Muslim girl. Her family had also converted from Mormonism when they had been on a different missionary mission when *she* was young.

Wallace ended up not being able to come out for the premiere, both because of the flood of work he had to wrap up before the holidays, and because of the *actual* flood that was tearing up all parts of Atlanta and the southeastern states in general.

Ronnie didn't have the money to come out, and what with four kids to take care of and that snowstorm wrecking Denver, it just wouldn't be happening this round. Milt was lucky to have been able to find a nonstop flight through the country's irrational rash of natural disasters that had befallen the land on his way from Boston to Orange County where his mom lived in a senior community after divorcing husband number three, Milt's step-father Dave.

Teddy Miller, one of the many Gil Gladly fanboy hangers-on that Milt, Wallace, and Ronnie had to contend with, had posted on the film's main Facebook page something along the lines of, **"Good thing I didn't work on this project; it seems cursed!"** when Milt had posted: **"Thoughts and prayers to our producer and his editing team Wallace Connors in Atlanta."**

Ronnie had deleted Teddy's comment without a word about it from Teddy. Which was pretty standard by now, after the boys had had to delete a few of Teddy's other less appropriate and ill-timed posts on their film's Facebook page. Milt had once asked Gil Gladly, who tertiarily knew Teddy from various conventions, whether or not Teddy might be autistic.

"Why does everyone keep asking me th-th-that?" Gil had answered, chuckling.

Milt had left it at that. He *had* at one point started asking Gil about his thoughts on a piece Milt wanted to do about the instances of autism in geek fandom circles, but Gil told him the whole idea weirded him out and he didn't want to have anything to do with it. It was something Milt had spoken with a few of his other journalist friends about, and it turned out more than one had been considering writing about the same possible phenomenon. But, yes, better let it lie for now, they felt. No one wanted to get in trouble for saying the wrong thing about mental illness, interesting story or not.

Wallace and Ronnie would be coming out to the Chicago event held by CineRanchero later in the month, if the company didn't totally fuck the whole thing up, which Milt still wasn't certain about. It would be the biggest of the screening events, with music, special guests, and a whole bunch of other crazy crap after the screening, so Wallace and Ronnie were *definitely* not missing that one. Besides, the one nice thing about working with a company like CineRanchero was that, even if they were disorganized as all hell, they were able to pay for flights and lodging for Gil, Milt, his small crew, and their wives.

Originally, CineRanchero's reps had said they were only bringing out Gil and Milt and wives, but Milt had thrown down the gauntlet, telling them they either brought out his guys who had worked their asses off on this thing too, or else his team would take the big event somewhere else. Milt still wasn't sure that was the right way to handle the CineRanchero people, but he didn't want to leave out Wallace and Ronnie.

Meanwhile, Milt would be on his own in LA. He'd have support from old friends and colleagues like Frankly, but ultimately, he was here now in Orange County, about to spend a few days with his mom before heading up to the town that had broken him in half so many times in his early twenties before he'd literally left for greener pastures.

No wonder Gil Gladly hated the place. They didn't call it HelLA for nothing.

While waiting for his baggage to come, Milt felt a twinge of discomfort at having left to California for an entire week so shortly after what had happened with Laney back in Boston.

Before getting into the Lyft on his way to the airport in Boston, Laney had kissed him on the cheek, and her lips had felt frigid. Milt knew then that he might be making a terrible, terrible mistake leaving her behind so soon after—

But goddamn it, he was here now, picking up his two pieces of luggage from off the swirling carousel flanked by a frenzied crowd of raggedy, pajama-wearing passengers.

He received a text from Gil that read, **"Looks online like they haven't sold enough seats at the Portland screening. DISASTER."**

Milt texted back, "Stop worrying about it. It'll be fine. They've sold a fair amount, we've got plenty of time til that one, and the rest will come through via walk-in sales. Try to get some sleep."

"Yeah, right," Gil immediately texted back. "Still haven't slept a wink. CAN'T WAIT FOR THIS ALL TO BE OVER!"

Luckily, the show that would be happening at the McMenamins Theater in Portland, Oregon would be the last fucking one, and it was Milt's hope that they'd draw in some of the crowds of families that might need some reprieve after a busy and bustling Thanksgiving.

Or not.

Milt stopped, slowly breathed in-out, and began walking toward the outer area of the terminal where his mom would be picking him up. He couldn't remember if she still had her white Sentra or not, but he'd find out soon enough.

No email yet from CineRanchero, but now that his notifications were pushing through from the post-flight wave, he also saw—*yesyesYES!*—an email from Unemployment! Though only to say that his last wire deposit *would* be going through at week's end, and that he'd have to attend one more of those ineffectual all-day "job training" seminars they had made him go to.

The one thing Milt had learned at the last all-day training was that Penny from *The Big Bang Theory* really knew how to handle herself during a job interview because she was "just being herself." Evidently, this was the real trick to consider during such an exchange, according to the clip the—ahem—"instructor" showed Milt's "class" three different times for analysis.

The same facilitator used the word "chubster" more than once to describe people she was talking about, and it was equally revelatory to Milt that such language was still considered acceptable in a professional/government setting. But hey, as long as that last check was finally coming through....

Milt thought it ironic that dealing with the bureaucratic vicissitudes of Unemployment, something he had become used to over the years as a freelance writer and producer in need of financial supplement between more substantial gigs (*hey, it was HIS money he had already paid into the system, right?*), could often become a full-time job in and of itself. He wondered what people who had families and real lives and all that did to cope with the circuitous maze of paperwork, phone calls, emails, and training seminars. Milt supposed those people would get jobs and get *off* Unemployment as fast as possible.

Ronnie sent his text next, having made sure to send this one to Milt alone, knowing Wallace wouldn't approve. It was a picture of some adorably hot geek girl he'd been scoping out through their film's Instagram account followers, this time in scantily-clad lubricious Luigi from *Mario Bros.* cosplay.

Mentally rolling his eyes, Milt wondered if he should text Laney again since he hadn't heard back from her after his last *"I love you"* before his plane took off from Boston.

Having collected his baggage—his black wheelie duffel bag with one wheel broken off that he basically had to drag—Milt made his way to the exit, through the crowd, which included the pixie girl from earlier, now hand in hand with the ersatz Seth Rogen. Milt saw throughout the rest of the crowd that there were in fact multiple young men who resembled the bearded, bespectacled, burly comic actor.

Welcome to LA.

The white Sentra pulled up. Milt locked smiles and eyes with his mom, and was glad he hadn't brought any cigarettes with him for a post-flight smoke. Being the good Jewish mama's boy that he was.

CHAPTER 5

Milton's mom was one of the three most important people in his life, along with his uncle (her brother) and grandma (her mother). Whoops, he supposed nowadays also Laney, his wife. Better make that one of *four* most important people.

Milt loved, respected, and on occasion admired his father, especially when he was younger. But Dave Siegel had always been more of a...close friend. Or, to put it in Kurt Cobain parlance, Dave Siegel was less a father, more a dad.

Even when he was younger and still exuded that extra-special admiration a young boy has for his father, if he was being honest with himself, Milt really would go those four or five times a year for a weekend or school vacation to visit Dad's new (and third, keeping up with Mom) wife, Marjorie.

Dad would stay in his office most of the time, working or playing the earliest wave of computer games back in the late eighties. Ten-year-old Milt would be left to his own devices, reading voluminously as he always had, or watching countless LaserDiscs courtesy of his dad's setting him up in the living room before going back upstairs to the office.

Or, as was much more often the case, Milt would spend his visit with Marjorie, who would become like a second mother to him during his preteen years before they drifted apart once he left Southern California on his Steinbeckian cross-country journeying of the past few years prior to his settling down with Laney in Boston.

There *was* something important going on during those infrequent weekend visits to Dad's. Supplementing ten-year-old Milt's salubrious diet of old school Balloon, Dad's choice in LaserDiscs tended to be wholly age-inappropriate ones like *The Terminator, RoboCop, Total Recall,* and various others that ensured Milton Siegel would never be able to embrace *Star Wars, E.T.,* or the other '80s sci-fi blockbusters that were so enjoyed by the rest of Milt's screen-onboarded generation. Frankly, such a cinema diet set Milt up to always be a little...*off* from the bulk of his fellow Gen Y'ers.

Which in turn set Milt up as a wide-eyed observer, a seeker of the new and different.

Yes, Milt had made a documentary about a pop culture subject as conventional as could be imagined. But the doc was nevertheless *strange*. Milt had purposely put it together with the vision of something that would be unique in the nostalgia industry, perhaps to the detriment of marketability. Or perhaps not. Hopefully not.

Gil Gladly was never a typical talk show host. In its earlier days, Balloon had not been a typical television channel. They deserved an atypical doc, not the meandering series of pseudo-celebrity talking heads rambling on and on about the subject, punctuated with 8-bit videogame music throughout and a reve-latory montage at the end; CREDITS. Milt wanted something different. The way he had been raised to see the world, if only indirectly, by his dad.

It was this contrarian mentality that led him to convincing Gil and the rest of Milt's small crew that they should circumvent the traditional indie film festival circuit and establish their own specialized national tour around the country. Milt wanted every aspect of the process of the doc from soup to nuts to be unique. *Special.*

He just hoped his instincts were correct and all of this extra work and overthinking would make for a nice distribution sale in the end.

In fairness, all of this at times did seem a little crazy. Perhaps going against the grain was something better left behind in Milt's fancy-free youth.

Dad never fully understood why Milt had chosen to leave LA, particularly at a time when he was making his way up the local media ladder at a relatively early age, to give in to his wanderlust and live all over the country. Milt once explained to the old man, "You set me up to seek out new frontiers, Dad." Dad replied by blowing raspberries in Milt's face, then suggested they go get some sushi.

"Your dad's got a good heart," Milt's mom, Sara, said while they were enjoying their third drink each and discussing such history as they did so often when they met up every two years or so. "But he was in sales. Business was his life before he retired. He was good at it. It had its own ups and downs, but it was what got him up in the morning, and I think maybe sometimes he's a little confused about what you've chosen to do with *your* life."

Milt nodded vacantly, knowing she was right. Especially since it was almost the exact same thing she had said three or four hundred times before.

"It's *your* life, Milt."

Sara was seventy but could have passed for fifty-five. Maybe younger. Milt always joked that his athletic mom would outlive everyone, including himself, and she had in fact once taken a job over another opportunity simply because the first was closer to a park where she could go on walks and hikes during her lunch hour.

There was a point when he was a kid where it became far too clear that one after another of Milt's friends had a crush on his mom. She wasn't only pretty, but also probably the only single mom in the area.

Everyone else's mom in Born Again Christian Southern Orange County was in a loveless marriage, most having long slept in separate bedrooms from their husbands, the tension in the houses palpable to all the kids who would come and visit for sleepovers and afternoon hangouts. Milt's mom varied from her counterparts by being, well, liberated...and happy.

Milt's dad and Sara had remained friendly after their early-on divorce. More importantly, they had been freed from a marriage that clearly didn't work as well as what would prove to be a lifelong friendship. It was a proposition Milt's childhood friends' parents never allowed themselves to consider.

This had the effect of allowing Milt's mom to be free and happy, his dad to quickly remarry, and Milt to live in a home that all the other kids wanted to come to far more often than their own.

Particularly those boys who had crushes on his mom, which was just about everyone. A factor that could at times be embarrassing. Like the time Milt, maybe around twelve, had to ask his mom if she could please stop wandering around the house in obscenely skimpy cut-off jean shorts and tight white baby t-shirts, both of which left far too little to the imagination, especially the imagination of those boys such as Milt's friends, who were all way too imaginative.

Mom could meanwhile be rather aggravating in how encouraging she was no matter what Milt did or said. She was that breed of Jewish mother (and, as Milt would discover from friends as he grew older, Italian mother) who would support their little princes a little *too* fervently. No matter what.

This was probably one of the reasons Milt never learned to watch his mouth and why he would, then and now, get in trouble for the failure to do so. Especially these days, when he could on rare but steady occasion find himself in the public eye with his articles, books, and film and TV work. Even at the tiny level he was at, there were always blog interviews and podcasts he'd be nudged into doing, and it was becoming more and more difficult to watch what he said. Another "sign of the times," as he would shrug it off as.

Ordering their fourth round of the night, Milt reflected on the fact that Mom had never been a big drinker in the past. But what the hell, they hadn't seen in each other in far too long and they weren't operating heavy machinery or driving anywhere in her "hip" senior community set up as a weirdly all-inclusive, Orwellian city of the future.

Round four arrived, and Sara asked why Milt was slowly shaking his head with a mischievous grin on his face.

"Oh, I was just remembering something funny about you," Milt said. "That time I played a game with you over the phone about whether or not I should go to grad school. No matter what I said—"

"I know," Milt's mom smiled mischievously back. "I would tell you you were right. Go to grad school? Fantastic! You'd make a great academic. Not go to grad school? Yeah! You're too busy and don't have enough money to take that on." Sara sipped her cosmopolitan, beaming. "That's something we Jewish mothers do. When we're not *kvetching* all the time."

"Speaking of *kvetching*," Milton said, "I just noticed they never brought us any water."

Sara took another swig of her cosmopolitan, spilling a few drops on her chin. "The drought."

"What drought?"

"The drought, Milt," Sara said. "The drought this year's been rough. They have to cut back on things like complimentary water at restaurants and bars. That we *can kvetch* about."

"The drought or not being able to drink tap water?"

"Were we *ever* able to drink tap water in Southern California?"

Milt shook his head slightly and leaned back in his chair, looking out to his right to the perfectly tranquil verdant golf course spreading out all around them from the second story of the clubhouse where they enjoyed their nightcaps. The tranquility of the SoCal "winter" desert-y night air breezed over him, and that was when he suddenly sniffed and sat forward, whispering to his mom, "I think I smell pot."

"Yeah," Mom said. "Pretty much everyone smokes here. I told you it was a cool place to spend the last years of my life."

"I think you kept saying 'hip,'" Milt laughed. "But close enough."

"Do you want some? I got some from my neighbor yesterday."

"You're smoking again now too?" Milt asked.

"Yeah, well, I'm pretty much transitioning into retirement mode," Milt's mom said. "I've probably got another five years in me. With the money I'm getting from the divorce settlement with David," (she always made sure to create a distinction between Milt's dad, Dave, and Milt's now-former step-father *David*), "I'll probably only need to work at the rehab clinic until that time, then maybe travel or start my own practice. Who knows?"

She guzzled down the last of her cocktail, and Milt's mind began reeling about the concept of doing a TV show or a movie about a senior community that defied convention, where everyone smoked weed, drank, and embraced life as some kind of Fellini-esque parade of *la dolce vita*.

This was how Milt's mind worked. It was partly why he had so much trouble sleeping. Partly why he *hated* sleeping. It reminded him of a favorite quote of his from—*who was it again?*—either Isaac Asimov or Arthur C. Clarke. When asked in an interview how (let's say Isaac) got so many ideas, the sci-fi pioneer had answered, "No, no. The real question is...how do you make them *stop*?"

A show about a "cool" senior community made sense, Milt reasoned. The hippies of yesteryear were now the senior citizens of today. The same ones gigglingly skulking around the dimly-lit AstroTurf green golf course over which he was looking at that very moment.

"Hmm, that's a good idea," Milt said to himself, slightly inebriated by now.

"What's a good idea?" Sara asked.

"Nothing," Milt answered. "Just thinking."

His phone vibrated and, being programmed properly, he checked it immediately. He looked at the screen.

"Gil again?" Sara asked.

"Yup," Milt said. "He's pissed-off that some new article promoting the film online is focusing on his stutter rather than on his career. He really hates when they do that."

"I thought that's what a lot of the movie was about?" Mom asked. "Isn't that a big part of his story? A guy who overcame his stutter to become a successful talk show host?"

Milt exhaled heavily and nodded as he texted Gil that he shouldn't worry, no one reads that site anymore, and even the most moronic fanboy will see all the misspellings and misinformation on the post anyway. Besides, they should be happy anyone is talking about the film at all. They could use all the press they could get, especially since so few people seemed to care a new movie about Gil was being screened around the country.

"Get some sleep, Gil," Milt texted.

"Yeah, right," was the response as always. **"Easy for YOU to say."**

"The stutter and some of the other things Gil has gone through over the years is a big part of the doc," Milt said, his eyes still on his phone. "But Gil doesn't want those kinds of things to be how he's defined in the eyes of the media and his public, I guess. Sometimes he's up to talk about it, and sometimes he's not. It's complicated. He's...a complicated guy."

"Guess that's why you made a whole movie about him."

Milt looked up, and there was a moment between the two that required no discussion. He turned his phone off and slipped it back into his pocket. "Sorry. It's off. I'll keep it off the rest of the night."

"I bet you turn your phone right back on again in less than five minutes." Milt's mom smiled. "You can't help it. Work comes first. You're just like your father."

CHAPTER 6

Milt smoked a joint with his mom when they got back to her apartment. The occasion marked the first time they had toked up together since she had gone back to grad school, back in the days when he would infrequently come home, surprised to see his former hippie flower-power mom was smoking again.

After Sara received her Master's in psychology, she'd stopped for a while. Apparently, being at this hip senior community had changed her abstemious behavior once more.

Milt meandered to the guest bedroom, pulled out the bed from the couch, and laid down on the uncomfortable, noisy mattress, trying his best not to spook himself with fantasies about all the terrible things Laney could be doing while he was away for the week.

Regardless of the drinks, the weed, and the late-night neuroticism, Milt woke up at his usual time, 7:30 a.m. His body never seemed to be put off by the time difference when he traveled. He began his day with a breakfast courtesy of Mom (when had *she* learned to cook?) on her way out the door to work.

By 8:00 a.m., Milt was receiving texts and emails from everyone about the screenings ahead. There was also a litany of progressively degenerate, drunken ramblings from Silverstein about how much he wanted to kill himself over how awful it was at the *Boston Star*.

Milt didn't have too much trouble ignoring such histrionics, but was sincerely concerned about Silverstein's nosebleeds from stress. Some of the pictures sent were pretty horrifying.

Lars von Trier, eat your heart out.

Between getting some more work done on his MC Phliphlop autobiography and watching the Lady Gaga documentary on Netflix (ugh, why not: part of the job to keep up with all the pop culture palaver), he answered his emails as swiftly as possible.

There had been one, at long last, from Sally Miranda over at CineRanchero.

Sally was the same age as Milt, thirty-six. But from her Facebook page, she looked a lot older. She looked like a mom. Not Milt's mom. Sally Miranda had the face and body of a *normal* mom. Like the weathered, put-upon moms of the other kids Milt had grown up with in Southern Orange County.

It immediately made Milt uncomfortable for some reason he couldn't put his finger on that from their early Skypes, it was clear Sally Miranda styled her hair in a way that (intentionally?) mimicked that of Daryl Hannah's Pris in the immortal sci-fi masterpiece *Blade Runner*, one of the many LaserDiscs Milt had watched over and over again in his precocious preteen years thanks to his father.

It was as though Sally was forever wearing a white fright wig that had been teased-out, almost like a female Andy Warhol or an albino version of young Uma Thurman's Mia Wallace in *Pulp Fiction*.

Milt had long been friends and worked with misfits, though, and certainly he wasn't exactly a chiseled work of art himself. As with so much else over the year, he had shrugged Sally's hairdo off as something not worth thinking about. Maybe, like him, she was the *good* kind of crazy.

As long as she got the work done.

"So, guess what?" Sally's email began. She wrote her emails as though Milt and she were forever embroiled in an ongoing conversation. Her email style was in fact that of a "Hey, guys!!!" blogger. **"Because they say pre-sales haven't been as good as they had hoped, CineRanchero is cutting the budget. This means there will be only one show instead of the two back-to-back ones we had been planning. Not a biggie."**

Milt shook his head slowly, as though Sally Miranda could see him. Even though she obviously could *not* see him, Milt for some reason kept the nodding subtle.

Gil would see this as a biggie. A really *big* biggie. A total clusterfuck. One of many Milt and Gil had been dealing with when it came to the massive CineRanchero event set for Chicago later in the month.

Milt and Gil cared very deeply about how the tour came off, and now Sally was telling him that CineRanchero had indeed been doing such a piss-poor job promoting the event that there weren't enough pre-sales to merit the back-to-back screenings Milt and Gil had already been advertising for more than six months.

To add fuel to the freak-out fire, Milt saw a second email had come from Sally while he was languishing over how he would explain the scheduling change to Gil who was already in disaster-preparation mode about screenings not coming together as smoothly as they'd hoped.

The second email explained that Sally would unfortunately not be able to be there after the screening to help run the various details of the live event aspect of the presentation. But, she promised, they would be in good hands with two volunteer interns from a local community college who would be filling in.

Milt closed his eyes. He did not want to make the call he'd inevitably need to make to Gil about this…and soon. He could hear Lady Gaga crying in the documentary onscreen that he'd earlier minimized while reading his emails.

Milt opened his eyes and read on about the "awesome" interns who would be helping out after the screening: **"They're both *huge* fans of Gil's. Maybe even as big as you and me!"** There followed a short PS about how bad Sally felt that she hadn't gotten in touch with him sooner, but the fires in her area that had been raging all month after two freak tornadoes were making it difficult for her to be as focused as she wanted to be on this project.

Christ. What was he supposed to do with *that* information?

He was gobsmacked by the emotional conflict. Maybe it wasn't Teddy Miller but *he* who was the autistic one.

Well, maybe there's enough room on the spectrum for both me and Teddy Miller.

Then again, maybe it wasn't Milt. Sally had been screwing up so much of how the event was coming together for months. There were times when he didn't even understand what it was she was doing as "producer" that he wasn't having to do himself. Yet, of the two of them, she was the one getting paid by CineRanchero!

Then again *again,* Sally's neighborhood was on fire. So, how angry could he really be at her during this tragic time?

Before he could reconcile his combating thoughts and emotions, he saw an email from Dillon Rogers, with a subject heading in panicky caps, punctuated by an endless string of exclamation points.

Uh, oh.

"**Turns out….**" Dillon's email began.

What "turned out" was the fact that Dillon hadn't been receiving any of the emails that Milt had been sending to the budding rock star and musical collaborator on a small handful of pilots that Gil was always trying to help his younger colleagues get off the ground (without success; but Dillon *had* made for a terrific interviewee in the documentary).

The problem, Dillon went on to say, in not having received these emails was that he hadn't bought his plane tickets to the CineRanchero show where he was supposed to be leading a local studio band for the promised live music segment of their event.

Dillon hadn't realized that by agreeing to perform two of his songs that were starting to go viral on YouTube, his expenses would be reimbursed and not taken care of outright. And since it was clearly too late to buy plane tickets that would be cheap enough for him to purchase, he *regrettably* wouldn't be able to make it.

He explained that he really, really, really, really wanted to come perform but that he didn't have enough money to supplement what he was supposed to have already spent buying cheaper tickets three months earlier. He had just dumped his life savings into a new album he'd be dropping in the new year.

He apologized at the bottom of the email, and Milt immediately pulled out his phone to text Dillon back.

Like what seemed to be just about everyone else he was working with on the tour except for Gil and sometimes Wallace, Dillon would never answer a call. But he was a diligent text message responder. Most of the time.

"Hey, man, just got your email and gotta say that I'm really worried about this!" Milt texted to Dillon, who responded seconds later.

"Yeah, I know. It sucks."

"If I somehow figure out a way to expand the budget a little, would you be able to make it?"

"No, sorry. Even a little wouldn't make a difference. I'm actually a bit worried about how I am going to pay rent at the end of the month."

"What about your song that's blowing up on Spotify? I heard it sampled in a Dunkin' Donuts commercial. That's got to be good."

"I'm not going to get paid anything for that project for another six months. Fucking lawyers, agents, and contracts, man!"

Milt slammed the table with his fist, jostling his computer screen and knocking over some of the papers he was going over for his ghostwriting project.

He leaned back in his chair, took a deep breath, and slowly let it out.

Okay. Let's solve this problem.

Dillon and he kept texting back and forth, with Milt reminding Dillon that CineRanchero had already been advertising the event on their socials and main website and (hopefully?) in some kind of local press. In the advertisements, it was made clear that the up-and-coming Dillon Rogers was going to be playing a short set as part of the proceedings.

Dillon *had* to be there. There *had* to be something that could be done. Right?

Milt went so far as eviscerating any kind of personal sense of propriety he had here in dealing with someone he kind of admired, was slightly intimidated by, and that—most importantly—he didn't really know very well, and asked Dillon if he could possibly hit up his old drummer who had been touring with Taylor Swift the last seven months for a small loan the production would pay back as soon as possible.

Dillon texted back that both Savion *and* he were in the poorest, most-nearly-bankrupt time of their entire lives. No matter what kind of modestly successful projects they were working on at that moment, neither was seeing a single penny. Not yet. Not for a while.

"Shit," Milt texted finally, resigned to the reality that Dillon Rogers would not be playing the CineRanchero event and that this hiccup could so easily turn into perfect fodder for online assholes. That meant bad press for the film; and worse, Gil Gladly as a brand, which Milt had indirectly been put in charge of protecting for far too long now.

Sure, the outlets speaking about the tour and the film were few and far between. But Milt knew how that community worked. He had been a part of it himself from time to time, especially in his twenties when he could afford to do so, when he didn't have quite the responsibilities he had now (read: Laney), and had to take on projects promising more substantial dividends.

As soon as something went *wrong*—something like a promised indie rocker not showing up after everyone paid way too much money for a ticket to a special screening of the Gil Gladly documentary—there'd be a deluge of so-called "articles" on what would be reported upon as a total mess, a disaster, with words like "backlash" in the clickbaitable titles. This would be punctuated by interviews with the hordes of fans who had planned on using the scant vacation time they had from work to fly out to Chicago and experience the full show as guaranteed.

Would these bloggers talk about the film and tour beforehand to help promote the goddamn thing and let the fans know what they could get in on seeing? No. Would the bloggers eagerly post about what a disaster the thing would be if Dillon Rogers didn't show up as promised? Of course.

Welcome to "the future of journalism."

It was time for Milt to hit up Gil Gladly, who was thankfully old enough to answer his phone.

Milt started dialing, breathing deeply. He thought about how he had been doing his best to keep Gil guarded from clusterfucks like these as the tour continued to come together. Beyond Gil's anxiety, the sexagenarian had his recent heart problems to keep under control, problems that Gil had had to keep out of the news for fear of appearing far too old and too frail to ever be brought back in front of the camera where he so desperately wanted to be again.

There it was again. The bulk of bloggers couldn't care less that the man was touring around with a new film, something that he and a cadre of young, hardworking, creative people had actually *produced*; but as soon as the same online scavengers caught wind that the old dude might croak because of a heart problem, they'd be all over it.

Without so much as a hello, Gil picked up and told Milt that he only had five minutes. Milt timorously revealed the Dillon Rogers problem to Gil. Milt could hear Gil's astonishment at the very idea Dillon was more or less broke. Milt did his best to sneak in something quick about how that was the kind of thing he himself and *everyone* in their bracket in the creative field were coping with these days, but Gil went right into how he didn't really want Dillon to play the show anyway.

WHAT?

Milt calmed down for a second and stood up, pushing his chair back with his butt. He began pacing nervously, clutching the phone to his ear like it was a seashell whose plangent ocean sounds he was trying to more closely hear.

He did what he could to explain to Gil about the whole advertising and "backlash" concern to no avail. Gil had to go and, besides, he said, *"They're coming to see me, not Dillon. His head's been getting a little too big since the Dunkin' Donuts commercial anyway."*

Gil clicked off. Milt was fucked. He'd get blamed for this. Gil would forget he had said this, as would happen from time to time in such situations. When everyone started ruthlessly attacking the film and tour, Gil would be unspeakably pissed at Milt for allowing it to happen.

Milt was also growing slightly alarmed at the ease and frequency with which Gil could so matter-of-factly offer his clandestine, often snarky commentary on other people around him. For a brief moment, Milt wondered what Gil told people about *him*.

But no time for that now. Milt *did* have to admit the amount of dirt Gil claimed to have on Matthew Broderick (for whatever weird reason) was startlingly impressive.

There had to be a way to expand the budget and make it work. He called Sally Miranda. He needed to actually *talk* to her. They needed to exchange words, not emails. He needed her to pick up the goddamn phone.

Her voicemail was a cheery, typical greeting followed by a statement about being reached more easily over email and text.

Knowing it wouldn't matter in the end, Milt didn't bother leaving a voicemail and instead texted Sally to see if she could talk. To Milt's great amazement and slowly ascending hope, Sally actually texted back. She claimed to be in a meeting and said they could text but not long. Milt asked if she could take a moment away from her meeting so they could actually talk; he'd keep it brief. Sally said she couldn't and that he needed to just text her.

Milt told her about the Dillon Rogers kerfuffle and that they needed to work out some plan, especially since CineRanchero itself had already paid for the instrument rentals and engineer for the show. To do so right, he would need to *talk* with her one-on-one.

She suggested emailing her; she couldn't keep texting because she was at the meeting and someone else was emailing her right then anyway and she had to answer that right away.

Sally ended the conversation by saying she would do her best to get back in touch with him soon. **"I PROMISE this time,"** she texted.

CHAPTER 7

"**I**'m pooing right now," was what Milt heard Melody Winston say over the phone.

"Thank you for your brave honesty," Milt said, his cell phone cradled between his right cheek and shoulder. "You're a regular Lena Dunham."

He was concurrently typing up an email and finishing a brief conversation with Melody, his ex-girlfriend.

Why his ex-girlfriend Melody would pick up the phone while she was shitting was a question he didn't bother asking her. He knew Melody quite well; Melody did things like this.

She would sometimes pick up the phone at her work and whisper in conspiratorial concentration camp tones, *"I can't talk right now; I need to call you back later."*

In those instances, Milt would always ask himself why the hell she would bother picking up the phone at all. Why not just let the call roll over to voicemail? Why not just text back, **"Sorry at work can't talk hit me up later"** like the rest of the people in her generation?

As was the case with a large number of interviewees he had spoken with over the years for his various articles and documentary projects (hence his relationship, such that it was, with Gil Gladly that had led to his nudging the man into allowing

78

him to make a doc), Milt had a peculiar tendency of staying in touch with his ex-girlfriends.

Milt had visited Melody once or twice over the years when she lived in Queens with her four hateful roommates and one recalcitrant toilet. Milt would on occasion have some sort of business or the indication of business in New York City, and he would either stay with Melody or would somehow devise a way for her to stay with him in whatever apartment he'd find on Craigslist or, in more recent years, Airbnb.

They usually shared a good evening together.

"I really enjoy my poos," Melody said, without a hint of childishness to her proclamation. She meant it.

"Ugh," Milt said. "This just keeps getting worse and worse, the longer I stay on talking to you."

Melody laughed uproariously on the other end. Though she never cackled, there was always something decidedly witchy about Melody's laughter. He could see in his mind's eye the uncannily wide smile on her face, eyes closed, and huge mouth laughing loudly. All this while she was on the shitter.

Melody had a kind of evil stepmother disposition. Something definitely prim and proper, almost sophisticated and patrician, yet with a twinge of malevolence about it. Like she was always getting ready to tsk you for some heinous wrong she believed you'd committed.

While Milt couldn't quite put his finger on it, it made sense in this incident that she was seemingly getting off on announcing to him that she was defecating at the very same time they were having a conversation.

For some reason, he couldn't get off the phone with her.

Melody was probably Milt's favorite ex-girlfriend. The one he had talked to and seen the most over the years. His guidance was often needed to help Melody out with whatever melodramatic soap opera situation she had gotten herself into *this* time.

There was no question Melody was doing much better now that she was a little older. She was only five or six years younger than Milt, but up until maybe a year or two ago, he had long felt that she was far younger than that.

Melody was always getting herself into dramatic scenarios, a kind of kid sister who constantly needed rescuing, especially back in her days living in Astoria. It was a breeding ground for young people like Melody and Milt, creatives trying to find their way in New York City...but ending up in, yes, Astoria.

"Milty, two nights ago I woke up in the apartment of some guy I didn't know, wearing his t-shirt," Melody told him over coffee when he'd been out there producing a short film about talking mice a few years back. "I'm not sure what he did, but he was asleep next to me when I got up, and I ran out of there before he woke up. Should I take his shirt back to him?"

"Not *again*, Melody!"

He felt confident being able to talk to her this way, at this point being more like a snotty older brother who could make her laugh like a witch, but who could also speak with her bluntly and treat her like a full-grown adult often making indecorous choices.

Milt felt a strange, familial duty to be as forthright with Melody as possible, considering all she otherwise had was a tiny coterie of minor fair-weather friends at the time, none of whom would ever dare say such a thing to her for fear of seeming insensitive or potentially opening themselves up to some kind of nasty statement made about their callousness via Melody's long-running blog, pieces of which would sometimes get picked up by lower-rank female millennial-oriented blogs.

This last idiosyncrasy was something Melody stopped engaging in right before she left New York in disgust about "the person I was becoming," as she had phrased it. Part of which revelation involved one of her pieces being so summarily distorted by the, *hmmm,* "editors" at Univision-owned Sweetie-Pies.net that she vowed from then on to keep her judgmental views on her dwindling group of friends to herself.

Since having left New York, Melody stopped blogging alto-gether and focused more on bettering herself and working on her career as a communications director for nonprofit organiza-tions, like the one she had found a few hours outside of Portland, Oregon where her mom and sister separately lived, and where she had been raised in her broken, dysfunctional home that helped forge her into the fucked-up person she was trying not to be any longer upon entering her thirties.

"What are you doing right now, Milty?" Melody asked, this time purposely intoning a childish timbre to her voice. *"Why aren't you paying total attention to me?"*

"I'm working," Milt said. "I'm always working. I'm trying to get all this shit handled for the tour, and I can't deal with some of these people much longer."

"Awww, poor Milty..." Melody said. Then, *"Whoops!"*

"What?" Milt asked.

"I farted, and I thought you might have heard me," she confessed.

"Christ, you really are disgusting," Milt said. "Dunham has *nothing* on you!"

"Awww, no, you love me," Melody said. *"You love when I'm pooing and farting."*

"Oy, sick," Milt said. "You're the most revolting ex-girlfriend I have."

"I'll put the phone up to my butt cheek the next time I feel one coming out, okay, Milty-Poo?" Melody chirped.

"Please don't," Milt said. "Hey, so are you going to be around when we're in Portland for the tour? I'd really like to see you. We've got a screening at McMenamins."

"Ohhh, we'll see," Melody answered, sounding adult, officious. It was as though she would have to "check her schedule" and maybe see about "fitting him in." No irony, except of course, the dramatic kind.

How quickly she could vacillate between goofy neoteny and the cold harridan act, Milt thought, quietly proud of the observation and his mental use of the word "harridan."

His neck was starting to hurt. He had completely stopped typing his email to Louis Bradley, his old friend and fellow filmmaker/writer helping him produce the upcoming Portland screening, which would be the terminus of their brief nation-wide preview tour..

He switched ears before saying, "Look, I know you want to see me and I want to see you too. It's been forever since we've hung out. You can grab some coffee or a dinner with me."

"Are you paying?"

"Duh," he said. "When have I ever *not* paid?"

"When we were still together," Melody laughed. *"You* never *had any money back then."*

"Yeah, because you were always making us go to sushi and shit, which costs a fucking fortune in New York!" Milt fired back.

"Oh, Milty-Poo," Melody cooed.

"Eww," Milt said.

"What?"

"That time I *did* hear you," he said. "I heard a plunk. You're sick."

"You love me."

"Yeah, yeah, just do what you can to be around when we have the screening at the end of the month, okay? It'll be a way for you to escape your mom and sister after having to endure Thanksgiving with them."

"Why do you want to see me so bad, anyway?" Melody asked, inevitably bringing up, *"Aren't you married now?"*

"Laney knows I still talk to some of my exes. You're not the only one."

"Ohhhh," Melody said. *"I'm not? Holy macanoli!"*

"Yeah, you can add that to your fucking blog," he said. "Just make sure to add the only reason you know 'Holy macanoli' is because I forced you to watch all those episodes of *Punky Brewster* when we were still together."

Melody laughed, and this time it *did* sound a bit like a cackle.

"I still have one of the VHS tapes you left at my apartment in Astoria," Melody said. *"You're right, they're better to watch all wonky and second-generation like that than the remastered episodes online or on DVD."*

"Totally," Milt agreed. "Plus, you get the commercials that were on back then as an added bonus. The Slip 'N Slide one is a classic."

Milt thought it best to pull back. He knew that Melody was the kind of girl—courtesy of her rather tenebrous upbringing—who had a tendency to recoil from advances. She preferred those who played hard to get, whether friend or lover. Or, as Milt had noticed over the years, even parent. There was nothing that made Melody complain about her mom or divorced, mostly estranged father as when they would actually attempt to reach out to her in the rarely loving way.

She had presented a valid point, though. Milt had to admit that. Why *was* he so fixated on seeing Melody when he'd be out in Portland for the screening? He *was* married, sure. And though over the years they'd been broken-up (even while in other relationships) they'd messed around a bit when he'd be visiting Queens, she'd never let him actually fuck her anyway. Not really.

Damn it, he *was* married. No matter what had been going on between Laney and he, he needed to calm down about all of this.

And yet, there was also an element of not backing down. The same drive that made him so adept as a producer and hustler in the creative realm was that which throttled him forward to accomplish and complete whatever mission he was on, including getting an ex-girlfriend of his to meet up with him even if it *was* just for coffee...or whatever.

It was a sense of not wanting to be rejected by Melody. Or at least not *feeling* as though he was being rejected. Who was Melody Winston, after all? Some nutty girl he'd met while writing for a bullshit clickbait content farm back during one of his tempestuous stints in New York? Some girl he'd dated on and off through an even more tempestuous "relationship" of mostly drinking heavily, tracking down and doing coke, fighting, eating food way out of their price range, and fucking their brains out til all hours of the night?

That was who Melody Winston was. Wasn't she?

And here Milt was, coming out to Portland—*the* Portland, like from the TV show!! Where the music came from!! Where everything was "craft" this and "artisanal" that!!—for a screening of his damn *movie* that he'd spent the last two years making through sheer panic and fervent will and calling in every single fucking favor from every single fucking person he'd ever met from all over the fucking country.

"Milty-Poooooooooo, where'd you go?"

"I was just thinking for a second," Milt said.

"Me too." Melody let out a loud, gut-wrenching fart, followed by a tremendous, truly impressive belch. *"Fuck, I'm so gassy!"*

"Yo, I really gotta finish up this email to Louis," he said. "Just do what you can to meet up. Or not. I'd really like to see you and I'd really like you to see the film. But it's up to you."

"Ohhhhkay," she practically sang. *"I'll do what I can. Say hi to Laney for me. Hey, why isn't she coming?"*

"We can't afford it."

"See?"

"I'm getting there," Milt said. "Don't worry. I've got stuff coming together."

"Yeah, yeah, you always do," Melody's voice intoned from the phone, dripping with syrupy sarcasm.

"Okay, love you."

"Love you too, byyyyye," Melody said with a toddler-like burp.

Melody hung up and Milt went back to finishing his email to Louis Bradley, asking him if the two bands they had playing the after-party of the Portland screening needed anything else aside from the riders he'd received two weeks earlier.

Louis immediately emailed back that he was handling it all for now, everyone at McMenamins was very excited about the upcoming event, and asked if Gil knew if the local TV station that was going to be hosting the event and broadcasting a live feed from the screening, Q&A, after-party concert, and all was merely "sponsoring" the event in name only, or if they were actually going to be putting any money in.

"You know," Louis had added at the end of his email, **"so I can let the bands know if they're going to be getting anything aside from a cut of the door."**

There was absolutely no way that Milt felt comfortable hitting up Gil Gladly about this right now. Despite the fact only Gil himself would know what the deal was here.

Then again, as Milt was getting used to throughout this whole quixotic enterprise, it was just as likely Gil didn't know the answer to Louis' question, even if he *had* been the one who had gotten WTDM involved in the event, courtesy one of his many former proteges who was now an assistant programming director there.

Either way, it was not something Milt wanted to deal with right now. Just as he did not want to deal with the fact that he had also seen an email come through from Ronnie Clark. The email had been sent to not only Milt, but to all the people involved in the CineRanchero screening, including Sally Miranda.

An email from Ronnie that could conceivably put a kibosh on the whole goddamn thing in Chicago.

Fuck!

For some reason, Ronnie had taken it upon himself to tell the folks at CineRanchero to provide him with all manner of props and assistance for a new "brilliant" idea he had had that would make the event that much more "spellbinding" and "fantastical for fans and newbies coming to the film alike."

Oy.

Milt shook his head, called Ronnie, upbraided him appropriately without sounding too much like an asshole, and emailed everyone to say there had been a communication breach and that they of course did not need to suddenly revamp the entire event a few days in advance solely because one of the crew members on the film had some grand flight of fancy about a whole other direction it could take...that would also make the whole thing twice as expensive to produce than originally budgeted.

Milt went so far as to text Sally, apologizing to her for the email mistake. Much to his surprise, she texted him right back:

"NO WORRIES! SEE YOU IN CHICAGO!"

He exhaled deeply, closed his eyes, and wondered if this would be a good time to meditate. Or perhaps go to the gym in his mom's Orwellian all-inclusive senior community. Or perhaps get some more much-needed work done on his ghostwriting project. His deadline was approaching before the holidays and he did need that next part of the advance that would come with delivery of draft one. And he needed it *soon*.

But no. He was exhausted.

He would do no more work. He would not go to the gym. He knew this to be true. He would head to the one bathroom his mom had in her one-story two-bedroom apartment, jerk off to Melody's fabulous ass in his mind's eye (without the farting... most likely), take a shower, and of course, get ready to go see Frankly, who was likely on his way from Costa Mesa even now.

Milt always loved jerking off to Melody's fabulous ass, what with its delicious and pristine half-eaten red apple tattoo on its right side. Something about that tat. He had seen a broken heart on another girl's ass he used to bang. He had seen the cliché cherry-red kissy lips in various porns before. But Melody's half-eaten apple was...*ripe*.

Yes, after another in a long line of blurred, seemingly dream-like days on the job, the adventure was at last about to truly commence. Milton Siegel knew exactly how he would spend a miniscule but essential tranche of that final, hard-earned Unemployment payment.

He couldn't wait for Frankly to arrive and take him away for a night they'd both wholeheartedly enjoy.

CHAPTER 8

Milt shooed away the offering of an extravagantly well-formed lit joint in Frankly's one hand while he drove his dented silver Honda Civic with the other. Milt was busy being an emotional punching bag for Gil Gladly's fulminating venting on the other end of the cell phone wedged to his right ear.

"C-c-c-can you b-b-b-b-elieve it?" Gil erupted through the cell phone speaker.

Milt glanced over at Frankly, leaning back in his seat comfortably as though in a Hawaiian resort lounge chair, poolside. Frankly had one hand on the wheel, the other clutching the smoldering joint, the only light aside from the *Matrix*-green cockpit illumination of the car dashboard in the near darkness as they sped forth on the traffic-less 405 North.

Milt tried to lock eyes with Frankly, but his compatriot's eyes were on the road and maybe veering off to somewhere else altogether. One never knew with Frankly, particularly when he was stoned.

"Yeah," Milt finally answered back to Gil on the phone. "That totally sucks. I can't believe they keep doing this to you. You're right, Gil. Yup."

"I m-m-m-mean, they call me up, they w-w-w-w-waste my time, they have m-m-m-m-m-m-me come all the f-f-f-f-f-f-fuck the w-w-w-w-way out to fucking New York, f-f-f-f-f-flake on the

89

m-m-m-meeting…twice…and…and—th-th-th-then finally have the goddamn meeting, no one is there except for f-f-f-fucking Rollins, and I know h-h-h-h-h-he has no idea what he's talking about. It's not l-l-l-l-l-like he can do anything at that fucking p-p-p-p-place anyway. They get me to consult on this new sh-sh-sh-sh-ow they're trying to do which is basically just KidTalk all over again…and n-n-n-now they're back to not answering my c-c-c-c-alls again when I ch-ch-ch-check in about it! Th-th-th-thanks for w-w-w-w-w-w-w-w-wasting m-m-my f-f-f-fucking t-t-t-time, motherfuckers!"*

Frankly looked over, somewhat interested, hearing bits and pieces of the rant, with Milt doing his best to communicate with his eyes, *Please stop smoking the joint, you know how much it makes me freak out in the car on the freeway,* to no avail. Instead of responding to Milt's telepathic entreaty, Frankly looked back to the road, scrunching down in his seat to allow himself to lean back a little further as he drove on.

"I don't really understand why you bother trying to deal with Balloon at all, Gil," Milt said, trying to sound practical without being out of his depth. Gil had practically *built* Balloon back in the eighties during his long reign, and so who was Milt to consult on how the minor mogul should deal with his old employer and near lifetime frenemy?

"What the fuck is he talking about?" Frankly stage-whispered without turning his neck.

Milt shook his head violently—*Please don't talk, please don't say anything, please don't reveal that anyone else is with me right now while Gil Gladly friggin' berates an entire billion-dollar global television network that, by the way, we all grew up on back when it was still good and the man practically ran the place.*

Frankly smirked that Frankly smirk of his, shook his head subtly, had a hit of his joint, and applied more pressure to the accelerator.

The truth was that what Gil was talking about was nothing new. This kind of exchange had been happening on and off between Gil Gladly and Balloon throughout the entire time Milt had known him, which was going on seven years now.

Why did Gil do it to himself?

Milt had written about and interviewed countless people from the "old days" at Balloon, the earlier administration, executives, show creators, and stars. This was how he'd met Gil Gladly in the first place.

Milt knew things about Balloon that no one knew, one of those things being that the network was a very different place than what it had been when it first started.

It had at one time been an art haven of sorts. It was once a play place for creative, young, innovative, wild, crazy, cartoonish people...like Gil Gladly. A place where they could run amuck and do whatever they wanted, because there wasn't much money, which meant there wasn't much risk, but also that there was a whole lot of needful, resourceful innovation going on in those small offices and studio sets where people made desks out of cardboard boxes and props in the executive offices.

These factors colluded into the production of what many believed to be some of the most unique, vibrant, irreverent, and strange children's programming ever seen...before, whoops, they accidentally did *too* well of a job and everyone who made the shit got bought off and rocketed off to their personal fortunes at larger, long-established "real" TV channels. No more kid stuff for them!

Meanwhile, back at Balloon, in came the new administration to fill in the staffing gap that was left, and by the mid-nineties, the channel had gone from being the "anti" to the "it."

When Milt would get asked in interviews why he never bothered talking to people who worked at Balloon now, he always pivoted with his pat response: "That would be like writing about your favorite Chinese restaurant you used to go to all the time with your family when you were a kid thirty years later now that it's an *Italian* restaurant. Same building, different owners, menu, and kitchen staff."

And the owners, menu, and kitchen staff that came to Balloon over the span of its later years? They were *not* fun, were *not* innovative or strange or irreverent. They were business. They were scared of rocking the boat. They were scared of losing their jobs. They came up with saccharine, antiseptic programming that at best merely mirrored previous successes, like this show they were developing in part with Gil, sort of, that was basically a reboot of *KidTalk*. At worst, the later programming on Balloon was the kind of baffling pabulum that the network had been trying to countervail in its "classic" days.

Nothing new here.

Even as a kid, Milt was precocious enough to read the trades, biographies, and autobiographies. It wasn't enough for him to watch *Looney Tunes* like the rest of the kids he knew. He had to read *Chuck Amuck*, the story of renowned series director Chuck Jones.

Milt had long understood how these kinds of things went: once again that simple and inexorable cycle of pop culture entities like Balloon, punk rock, hip-hop, and *Saturday Night Live.*

For some reason Milt didn't understand, Gil Gladly still thought he could fight the ineluctability here and find those at the current Balloon who would actually listen to what he had to say about remembering to make these shows special, weird, different. As though they cared about the content, and not just the commerciality. Gil was going off of tradition, gut feeling, and word of mouth.

Yet Balloon would never swerve from their hidebound analysis of paid-for stats and *data. "According to Twitter..."*

Milt thought of John Henry, the mythical folk hero who had tried to prove man could still defy machine, winning in the end but losing his life along the way.

Why was Gil still fighting so indignantly with the network to get back there? Gil knew what they had become.

Then again, Milt did know Gil, who often operated on a volatile cocktail of stubbornness and pride, hadn't exactly endeared himself publicly to the current administration of Balloon.

A quick Google search of Gil led directly to two kinds of entries: those in which Gil horribly berated the network to anyone who would listen, and in which he was essentially begging the channel to bring back *KidTalk.*

This Chad Rollins character was the latest exec over there with whom Gil had been locking horns. Rollins was one of Balloon's many new "development directors" (sometimes "programming supervisors," sometimes "directors of programming/development"; the titles changed more frequently over there than the rapid turnover, as the channel continued to hemorrhage money for staff who were experienced as opposed to simply subsidized by Mom and Dad right out of NYU, UCLA, or USC).

The tenuous relationship Gil had with Rollins exemplified the bipolar love-hate relationship Gil had with the network as a whole. There were times when Gil really *hated* Rollins, and would make that hatred clear. A little too loudly in public places, Milt worried.

Other times, Rollins was, according to Gil, "The only one th-th-th-there wh-wh-who kn-kn-knows what h-h-h-he's d-d-d-doing."

More than once, Gil had brought up the fact that Chad Rollins also happened to be one of the few black people at Balloon. But even Gil wouldn't dare bring that up in public. Milt didn't have to worry about *that* hornet's nest.

The network employee pool was and always had been filled to the brim with women, but it still wasn't quite the diverse population that made for such a hot topic when it came to media/entertainment/tech companies over the past five or ten years.

In those rare instances when Gil would talk in this way, Milt would chalk it up to Gil's sense of Rollins being something of a so-called "diversity hire," someone who would make the otherwise blindingly lily-white Balloon appear more colorful in the public eye.

Milt's phone vibrated and he pulled his phone away from his ear, checking the screen to see who it was. Jessica Chen was hitting him up with screenshots from her contact sheet of new headshots she was hoping to bring to the premiere of his Gil Gladly documentary.

He saw he apparently hadn't felt the vibrations from the slew of texts waiting for him from Silverstein complaining about the job, nosebleeds, Shitsmelled, life.

Milt couldn't help but scoff. How very Victorian. A thread of his ectoplasmic snot flew onto the scratched-up glovebox. Frankly turned his head to Milt, said nothing while shooting daggers with his eyes, took a drag of his joint, and turned back to the black void of spot-lit road ahead.

Milt leaned forward to wipe the glistening snail-line of snot from the black glovebox with his right sleeve before leaning back into his seat and placing the phone against his ear once more. "Gil, look, this isn't something you should be worrying about right now. We have the LA screening and that needs to be the one thing we're thinking about. Don't worry about Rollins or Balloon. They do this shit to you all the time. Try to let it go. For now, okay?"

"Yeah?" Gil said, winsomely timid, almost imploring Milt to give him the security he needed so often during such calls.

"Yeah. Look, we're about to have this huge screening at this great spot in LA, where you will be fucking surrounded by all of your fans who can't wait to see you, meet you, get autographs from and pictures with you, see your film, and learn things about you they always wanted to know. This is a good thing. This is a good time. We all love you, Gil. Screw Rollins and Balloon. Who needs 'em?"

"Yeah!" Gil said. *"Who needs 'em? Fuck 'em! Piece of shit network going down the toilet anyway. Ticket sales are doing better for the other screenings?"*

"Uhh," Milt sputtered, taken aback by Gil's car-crash timing. He turned to Frankly, who was looking right at him with that Frankly smirk, clearly having overheard this part. "Uhhh, yeah. We'll be fine."

"Fine? Or sold-out?"

"Uhhh," looking back at Frankly who was somehow driving with one hand, holding his now nearly extinguished tiny joint with the other, and looking right at Milt as though expressing nonverbally, telegraphing, *Just tell him the truth, you asshole.* "I told you already, walk-ins should fill in the gaps. There's still time left before the ones after LA. I gotta run, but do your best to get some sleep, okay? I know you hate when I bring it up, but you gotta take care of yourself with your heart and everything."

"Why? If I die, the cost of the doc goes up significantly, and you and your crew will be famous."

Frankly nodded his head, smiling.

"Shit, Gil, I didn't think of that before!" Milt said. "Never mind. Go run a marathon and get in a fucking street fight!"

"You got it, fook-fah-shay," Gil said. *"Just make sure those sons-of-bitches at CineRanchero start doing a better job getting the word out. That one has to go big or we'll all be dead. See you Sunday, you crazy schmuck."*

No goodbye, of course. Conversation over.

"Jesus," Frankly said, opening his window and flinging the infinitesimal bit of paper and ash out the window before pressing the button to roll it back up. "Is he *completely* nuts?"

"He's been joking that anyone who's wondering that should watch the film," Milt said. "I'm telling you, man, all that counts is the movie is good. We made some last-minute tweaks since the last cut I sent you. Right in time before the DCP conversion, thank God."

"Yeah, like what?"

"Some minor tweaks here and there, some stuff none of us really liked but no one who's seen the last version will notice. Ronnie and I flew out to Jersey to shoot a few more interviews with Gil. Wild stuff. Got that fucking dude to fucking *cry*."

"Buhhhhhhht...I mean, is he *nuts*? Or not?" Frankly asked while Milt peered out the closed window to the passing buildings beyond the freeway, illuminated squares of offices blurring in the distance.

"Everyone is nuts," Milt said. "You're nuts, I'm nuts, Gil's nuts. He's human. He stutters. He's got this heart shit he's been dealing with lately. He's getting old. He has his family stuff. He's not a cartoon character, even if he seemed like one for all those years on *KidTalk*."

"He seemed pretty normal at the comic-con in San Francisco," Frankly noted.

Gil had been on pretty good behavior there. He had turned on the juice and became the character the crowds remembered from TV. The character who really wasn't a "person," who wasn't a three-dimensional, flawed, typical, fucked-up human being like everyone else. He was Gil Gladly from *KidTalk*.

It had been a summer ago, the thirty-fifth anniversary of the show. Balloon had put together the whole event at the San Francisco Comic-Con that Milt, Wallace, and Ronnie had gone to in order to acquire some behind-the-scenes coverage for the documentary.

Milt had known he'd need some extra help, someone to run around getting releases from people they shot and interviewed, someone to help as a kind of all-around production assistant, and so he had enlisted Frankly, who was always up for these adventures and could take days off nearly whenever he wanted from his day job managing a Barnes & Noble that paid the bills while he continued pining over wanting to be involved in film productions.

For this particular shoot, Milt had also brought on an old friend who was working freelance in San Diego. Bobby Taylor was, like Frankly, someone who was happy to come to the San Francisco Comic-Con to be a second camera operator at what was supposed to be a kind of "comeback" for Gil Gladly. *FINALLY! Gil Gladly returns to Balloon for a very special live event at one of the biggest pop culture hubs in the country!*

Milt, Ronnie, Wallace, and their ad-hoc team got plenty of good stuff for the doc. In the end, however, both Gil and the reps from Balloon disallowed the boys from using all but a few seconds of their three days of full coverage. Wallace would, in fact, have one of his assistants simply cut together a montage of "best of" clips from the event, which ended up not going as originally planned.

For some reason, likely economical, Balloon had put a gaggle of goofy, green, and giggly recent college grad girls in charge of everything. After meeting the first director in charge, Ashleigh (who made sure to mention the spelling of her name every time Milt had to talk with her about anything), Milt brought up his concern privately to Gil that there might be trouble ahead. Things worsened when the more Milt talked with the gals in charge, the more he realized they were *all* considered "directors," and *all* girls from the upper crust of their generation with nontraditionally spelled but still traditional names.

The large-scale *KidTalk* panel Gil took part in was scheduled for a different room than what Balloon had been promoting all around the con, so almost no one showed up, and those who had were there to get in early for the next panel with some of the minor stars of *Firefly*.

The man-on-the-street interviews the Balloon girls had set up for Gil to do as spontaneous, YouTube friendly bits didn't work out because no one had bothered to get permits, and one of the restaurant owners outside of which some of this spontaneous footage was shot came outside screaming and yelling, threatening to sue for the foot traffic blockage the shoot was causing.

The main event itself—a small mock-up of *KidTalk*, hosted by Gil and featuring a handful of minor celebrities, none of whom Milt and his team recognized—had so many technical problems it was amazing more audience members didn't complain afterwards on social media.

There had been a *few* complaints, but none made by anyone with any real social media clout, and as the larger media outlets didn't seem to care the event was happening at all, there was no real coverage anyway.

Milt couldn't believe that even at such an extremely high-profile event, there could be so many fuck-ups. Dealing with CineRanchero was one thing, but this was *Balloon,* at the

San Francisco frickin' Comic-Con, for goodness sakes. How could they have let this happen?

At one point at the end of the whole goddamn thing, Gil had called Milt and the guys from his hotel room.

"Are you sitting down?"

Uh, oh.

Milt's first thought was that Gil was about to say Balloon wouldn't let them use *any* of the footage, especially since a lot of what Milt and his team had been capturing was fuck-up after fuck-up.

But no, that wasn't it. Turned out the camera guy who had been brought on to shoot everything for Balloon itself hadn't properly initialized his camera's memory card, and so they'd gotten *nothing* for the entire day. Tens of thousands of dollars, not to mention their time, had been totally lost.

Who knew why Balloon hadn't hired more than one camera man? Who knew why the girls in charge never bothered to check with him throughout the day if everything was going all right? Who knew why he never checked himself?

None of this mattered. What mattered was: A. Balloon would have to figure out a way to pay Gil his $45,000 appearance fee for an entire day to shoot everything all over again, B. Gil would have to fly back home a day late, and C. Milt would have to convince Bobby Taylor, who *loved* this kind of industry fuck-up intrigue, to *please please please NOT* post anything on his fairly popular Facebook page about how horribly Balloon had screwed up this huge event.

If Bobby spilled the beans, Balloon would never approve anything else that Milt and his team did on the doc, something he also knew he'd need later down the road when he'd need to license *KidTalk* footage from them for the finished film.

It hadn't been very easy for Milt to convince Bobby to keep his online mouth shut. Bobby was the kind of person who thought it his *duty* to let the world know about the problems Balloon had had at the event, something that would hopefully get them to do better next time, to see this as a "teachable moment," blah blah blah.

Bobby Taylor was one of those people who took Yelp *really* seriously.

Since Bobby and Ronnie had gotten great footage of everything over the day, Gil said Balloon was interested in potentially buying their footage for a handsome fee. This could go back into the budget of the doc and then, hey, maybe everyone could be paid for the days shooting the event.

In the end, Balloon buckled down, paid Gil his fee, and shot all over again, with background extras to fill the audience this time, also paid for by Balloon. Clips from this version of the event would later be shown on Balloon, and anyone watching could see that something about the whole thing felt inauthentic and plastic. Because it was. It was still out there though, Gil Gladly having his teaser for a semi-reboot of *KidTalk*.

As with so many of these kinds of things, the viewers watching at home would never see the real show behind the Great Oz curtain. It certainly wouldn't show up in Milt's documentary.

Frankly, sitting there in the car, eyes on the road as they went under an overpass, the sci-fi green luminance from his cockpit dashboard gleaming eerily, had been right. Through it all, Gil Gladly had acted great in San Francisco. He hadn't blown up. Except for the one or two times he'd fought with one of the young directors of the event, something else that would never make it into the doc.

Actually, how those golden moments had ended up on the digital cutting room floor made for a humorous and all too telling moment in the production history.

An executive at Balloon had seen an early cut Milt had sent to make sure everything was approved. She had called to say everyone there loved the film...*but* there's that *one scene* where Gil was fighting with one of the Balloon directors, and could they *please* cut it out before screening it on the tour?

The executive had tried to explain to Milt that she had been at Balloon for over *ten years* and "we don't act like that at Balloon. Everyone is nice and friendly, generous and gentle over here, and we don't want that scene going out to people thinking that people at Balloon talk or act like that."

Which, of course, Milt knew was total and complete bullshit. As though people at Balloon, Disney, Nickelodeon were all sweet, magical little pixies with no human emotions. As though just because they worked in children's programming meant they weren't all young, fiery, often frustrated, underpaid *artists*— often totally screwed-up and hence why they were making TV instead of being lawyers or something—who fucked and fought and did drugs and argued and did everything every other normal person, *especially in Hollywood,* did.

Milt had wanted to say, "Lady, I've written about your network for *years*, and mostly with folks who were there *way* before your fucking ten-year tenure. I know the people who *made* your goddamn channel and left because of how fucked up things got once all the money came in...."

But instead Milt had said, "Sure, you got it. Thanks, and glad everyone likes the film over there!"

"You know, it's funny," Milt said, pondering.

"What's that?" Frankly asked, still driving with one hand, his other relaxed at his side.

"When I look back on the San Francisco Comic-Con, I think about how there we were at one of the biggest, most popular pop culture things in the country, maybe the whole fucking world, with our backstage passes and full access, and—"

"We didn't do shit while we were there except work and drink," Frankly cut in.

"Yeah," Milt said. "Exactly. It's weird, isn't it? So many people would have *killed* to have that kind of access. But we didn't even think about it. It was just a gig. To all of us."

"*Most* of us," Frankly corrected.

Milt knew what he meant. Frankly, Bobby, Wallace, and he shot everything they could for three days straight, got all the releases and permits signed, and did everything one must do to stay afloat during all the chaotic madness of such a 24/7 event going on with hundreds of thousands of people running amuck, dressed in full cosplay regalia and handing out flyers, posters, memorabilia, and God-knows-what right in your fucking face the whole time. So *loud* and so *crowded*. One huge blaring commercial. Only in *real life*.

"Nothing! I want nothing!" Milt would want to shout into the faces of these clone drone trolls shoving paper garbage

into his face, repeating the line from the analogous Bazooko Circus scene in Terry Gilliam's *Fear & Loathing in Las Vegas.*

Every time there was a short break, when Gil would go back to his hotel to take a nap or FaceTime with his wife and granddaughter who lived with them back home in Jersey, there was not even a question asked of where Milt and his crew would go. Inside the actual convention itself? *No way!* They were off to whatever bar they could find until it was time to go shooting shit again.

Then there was Ronnie Clark. Ronnie was something of what Wallace and Milton had referred to affectionately as a "daywalker."

Ronnie, despite sometimes making a gaffe like the email he had sent to the CineRanchero people, was unmistakably a pro, and one of the best shooters Milt had ever worked with. Frankly could see it for just the few days they all worked together too. Ronnie Clark was a fantastic cameraman, a fantastic director of photography, and a fantastic crew member.

But he was also a fanboy. A geek. *Or was he a nerd?* Frankly asked.

To answer, Milt invoked novelist Douglas Coupland's assertion that "a geek is a nerd who knows he is one," that a geek was the *new* nerd in a way, that a geek was more like Comic Book Guy on *The Simpsons* (loud, at times abrasive, vying to "collect-em-all," promoting his geekiness). Whereas a classical, old school nerd was more like Lisa from *The Simpsons* (quiet, introspective, so passionate and obsessive about her interests that she didn't necessarily consider herself a nerd). She did what she did for the love of it, not for the connection to a larger community as with the geeks.

So, perhaps Ronnie Clark was more of a nerd than a geek. Ronnie was a nice guy. He wasn't trying to push his nerdiness on anyone like the geeks at the San Francisco Comic-Con or elsewhere offline and on.

Whatever the case, Ronnie *was* something of a daywalker who, as one-part pro and one-part fanboy, kept trying to get everyone to actually go inside the mad beast of the comic-con's stomach, churning and overflowing with geeks and advertisements and loudness and outrageousness, and all that came with being a true, live incarnation of pop culture at its best (or worst, depending on if you were a geek, nerd, or miscellaneous).

"What was *with* that guy, anyway?" Frankly asked.

"He's one of the best people I've ever met," Milt said without a shred of hyperbole. "One of the things I'm really grateful I got out of all this nonsense is the bond that Ronnie and Wallace and I have now by having gone through all of this together. I hardly knew those guys beforehand, but we went through so much together out there, that even at one point when Ronnie and I got in some stupid fight over whatever, the very next morning you know what he said over breakfast?"

"What?"

"He said, 'Brothers fight.' That's what he said. I'll never forget that. That's what I think about when I think about Ronnie."

"That sounds *rrrrrrrealllllllllyy* gay," Frankly said, doing a terrible impersonation of Ed Sullivan.

"Nah, I'm serious. Ronnie, Wallace, and I are so close now. It's strange. I've spent so little time with them, but the time we have spent over the past few years was going to war together. Like we were in the army."

"That's what most shoots are like," Frankly said, getting serious. "I guess it's part of why we do this kind of work."

"I guess," Milt said. "It's definitely not the money."

"*What* money?" Frankly said with an extremely rare laugh. He was clearly uber-stoned now.

"Right," Milt conceded. "That's just it...."

"What?"

"I'm supposed to be doing this shit *for* the money."

"So? You make some...sometimes."

"Yeah, but there's so much easier money made elsewhere. There's a lot of things I could do."

"Well, I don't know about *that*."

"No, really," Milt intoned, sitting up in his chair. "Why do I do *this* shit? Go on shoots at San Francisco Comic-Con with fucking Gil Gladly in partnership with Balloon. Without even getting *paid*. I mean, I'm not a fanboy, a geek, or a nerd. Not really."

"And?"

"And, I don't know. Sometimes it makes me feel bad about the whole thing," Milt said.

"Why?"

"Because it's like I'm an outsider. Not really a fraud. I mean, I guess I'm into this shit. Obviously. I watched Balloon when I was a kid. It's fun hanging out with people like Gil. Most of the time."

"Obviously."

"I wouldn't be able to put so much time and energy into these kinds of things otherwise," Milt said. "But is it a *job* or a passion? Or a hobby? Or what the hell is it? I don't really get that much money, considering everything I always do on projects like this."

"Especially on *this* project."

"Yeah, I mean, aside from the money Gil dropped in my account for the budget in the very beginning of all this nonsense, we haven't gotten shit. I've been paying for most of the last six months' worth of stuff out of my own pocket, and people like you, Wallace, Ronnie, and everyone else have just been working as a labor of love type deal."

"Yeah, sure," Frankly scoffed with his own unique version of a subtle laugh. "'Labor of love.' Keep telling yourself that."

"Then there are people who really, really just want to *touch* Gil, or be around him, or talk to him, or get a selfie with him, or autograph, you know?"

"Now *they* are *really* nuts."

"It makes me feel weird sometimes that they would do anything to be around Gil, and I'm sitting here complaining about how he's always hitting me up on the phone about shit he's freaking out about, or I'm having to tell him where to go or what to do next to get ready for this tour or whatever else." Milt sighed.

"Maybe that's why you're so good at this stuff. You're *not* a fanboy, so you can take it seriously and ask good questions during interviews and take care of business instead of being one of these frothing-at-the-mouth bloggers squeeing out on your interviewees and whatnot."

"Yeah," Milt said. "That's me. The Margaret Mead of eighties/ nineties pop culture."

"Now if only you could figure out some way to get a whole lot more Twitter followers than Margaret Mead," Frankly said with a wide crocodile grin.

"Sorry, I'm one of the eighty-plus percent of Americans *not* on Twitter and that's where I'm stayin'!"

"Yeah, yeah," Frankly said, tired of hearing Milt's statistic for the umpteenth time. "I know, I know."

They both laughed now. It felt good. It was one of those moments when Milt realized all at once just how stressed out he had been.

They were both quiet for a few minutes. Milt rolled the window down, and laid his head on the black rubber of the door into which the window had disappeared. Felt the rush of the silver-chilly wind on his face, through his crinkly Semitic hair.

Something dawned on him. He sat back, rolled up the window.

"One thing about those geeks, though," Milt said, more serious, staring out the windshield to the eucalyptus trees in front of him lining the parking lot into which they were now entering, having almost reached their destination. "They're spending all this money on old boxes of Nintendo cereal they find on eBay or go to these elaborate *Ghostbusters* conventions or whatever it is...."

"Yeah?"

"It all seems so silly and it's easy to make fun of."

"Oh kaaaaay...." Frankly said. "Your point being?"

"So many of these people, they still, like, have a family of their own. Wife, kids, and a day job, and..."

"Normal, you mean," Frankly said.

"Yeah. They have real lives. They're weird and strange and obsessed with the eighties and nineties, but then they go home and have a house and a car, two kids, and a wife. A job. A real job. Not just—"

"Not just writing and making movies about these things like you do."

"Yeah. They wear the costumes and buy the old boxes of cereal and spend their two-week vacation going to these conventions I fucking *hate* having to deal with, but they're the ones with lives of their own. For right now, I just have Gil Gladly's. It's not even mine."

"Hmm."

"Yeah, then half the time I'm basically just traveling around behind him sweeping up the shit he leaves behind, so that I smell like fucking shit myself. *That's* fun."

Frankly parked, keeping the car running.

He pulled out another joint from his jacket pocket to light up, offering the stuff once more to Milt, who once again shooed it away. Frankly opened the window, let his arm with the joint hang out there as he smoked and exhaled.

Frankly was totally and enviably at ease. Milt worried about getting caught in a car with the joint, but Frankly smoked like none of this mattered.

Frankly finished his joint, flicked it out the window, turned off the car. Milt picked up the hat he'd been keeping on the floor at his feet and put it on.

They both opened their doors, then they were out in the Southern California night, an unseasonably warm breeze blowing across them both and through the trees lining the parking lot as they turned to the pink neon-lit sign ahead.

"I don't want to stay out too late, so just get the coke from your girl and we'll head to the beach to do it, okay?" Milt asked, handing Frankly two hundred-dollar bills as their sneakers crunched on the gravelly path leading up through the near-empty parking lot toward the strip club.

"Well, we gotta hang for a bit and have a private dance, or else the bouncers might think something is up," Frankly said.

"All right," Milt said. "Just as long as we can get out of there early enough to go to the beach, do the stuff, and get back to my mom's so I can get up early and get some work done tomorrow. I'm behind."

"Jesus," Frankly said, opening the door to the strip club with a blast of distorted hip-hop music pummeling them, "you're so Jewish."

CHAPTER 9

It wasn't a hard choice.

As soon he locked eyes with the olive-skinned, pocket-sized Devlin standing across the way, Milt was transfixed. He sat in his chair in the dim mauve lighting of the Santa Ana strip club Frankly had taken him to so they could procure some cocaine from his stripper "friend." Milt was in.

Devlin would make for an ideal way to kill a few minutes while Milt waited for Frankly to conduct his business.

Upon entering the modestly sized and fairly empty strip club a few minutes earlier, Frankly and he had moved in that quiet, strange walk one does while entering such an establishment. Slightly embarrassed, slightly guilty.

But only slightly.

They were here for the coke, sure. But without needing to say anything aloud, Frankly gave Milt the look which said, *"We need to hang here for a bit and we need to get dances so it doesn't look like we're just here for the illegal drugs, okay?"*

"Okay," Milt silently communicated back at Frankly.

Into their respective chairs they plopped, turning off their phones as signs requested.

Frankly flattened out comfortably, his whole body becoming one of those beanbag stuffed animal toys, languid and inhumanly relaxed.

Milt had never really liked strip clubs. He always felt particularly bad about the people who would go there. The clubs themselves seemed scuzzy and strange to him. They smelled, and tended to be balmy, like a fenny bog. The walls seemed to sweat and were for some reason always lined with a kind of pubic black carpet.

He'd go to strip clubs with friends, and had gone a few times by himself, though he never really felt very good about it. Afterwards, the experience would leave him hollow, like he'd wasted both his time and his money.

But here he was now. Might as well make the best of it. Drugs were on the way, time would pass.

The music pulsed, muffled and distorted to the point of being white noise nearly drowning out the distraction of these intrusive thoughts as Milt sat in his chair a few feet from Frankly, who raised his hand to motion over some drop-dead young swain in a see-through gold lace nightie that would have better fit her much younger, smaller sister if she had one.

Frankly whispered in the girl's ear, and she flitted over to Milt, leaning down so he could smell her breath of whiskey, harsh spearmint gum, and gritty charcoal cigarettes.

"What can I get you, sweetie?" she asked sultrily.

"Uh...I'm fine right now," Milt replied.

"We don't have a cover here," she said, "but you do need to buy two drinks, love, okay?"

"Oh...."

"You want me to just get you a couple bottles of water?" she asked, knowing that "oh" really meant, "I'd rather not drink tonight," being totally in tune with the lingo of the various species of men who came through here.

"Yeah," Milt sputtered. "Sure...."

He didn't know why he was so fucking nervous, why he couldn't keep it together. She must have seen that he was clenching the side of his chair hard, because she put her soft, surprisingly icy hand on his and leaned in closer to his cheek to whisper, "I'll be right back."

The bottles of water, Aquafina, were nine dollars each. Milt wouldn't drink the water. Ever since he had helped write the memoirs for a dowager of a well-known Pepsi executive who had told him, "Never drink Aquafina! It's the excess water we don't use for production of the soda!", he never had a drop again.

The distorted white noise of the music, some kind of clubby hip hop track that briefly sounded as though it were a skipping CD—*What-what-what-what-what-what Yeah-yeah-yeah-yeah-yeah Ungh-ungh-ungh-ungh-ungh*—ensconced Milt in his own sonic bubble until...

"Hey, how's your night going?"

Another silky-soft icy hand rested upon his own still clenching the right side of his chair. It wasn't a girl, it was a woman. She must have been in her forties. At least. He'd seen strung-out before, but this was not it. Just tired. This was probably one of her many jobs. She was probably back in school, probably had more than two kids. The light streaks in her otherwise auburn, wavy, shoulder-length hair loudly advertised she was trying to fit in with the five much younger girls who were tomcatting around, or the two up on the dance floor clicking their oversized clear plastic shoes and writhing around naked with glittery bodies lined with a patina of telltale baby fat.

"I'm fine," Milt said. "How are you?"

It was a reflex. He immediately felt silly saying it. But that's what came out of his dry mouth. He wished he could drink the Aquafina, but would *not*.

"Oh," she leaned back in her chair, presaging her pitch to come, "you know. Just starting my night. Man, it's been slow."

"Yeah, Thursday night! It'll...uh, probably pick up soon, right?"

"I hope so. I don't want to be here too late. I have class in the morning."

Bingo.

"Oh yeah?" Milt said, keeping the conversation going out of politeness. "What are you studying?"

She sat up and looked at him with a sudden crack in the veneer, punctuated by a confounding smile. "I...don't really want to say."

"Mmm," Milt said, looking around the room for alternatives. If this was the game, he wanted to make sure he was with the right partner. And she wasn't it.

"What do *you* do?" she asked.

"Whatever pays the bills," Milt replied, his standard superficial response.

"Nice," she said. "That's why I'm going back to school. This *doesn't* pay the bills. Not all of 'em, unfortunately."

The music changed to something similarly indiscernible. Milt heard that generic fast-talking boilerplate mumbo-jumbo of the unseen DJ announcing a changeover of girls (Missy and Lihhhhhhhh-dia were up next, with Daisy on deck), and saw Frankly escorted hand-in-hand by an extremely tall Thai girl with short, silky black hair and a silver bra, silver G-string, and matching silver fuck-me pumps toward the private dance booths on the other side of the club beyond the stage.

The tall Thai stripper strutted slowly, holding Frankly's right hand over her shoulder, leading him like a dog on a leash to her secret lair where she would fleece him of whatever money he could muster, and where Frankly would presumably make the buy.

Squinting, Milt was fairly certain he could see Frankly's supernumerary earlobe twitching as he disappeared with the stripper beyond the black velvet curtain to the private area.

His attention stolen away from the woman sitting with him, Milt could tell she was getting impatient, that she knew it was now or never, and likely the latter.

She sat up straight. "Do you want a dance like your friend?"

Milt took another survey around the room with his eyes, doing his best not to be too obvious. He really did feel bad for the stripper pitching herself to him. But he also didn't want to spend a hundred bucks or more on her. Wasting money on a stripper was one thing. Wasting money on one he didn't really want was another.

"I...uh, I *might*..." he said, almost stuttering like Gil Gladly.

The look in her face changed again, this time to "fuck it," and she sat back, resigned. "Sweetie, this is the time when you can be honest, okay? You can tell me if you don't want a dance. It's all right."

"I don't want a dance," Milt blurted, relieved she had granted him permission to do so.

Without so much as a "buh-bye," she was on her feet and off to one of the other scant patrons who had come through the door since she'd sat down with Milt.

There was a brief moment where he thought he'd simply sit it out, wait for Frankly to finish his business, actually get their night started. It was a simple plan ahead. Get the stuff, go to the beach, enjoy the stuff, grab some drinks at a local bar, head back to Milt's mom's, pass out. Wake up early in the morning, have some breakfast, and head up to LA where Frankly and Milt would prep for the premiere, camping out at the apartment of a mutual friend from UCLA, Gabe Martinez, one of their few former classmates who'd remained in LA and was actually working in the industry.

Then Milt locked eyes with Devlin.

There she was. Perfectly tanned, olive-colored skin, as though she had been lovingly burnished by some master craftsman with the most enviable job of rubbing oil up and down her near-flawless body. Large, startlingly green Kewpie doll eyes (Milt's favorite); a tiny button nose, the kind he loved to pinch when granted access; cotton candy pink lips glistening with gloss in the low light of the dank place. She wore a translucent yellow bra—simple, ascetic, no flares—and matching diaphanous lingerie underwear.

Along with her light brown hair, she looked soft, cuddly, adorable, innocent. The only part of Devlin (whose name he would learn quite soon) that screamed "I will dance naked on

SELLING
NOSTALGIA

top of you for money" was her requisite overly-high heels that showed off her manicured toenails and their pale pink polish.

She saw he was looking her up and down and grinned hungrily. Her tiny, endearingly misshapen Chiclet teeth immediately reminded Milt of that indelible line in Jeffrey Eugenides' *The Virgin Suicides* in which the anonymous, omniscient narrator similarly admires the misshapen Chiclet teeth of Lux, the main sister of the book's adoration, played in Sofia Coppola's luminous film adaptation by the hauntingly lovely Kirsten Dunst.

Devlin stepped right up to him, leaned over him in his seat, and said simply, "Hey."

"Hey," Milt said back to her, looking up at her, aching to smell her hair.

"I'm Devlin. Do you want a dance?"

"Yes." He stood up, allowing her to hold his hand and walk him away from his two unopened bottles of Aquafina.

Milt was not so much walking behind Devlin as hovering across the dark-brown carpeted floor on tiptoes, dragging his feet as though he were ensorcelled a la Fairuza Balk's Nancy in *The Craft* or fellow femme-fatale witches from Disney's *Hocus Pocus*.

He *was* floating, hand held by Devlin's as she walked forward, glancing back at him once before entering the private area. That beaming, soft smile made it clear he was about to enjoy himself.

He gripped her hand, which was warm, and they entered beyond the black curtain to one of the private booths. She helped him sit down, his eyes not leaving hers. She radiated with a wide smile. She went to the door, closed it. The room was empty, not decorated. A soft pink lightbulb dangled from the low ceiling, barely luminating everything.

It was a dreamy, comfortable place unaffected by the physical and mental limitations of time and space.

Milt could see her body, her face, her smile as she turned to him and slowly unbuttoned her yellow bra. She closed her eyes in ecstasy (real or fake, it didn't matter), and wiggled her hips, pulling down her nearly transparent lacy daisy-colored underwear around her high-heels—which would stay on, of course—and was otherwise mercifully, blessedly, miraculously, completely nude before him.

Devlin was unquestionably beautiful. Her gentle voice was at once reticent and firm, and Milt no longer felt the need to clench anything with his hands. He was not nervous. He was disarmingly mesmerized.

He sat on the bench and licked his dry lips as she motioned toward him, her high-heel shoes clacking on the cold concrete floor of the cubby-like room doused in roseate light.

There was not a strand of hair on her body, with a helpful amount of baby fat on her to keep her so authentic and approachable. She flashed those achingly wondrous misshapen Chiclet teeth and stepped right to him, looked down on him, leaned into him, asking that most ordinary of stripper questions: "So, what do you do?"

She was close enough now that Milt could smell the redolent scent of body lotion and candy-like perfume. He'd always hated the scent of Jolly Ranchers and the taste of Twizzlers, but

Devlin's scent was somewhere in the middle, and he didn't mind at all.

"I'm...uh, a writer-producer," Milt said. Her emerald saucer eyes revealed nothing. She'd heard this kind of thing before, and he knew it.

He was surprised at himself that he'd let it out so effortlessly. No snide riposte to her question, no guarding of his true vocation. The lotion-candy smell of hers was ostensibly rather like Sodium Pentothal to Milt, and likely any other man who came in the room here with her.

"That's nicccccce..." Devlin cooed sibilantly, gently blowing into his ear with warm Bubblicious gum breath, leaning into him further so that her small, pert breasts brushed against his face. His nose delved deeply into the wide, buttery crevice, her nutbrown nipples pointing accusatorily into his cheeks.

She placed his hands on her hips, making it clear he could touch her, and she slowly, steadily straddled him. There was nothing now between her bald nether region and his crotch, but for his underwear and jeans. Without them, Milt and Devlin would be fucking.

It was more than the sexual arousal now, Milt at once felt. He had let the cat out of the bag and something inside of him wanted more. "Yeah," he went on, "I'm actually back in SoCal for a screening of a film I made with some friends."

"Oh, yeah?" Devlin said, tightening her knees around his waist and gazing deeply into his eyes. There was a shock of recognition in her face.

Wait, this guy is for real?

"Yeah," Milt said, firing up. "We're doing a full tour around the country, actually. You'll be seeing some articles about it in a few magazines and some TV spots soon, especially around here. Our premiere is in LA this weekend."

"Wow," Devlin said, seeming to be honestly into it. "So, you, like, make movies?"

"Sometimes," Milt said, feeling he'd earned a squeeze of her haunches, which led to her closing her eyes, leaning lustfully back, her breasts and brown erect pencil eraser nipples pointing toward his face, only centimeters away.

"That is *so* funny," Devlin said. "I was just gonna say that you look so much like Seth Rogen. Do you like his stuff? I *love* him."

"He's...pretty funny...sometimes," Milt grunted.

"I'm thinking about getting into movies," Devlin said, pulling herself back toward him, opening her eyes, talking to him now as though they weren't practically in the throes of sex.

"Yeah?"

"Yeah, porn, you know?" she said as though it were as simple as that. "A lot of dancers do it to help advertise themselves and get jobs at other clubs. I'd love to go work in Vegas someday. I only just started at this, but I think I'm doing pretty good for twenty."

Twenty!

Milt did the math and quickly realized she *wasn't even born* when Kurt Cobain killed himself.

"Do you think I look twenty?" Devlin asked, spinning herself around on Milt, shoving her labia deeper into the concrete denim-covered erection poking up underneath his jeans. She leaned back and placed his hands over her b-cup breasts, her erect nipples rubbing against his palms, sending lightning bolts of tremors up and down his back.

"I guess," Milt said, trembling slightly. "I think you look beautiful."

She turned her head slowly and looked in his eyes. "Thank you." It almost seemed sincere. "Do you think I could be in porn?"

"Uh, yeah," Milt said. "I think a lot of people would want to see you."

Aside from the very real urge to see her fucking on screen, Milt did feel as though it was a kind *mitzvah* he was engaging in here, encouraging her into what could be a potentially lucrative career path. She was a young starlet on the rise asking a seasoned pro what his thoughts were regarding where she should go next.

"Beats waitressing," she snickered. "The customers hate you, the kitchen hates you, the owner hates you. I tried doing it before I dropped out of high school to come work here last year, but it wasn't for me. Everyone was so *mean*."

He was delighting over rubbing her breasts and feeling her nipples, breathing in the smell of her silky brown hair brushing against his face as she rhythmically rocked her bottom over his pointy, hard dick poking up into her soft flesh from beyond the tightening denim between them.

Obviously, this girl really *could* be in porn. She would likely kick ass in it. The whole miscellaneous-race thing would be a big help. She was exotic without being alienating to any specific demographic. He almost wanted to ask her what she was, but thought better of it. Besides, she was already getting up and off him, her heels clicking on the concrete floor. She leaned into him, kissed him softly on the cheek, and asked, "Do you want another song?"

Song?

He hadn't realized music had been playing throughout their faux courtship. He did know from the three or four times in the past he'd actually bothered to have a private dance at other strip clubs that the cost was typically measured by song. But Devlin had not been clear about this, or the amount per song, when she'd first lured him into the booth.

Devlin and he had a special connection, didn't they? He was giving her career advice, for fucksakes. Would it just be a friendly, nominal fee at the end? He wanted to keep talking to her. It wasn't only about the way she looked and sensually moved up and down and all around and on him. It wasn't. He *knew* that.

"Uh, yeah, sure," he said. "A few more songs. I...like talking to you."

"Well, we can just talk, if you want," she said, smiling. "Some guys do pay me just to talk."

"No, no," Milt fired back, worried he'd flubbed it. "You can keep doing what you've been doing."

She smirked and he almost fainted from the power of it. She took off his hat and put it on her palm-sized head. The hat dwarfed her, but it looked good and she knew it. She winked and turned around, wiggling her ass in his face.

He looked down to her short crack and saw there a typical tramp-stamp tattoo, only it read as a romantically gothic scrawled

quote: *What matters most is how well you walk through the fire.*
He took note of it, liked it quite a bit. It was a guidepost from
the universe confirming that he needed to stay here with Devlin.
That was *exactly* what the ass-crack tat was.

She placed his right hand on her right buttock and lightly
patted it, giving him permission to continue. He gave her a
little spank.

"Mmmmm...." she said.

It was incredible. It was exactly what he needed. He had
earned this. He had been under so much pressure lately. The
money, the weight gain, the shit with Laney, the shit with Silverstein, the awful awful awful shit with CineRanchero, keeping
everything going with the fucking tour and film, and....

Devlin turned back around and leaned into his right ear,
blowing into it with her sweet-smelling sirocco breath. He loved
when strippers did that. *How did they know to do that?*

Then she purred, and Milt thought he wasn't going to
be able to control his animal instincts anymore...but a large
bouncer opened the door, looked inside, and exited, closing the
door behind him.

"Don't worry about it," Devlin said. "Carlos is just making
sure I'm not giving you a blowjob or something."

"Do you ever do that?" Milt asked.

"I don't, but a lot of the other girls do. Do you like drugs?"

The drugs. Frankly. The coke. How long had he been in
here? How many songs? "Uh, sure," he confessed.

"Do you have any coke? I'd love to do some coke with you
right now."

"Not right now," Milt said. "But we might be getting some...a
little...uhm...later."

"Oh, cool." Devlin danced around the room as though she were one of those girls back in high school rehearsing for a routine she'd be performing during lunch assembly. "Maybe we could hang out again the next time you come and we can do some together."

Milt knew he'd never come back here. But he wanted nothing more than some cocaine right now to do with this enticing little minx.

"You're married?" she asked, coming back from spinning around the room. She picked up his left hand with his large silver ring on his wedding finger and kissed it.

"Yeah," Milt said.

"What's that like?"

"It's all right." Milt was surprised at the conversation that followed, his revelations, concerns, and fears about his marriage to Laney. The admission that they had both messed around with other people already, that they both questioned whether or not they had gotten married too fast, that they had "only" gotten married at a courthouse with a few random friends who had happened to be off early from work that afternoon, that both Laney and he had been having some extremely tough conversations about this right before he had to leave for the tour.

Laney and he were still so new, see, and things would probably get better, right?

He couldn't believe he was unloading like this. More to the point, he couldn't believe that Devlin was not only listening but was seemingly interested. *Really* interested. And wearing his hat through it all, while she listened and soothed him, and grinded her crotch against his denim-encaged dick.

It had become the very best therapy session he'd ever had.

Devlin decided to lie down and stretch out on the floor. Alluringly coiling and uncoiling snakelike, she asked, "Why did you get married?"

"Because we loved each other," Milt said as easily as if she had said something like, *Do you want to just stick it in me real quick and no one will ever know?* "We still love each other. Very much. We're glad we're married. We both want to have kids. But..."

"It's complicated."

"Yeah," Milt said. "Marriage wasn't what we thought it would be, what everyone else said it would be. It's not like the movies."

"It's weird how many times I've been saying things are 'complicated' lately," Devlin said. "Or 'people are complicated' lately. When did everything get so complicated?"

He was impressed by her worldliness. Then again, she'd probably heard it all before. He really did love Laney, and he knew she really did love him. They *had* made the right choice. He knew it. But it was a matter of figuring it all out. He knew they would when he got back from LA, or maybe after this whole fucking tour was over and they could get back to normal.

Milt and Devlin continued speaking about love, relation-ships, and what it meant to grow up.

He smirked, and Devlin asked what was up.

"Nothing," Milt said. "This whole thing is just reminding me a little of that scene in *The Catcher In The Rye*."

"Oh, yeah," Devlin said, the childish waif of her surface-self fading almost entirely away. "When Holden's talking to the hooker in the hotel room?"

"Yeah," Milt said, surprised at her recognition. "I never really liked that book."

"Oh, I know!" Devlin blurted. "It's like, who wants to listen to some spoiled, whiny rich kid complaining about how horrible his spoiled rich kid life is? Who fucking cares, right?"

"Right!" Milt said, always glad to meet another hater of a book that had been thrust on him throughout high school and college by teachers and Salinger fans who for some reason thought the boring, whiny thing was a literary masterpiece.

Milt and Devlin nodded their heads, smiling at one another.

"Ha, I guess that makes *me* the hooker then, huh?"

"I have to tell you," Milt said to avoid the question and elephant in the room, "the thing about being married, is that it's so special. We're no longer just boyfriend and girlfriend. We're not dating. We're not 'together,'" he said with air quotes.

Devlin looked confused. "What do you mean?"

"I can't really say. And I think that's the point. Why am I married to my wife? *I don't know.* I think that's the best reason of all. It's indescribable what we have. She'd call this 'kinda gay,' but the truth is that there's something there we can't define and that is so unique between us, we *have* to be married, because we don't have it with anyone else. Even though both of us have had a lot of other relationships and have fucked plenty of other people. Some of whom, that's all the 'relationship' *was*."

"Yeah, I know what that's like," Devlin said. "And not just because I'm the hooker in *Catcher* here."

"There's this movie called *My Dinner With Andre*—"

"I *love* that movie!"

"No, you don't!" Milt laughed. "No way!"

"Why, because I'm naked and dancing for you?"

"No, because you're like twelve!"

"I'm twenty!" Devlin laughed, pretending to slap him. Milt put up his guard and blocked her. "I'm really into movies. *My Dinner With Andre* is rad."

"Rad?"

"Yeah!"

"Well, anyway," Milt went on, "there's that scene toward the end where Andre tells Wally that the reason he thinks people have affairs is because they're searching out the next kind of adventure or thrill, basically."

"Sure..."

"As he goes on with that line of reasoning, Andre says that what makes for a good long-term relationship—you know, like a healthy marriage—is the realization that *that* can be an adventure or thrill too. The unique experience of actually being with someone, the same someone for a record-breaking amount of time. You know? What is *that* like? Actually being with someone for that long and not breaking away. I think that's what Laney and I have going for us. No matter whatever other problems we might have, individually or together, we're *married*. We're best friends."

He wasn't sure, but Milt may have caught a brief, glittery seed of a tear in Devlin's left emerald eye. Then it was gone. "That's...beautiful," she said.

Devlin, still on the floor, closed her eyes and went back to writhing around. Then it dawned on Milt. "Uh, I think we'd better call it a night."

The mood completely shifted. Frostily.

Devlin's face registered a haughty *Oh* and she stood. "Are you sure?"

"Yeah. I really better get moving. My friend is here, and I don't know if he's waiting on me or what, and we've got other stuff going on tonight."

"Oh," she actually vocalized this time. She placed the hat back on his head and walked, clacking her heels, toward her bra and underwear over by the door. She put them on hurriedly like she was rushing out of her boyfriend's room before curfew. The illusion was over. It was time to leave.

The quick change in atmosphere sent a new set of lightning tremors up Milt's back. *Wait a second. How long had they been here?*

There was the part of him that assumed what Devlin and he had been doing had been...yeah, special. That she would maybe give him some kind of discount on the whole experience.

But as he followed her out the door, through the club—where Frankly sat sunken into his same chair from before and giving Milt a strange "WTF?!" look as he passed by—and toward the cash register area with two very archetypically business-like young men who were *definitely* not here for fun or therapy purposes, Milt experienced a frisson of brutal reality.

"Okay, fourteen songs, at sixty-five dollars apiece, that'll be—"

Holy shit.

"—nine-hundred and ten dollars."

Devlin was standing next to him. Why wasn't she saying anything? Why wasn't she coming to his defense? Why was there no, *"Wait, this guy is different. This guy shouldn't have* to spend $910 on a forty-five-minute hangout session with me because we had a real connection I don't have with any other customer?"

She said nothing.

Because she wasn't his friend. She wasn't a therapist. She was a stripper who aspired to be a porn star, and that's that, Mattress Man.

Fuck. $910. Plus tip.

Like a large church bell pealing over and over again in Milt's head, it repeated, crushing his brain. That was more than half his monthly rent.

Laney! What would she think? Would he be able to keep this colossal fuck-up from her? FUCK!

$910.

Plus tip.

Milt could tell the two business fellas behind the cash register who were not fucking around caught the fear in his face. One cracked, "Do you need to use the ATM, sir?"

Devlin feigned a modicum of theatrical concern. "Oh, I'm sorry, baby. I thought you knew how much it was."

He turned to her and tried to lock eyes again, tried to bring back that special connection. But the problem was that there had never been one. Maybe she could be more than a porn star, he figured. She had been an excellent actress.

$910.

She hugged him. She actually *hugged* him. "Are you okay?"

God, but she did smell good.

Milt was too embarrassed to say anything about how the price had never been mentioned earlier, that he had had no idea that it would work like this, and that he had thought that maybe it was going to be one solid *reasonable* price. So he said nothing, paralyzed with fear and anxiety.

Like a malfunctioning automaton, he fumblingly moved over to a young lady who looked almost identical to the two gentlemen on the other side of the cash register area where she stood by an illuminated computer screen. "Do you want to use a credit card instead?"

He did. He would have to. He hoped there was enough on his Discover Card. Or that they would *take* Discover Card. Did anyone take Discover Card anymore? Why did he *have* a Discover Card?

The church bell again: BONNNNNNNNG. $910. BONN-NNNNNG. $910...

Devlin was already moving on to another mark, Milt saw to his left, beyond whom Frankly sat shaking his head disapprovingly but with a contrapuntal smile that clearly communicated, *"Can't take you* anywhere, *son."*

"All right," the business lady by the radioactively lit-up computer screen said, handing Milt back his card and a receipt (a *receipt!*). "We had to charge you ten percent for the credit card usage, is that okay?"

What would have happened if it *hadn't* been okay? He remembered that bouncer peeking in earlier on Devlin's and his session. Carlos was *big.* Milt decided to continue to keep his mouth shut. "Uh, yeah, sure."

"All right, thanks!" the woman chimed, turning back to her computer screen, typing something up on the keyboard, then going back to fucking around on her phone behind the counter while she waited for her next customer.

Milt walked over to Frankly. "Did you get it?"

"Yeah."

"Can we please leave. Right now?"

"Sure."

Milt and Frankly fled out the door, a flushed look of ignominy on Milt's face. If he could have seen himself, he would have seen the face of one of the very guys he always thought so pathetic at a strip club.

$910, Milt thought over and over again. Almost chanting it in his head. *$910, $910, $910*....

"Nine-hundred and ten dollars," he vented aloud, as he entered Frankly's car in the parking lot.

Frankly got in, shut his door, dropped a miniscule bag of white powder and pebbles on Milt's lap, and corrected his friend. "With the credit card fee, you mean one thousand and one dollars."

Milt dropped his face into his hands, moaning, "With tip, eleven hundred and one."

"Jesus," Frankly said, peeling out and getting them back on the highway. "Maybe you're *not* really Jewish."

Off they drove. Milt decided he would leave his phone off for the duration of the evening so he could better embrace the evening still ahead that would be fueled by the most expensive cocaine he had ever purchased.

CHAPTER 10

Everything's going to be fine / Everything's going to be fine / Everything's going to be fine / Everything's going to be fine....

Milt was repeating this incantation *ad infinitum* in his head, lying on the couch of Frankly's and his UCLA alumnus Gabe Martinez's dark, cramped Los Feliz two-bedroom apartment.

Milt would not turn on his phone to check the time, knowing it would only get him up all the way, then he'd be a disoriented train wreck all day long.

He lifted his neck from the lumpy pinkish pillow and craned his neck to the right. Through the darkness, he could barely see across the small living room, overstuffed with Basquiat-esque paintings in various styles of frames and sizes, most of them lying on the yellowish, brown-blotch stained carpeted floor. Across the room, the sliding glass door leading to Gabe's balcony was obscured by a dust-covered, beige canvas floor-to-ceiling set of curtains hanging loosely from the top of the doorway.

Milt could glimpse a sliver of radiative light blasting through the left side of the curtain and was relieved to know that his hours of lying there on that obnoxiously uncomfortable gray couch Gabe probably found on the street, overanalyzing everything in his life to the point of pseudo-bad-trip panic, were nearly at an end. It was still early, but Frankly would probably be up soon.

Milt knew Frankly's circadian schedule from the time they had lived together, and knew that, like himself, Frankly was a morning person.

He was going over and over again thoughts about money, about his looming deadline on his ghostwriting project, about money, and more about money.

How much was on his credit cards again?

Milt did have money in his pocket, he forced himself to remember. He had money in his checking account. They would very likely be selling the Gil Gladly documentary at some point. Netflix was blowing oodles of money on anything they could get their sweaty hands on like this was Silicon Valley right before the tech bubble burst in 2001.

Granted, Milt knew he wouldn't get much for the fucking thing—most of the sale would go back to Gil, the project's main investor. The rest would be deservedly split amongst all the guys who had worked so hard on it.

More importantly, Milt considered, it would open more doors for him in "the industry," as they say. Wouldn't it? He knew too many people who had made documentaries or indie features, sometimes with fairly big name "stars" who had gone to Sundance, Cannes, SxSW, Tribeca…and returned empty-handed. Or with some shitty long-term deal with a payment broken up into too many tranches over, say, a five-year period with a streaming service like Netflix, et al.

No, Milt. Don't think like that. Stop self-sabotaging.

The money would come. Not much, but it would come. It had to. His crew and he had spent so much time and energy on it, and a lot of their own money besides Gil's initial investment. So much extra traveling, so many pizza lunches and dinners.

The important thing was they had made a good film. Even people who couldn't give a shit about Gil Gladly would probably enjoy it. Those people had *better* like it. This tour wasn't exactly paying for itself and Laney and he couldn't stay in their Boston studio apartment forever. Shit, he'd be forty in four years, and at some point they wanted to start having kids. Sooner than not, she'd be thirty-five....

Guessing it was likely around six, Milt set his head back down on his pillow and stared up at the French vanilla-colored cottage cheese ceiling that, mystifyingly, may have had more brown-blotch stains on it than the floor.

Milt's imagination concocted a strange, troll-like man who lived upside-down on the ceiling, drinking his morning coffee, spilling it everywhere.

Milt briefly considered jerking off to Devlin bumping and grinding up against his crotch from behind. Or perhaps Melody's apple-tatted ass once again. He thought better of it when he turned his head on the pillow to see that Frankly was in the cluttered living room with him, passed out on the ratty old yellowish corduroy easy chair a mere five or six feet away.

Milt wondered all of a sudden if he should text or tell Melody that he jerked off to her sometimes. Did girls like that? Would she be flattered? Offended? Disgusted? Indifferent?

This somewhat spiraled Milt down a madcap rabbit hole of thoughts involving identity politics and the Russian Revolution

(October) and then the French Revolution. Then the image of tumbling down such a rabbit hole made him think about *Alice in Wonderland;* the book, not the animated Disney film. Then he thought about the differences between the animated Disney film of *Alice in Wonderland* and the book that he knew actually had a slightly different name than the film(s). How interesting was *that* to contemplate?

Milt pulled up the scratchy, unwashed Garfield bed sheet Gabe had left for him when Frankly and he had come in with a key he'd left under the mat for them the night before around 2 a.m. They had hoped to get up to LA during the day after breakfast with Milt's mom, but that was simply not what happened.

Frankly and he'd been pretty coked-out and they were still reeling from the horrendous bill at the strip club Milt had rung up, but they were also both exhausted and neither ever had much trouble sleeping after a coke binge. Milt's body reacted differently to the drug, in fact, than the stated purpose. Oftentimes, the stimulant just put him right to bed.

Many a time, he recalled fondly, Laney and he would do some when they were still in their wondrously wild peacocking courting phase and still did things like coke back where it flowed like water in Lincoln, Neb. Milt would go right to bed and Laney would spend all night cleaning her house until six or seven in the morning, blasting Tool on one of her roommates' record players, said lucky roommates were always gone at their own boyfriends' houses. Those were the days! Little to no worries at all, before all this nonsense with the doc and tour.

This amusingly pleasant memory, combined with the silly kissy-face emoji Laney had sent to him at some point during the night that he couldn't recall, led Milt to realize—still staring up at the cottage cheese ceiling above, listening to the small fan he brought with him everywhere to emit the white noise he required to sleep for whatever few hours he could get at a time—that he was pretty fucking lucky. "Blessed," as some would put it.

He had (some) money. He had a wife who would send him silly little kissy-face emojis, ones about which she would sometimes say, "Well, I send them just because I think that's what you expect me to do," to which he would respond, "Well, we both know how stupid they are, but it's nice you're thinking about me at all like that, and that you still feel the need to basically say, 'Hey, you're in my thoughts.'" Milt had friends. He had his health.

Why was he fretting so much about his life? Things were pretty good, weren't they?

He began to feel guilty about all the struggles and tribulations of folks like Wallace and Ronnie who were dealing with all the same struggles about money, the doc, and figuring out adulthood, all the while being bitch-slapped by Mother Nature's wrath taking revenge for all the centuries of being bitch-slapped by humans and their pollutive industrial ways.

Oy!

He even had another fleeting moment of guilt about what Sally Miranda—incompetent or no, raging bitch wearing an Andy Warhol fright wig hairdo or no—was going through with the fires in Chicago.

And here was Milt, worrying about stupid things he had far more control over than things people around the country were going through *real* problems like *fucking natural disasters!*

Gabe's place might have been absolutely disgusting. So much so that as much as Milt wanted to get on the floor and meditate for a bit to calm himself, he would not. Just as he would *not* use Gabe's filthy, disgusting bathroom. Made more disgusting by the smell, what with Gabe having left a sloppy note on the door explaining they'd need to limit their flushes to three a day, collectively, due to temporary conservation restrictions set by his landlord courtesy of the statewide drought.

Yet, how lucky was Milt that he had a friend who had a place right up in Los Feliz, not too far from where the premiere would be for his film? A place he could stay at for free.

"You okay?"

Milt turned to Frankly, who was stirring on the easy chair (*also* very likely purloined from the street) on which he had been sleeping all night.

"Yeah," Milt said. "Just been having trouble sleeping the last few hours. But I think I'm okay now. You up?"

"Yeah," Frankly said. "Man, you worry too much about things."

"That's anti-Semitic," Milt snickered, smiling. "You wanna go get some coffee?"

"*Obbbbbviously*," Frankly said, stretching his short arms in his blue rain slicker. "Let's go, Jewboy."

By the time they were out on the sidewalk in the quiet, vacant streets of Los Feliz, Frankly was asking a simple question. "Why did you bring your toothbrush and toothpaste with you?"

"Are *you* going to use Gabe's bathroom?" Milt asked. "I'm using the bathroom at whatever coffee shop we end up at."

"I see your point," Frankly said, pressing on past two thread-bare homeless people who may or may not have been asleep. Their surprisingly purebred yellow Lab appeared to be dead.

Milt stepped around the dog, the two men and/or man and woman sprawled out across the moist, cracked sidewalk, and nodded at a coffee shop that was likely one of the only establishments in the sleepy hipster enclave open at the early hour.

Frankly stepped inside, ordered a cappuccino and a break-fast sandwich, then added, "And whatever this guy wants."

Milt felt terrible about having Frankly pay, but not terrible enough to decline, ordered a latte—calculating the calories in his head—and asked if they could give him a side of lox and a side of sausage.

"We don't really do that here," the lanky, nose-ringed, purple-haired, tatted androgyne in Woody Allen glasses retorted. "Everything is pre-made."

"Oh," Milt said, calculating again—*carbs, carbs, carbs.* "I guess I'll do the breakfast sandwich, then."

Frankly paid and said he'd bring the food to one of the tables outside, and away Milt departed to the bathroom so he could brush his teeth in a place that wasn't the cleanest spot in LA but did beat the fetid petri dish that was Gabe's bathroom.

When Milt came out to Frankly, already noshing on his breakfast sandwich, he asked, "How you feeling?"

"You know me," Frankly said. "The same. Always the same."

"Cool."

Frankly took a sip of his cinnamon-speckled, frothy cappuccino in its white alabaster mug. "Hey, by the way. You missed it."

"Missed what?"

"Celebrity sighting while you were in the bathroom."

"Oh, yeah?" Milt sipped his own coffee, not really caring one way or the other, inured to the excitement of celebrity sightings in LA after his tenure in town years before.

"Yeah, Danielle Fishel," Frankly revealed.

Milt brightened up at this. "Topanga? She came to the coffee shop while I was in the bathroom?"

"Yup," Frankly said, smirking knowingly. "She didn't buy anything. I think the barista is her roommate or something. She came to say something to him...or her...or whatever."

"Oh, shit! Topanga! That's kinda cool. Did you say anything to her?"

"Yup," Frankly said proudly.

"Did you ask her what it was like to know you're the first girl an entire generation of guys jerked off to?"

"Nope."

"Awwww, booooooo-urns."

"She had this weird black shape tattooed to the back of her neck and I asked her what it meant."

"What'd she say?"

"Nothing," Frankly said, leaning back in his chair. "She just turned to me, flashed a smile, then said bye to her roomie, and left."

It was still quiet out on the street that reminded Milt at once of the days when he lived here as a starving young filmmaker/ writer and of the times he lived in similar areas in Brooklyn. A narrow street, wide sidewalks, vintage stores. An absolutely *adorable* pie shop.

It would have been gray out even if it were not *what? 7:30 a.m.?* Milt didn't wear a watch, wasn't ready to turn on his phone or ask Frankly. He kind of liked not knowing what time it was.

"So..." Milt said.

"Mmm *hmm.*"

They sipped their coffee, finishing their sandwiches. Milt's hands twitched. So did his brain. He couldn't fight it any longer. He pulled out his phone from its denim pocket home in his pants, and turned it on.

It immediately began vibrating in his hand. He placed it to his ear and turned away in his chair from Frankly. "Hey, Deborah, what's up?"

"Oh, doing just fine, Milton," Deborah Goldflab said, sounding slightly concerned.

It was a tone of voice Milt never liked hearing. It also unnerved him slightly that Deborah used his full first name, something typically reserved for his parents or past girlfriends when they were mad at him. Laney never once called him by his full name, he realized, even when she was mad at him. Unless she was doing it mockingly: *MilllllTON.*

Then again, Deborah Goldflab was older, late forties, maybe early fifties, and was the director of operations at the Boston arts and culture space where they would be putting on the Gil Gladly doc screening back home.

"Good to know," Milt said, essentially trying to get Deborah to actually state what her business was here.

"So, I don't want to make a big deal out of this, but we had a few complaints from some people out here who were wondering

about *Tad Willoughby from* Round the Clock *being a part of the screening event."*

"Mmm hmmm," was all Milt could say, starting to tremble. "You guys seemed pretty excited about Willoughby when I first brought him up as guest moderator. He's a big name." Milt turned back to Frankly, who tweaked his head with curiosity.

"Well, you know the art center here is all about inclusivity and expressing everyone's opinions," Deborah continued. *"We just the other day had someone from the local Young Republicans chapter—"*

"Right...."

"But, well..." Deborah paused. *"There have been some... mmmm, concerns about Mr. Willoughby's recent tweets, and we just wanted to make sure that...ummmm, Mr. Willoughby's going to be totally...mmm...professional while hosting the event and doing the Q&A with Gil Gladly."*

"Ah," Milt said. "Yeah, I don't know Tad and don't keep up with his social media stuff." He laughed, trying to comfort Deborah. "I'm not *quite* a millennial, so I'm not much for social media in general. You know what I mean, right?"

Deborah laughed as well, placatingly. *"Right, well...uhhhh, there's just been some...concerns,"* she repeated. *"Concerns."*

"I'll ask Gil about it," Milt said. "But since Tad is such a big name and we were lucky enough to be able to get him for the event, since he happens to have a house in the area and is old friends with Gil, I would hate to lose a lucky break like that, especially so last-minute, you know? How would *that* look? Plus, he's just...he's a *big name*. I really think it will help a lot to sell tickets."

"Sure, sure. None of us here are saying he can't come. We just want him to be—"

"Professional," Milt said. "Right."

"Yeah," she laughed placatingly again, clearly still nervous.

Frankly raised his hands, nonverbally inquiring, *The fuck?*

Milt shook his head at Frankly and finished up the call. "Look, I'll call Gil Gladly right now and will let you know what he says about this, okay?"

"Sounds good," Deborah said. *"Thanks, Milton."*

Milt hung up and drank some of his now tepid latte.

"What's going on?" Frankly asked with a tone that suggested he didn't really care one way or the other.

"Eh, the usual," Milt said, dialing Gil's number.

"Hayyyylo," Gil chimed loudly on the other line.

"Hey, Gil," Milt said. "Uh—"

"I've only got about thirty seconds, so make it quick."

"What? It's not even eight in the morning."

"And I'm a b-b-b-busy m-m-m-an, M-m-m-ilt. What's up?"

"Yeah, so Deborah just called and—"

"Who the fuck is Deborah?"

"Deborah Goldflab, our contact for the Boston event?"

"Ohhhkay...."

Milt cleared his throat. "She's worried about Tad Willoughby hosting and doing the Q&A with you."

"What? Wh-wh-why?"

"Uh...she said some people saw some of the stuff he's been tweeting lately, and—"

"Tell those people over there I don't give a fuck about that and that Tad Willoughby is a f-f-f-f-fucking p-p-p-p-

prof-f-f-f-fesional wh-wh-who's been at this longer th-th-than most of them have been alive. I g-g-g-g-gotta go. T-t-ell th-th-them to g-g-g-go f-f-f-fuck th-th-themselves."

Conversation over.

Frankly widened his almond eyes, his eyebrows rising cartoonishly. "Hmmm??"

Milt called Deborah back, told her that Gil said Tad Willoughby was a "pro" and wouldn't need to be worried about. He made sure to leave out the last part of Gil's message and hung up after Deborah nervously acquiesced that it was going to be an *amazing* event and that *everyone* was *really* looking forward to it.

Milt placed his phone back in his pocket, stood up, drank the rest of his latte, and left the crumb of breakfast sandwich on his plate. "Let's go."

Before they were even away from the table, Milt's phone vibrated in his pocket again, and he answered.

"Wh-wh-what's this f-f-f-f-fucking shit with where they're p-p-p-putting m-m-m-e up in Boston, b-b-b-by th-th-the w-w-w-way?" the disembodied voice of Gil Gladly bellowed into Milt's ear.

"Gil, we went over this a few times already," Milt said calmly, walking side by side with Frankly up the sidewalk where they saw a few store owners and service people readying up their storefronts, opening their metal screen doors, flipping over their OPEN/CLOSED signs.

Milt knew that Gil had certain...*exigencies* that required minding. Milt had known that Gil needed a particular kind of hotel and a particular kind of hotel room to be comfortable or else, well, he'd call ranting and raving at Milt about it.

Which was why he had worked with Gil and Gil's personal assistant to find the right place in Boston for him to stay. That was four months ago. Milt had even worked it so that the art center there would actually *pay* for Gil's trip from the screening at CineRanchero in Chicago two nights previous to the Boston screening.

And Deborah had agreed! Nervously, of course...but still.

"I looked this place up on Yelp, and it's got the worst fucking reviews!" Gil hollered, so livid he wasn't even stuttering anymore.

Not good.

Frankly and Milt kept walking forward as though Milt wasn't being upbraided loudly over the phone by an aging eighties icon. An absolutely stunning woman jogged by them, tight ponytail bouncing up and down against her neck, her tan, glistening belly out for all to see under her black sports bra and above her tight black yoga pants, capped by her highlighter pink running shoes with black laces.

Frankly turned his head, watching her go around them. Milt's eyes stayed locked on the sidewalk pathway ahead of him, determined.

"Gil, we went over this months ago, man," Milt pleaded. "I can't ask them to change it *now*. The cancellation fee would be horrendous and so would the difference of getting a new room so close to the date. Don't forget, they're one of the only places paying for *everything*."

"Th-th-they're paying for everything?"

"Everything, Gil. Come on, we gotta cut them some slack, okay? The hotel they're putting you up in is fine," Milt said. "Laney and I were going to put my dad and my stepmom up there when they were going to visit a few months ago before their plans changed. My dad wouldn't stay at a shithole any more than you would."

"Your d-d-d-dad, huh?"

"Yeah," Milt said. Frankly caught up with him and gave him one of his Frankly looks: *The fuck is going on NOW?*

They passed a used bookstore opening its doors to their left. Then they turned and Milt froze, staring up at the concrete wall to his left. Frankly saw this and stopped as well, confused. Milt stood still, gazing upward, mesmerized.

"All right," Gil relented. *"I'll tell you wh-wh-what. You're r-r-r-right: I d-d-d-on't want to bug Dana or whatever her n-n-n-name is over there in Boston. I'll j-j-j-ust get a different h-h-h-hotel myself."*

"Gil, you sure? I can ask *Deborah* if you want," Milt said, playing child psychologist now.

"No, no. It's f-f-f-fine. They're b-b-being very nice, but I c-c-c-can't stay at a place like that. I'm a h-h-hotel snob, I'll admit it."

Milt emitted a faux laugh, still gazing up transfixed at the wall. "Cool, well just let me know where you decide to go so I can get everything arranged with picking you up and whatever, okay?"

"Sure thing, fook-fah-shay," Gil said, hanging up.

"Jesus," Frankly said. "It's like working for Howard Hughes from *The Aviator.*"

"I *wish* Gil had that kind of money," Milt said.

"Huh, yeah."

"Seriously, though, this is a lot of what we talk about in the documentary. I mean, Gil's stuff with his stuttering and whatever may have been as big a part of why he was successful as Howard Hughes' OCD and anxiety stuff," Milt said.

"Yeah, I know what you mean, like in that Malcolm Gladwell book talking about producers and lawyers with dyslexia and how they had to force themselves to be better when they were younger in order to overcome their shit, right? Their fucked-up shit forced them to figure out special ways to become awesome, and then they did."

"Right," Milt said. "I don't know if it's always a good idea to quote Malcolm Gladwell, but yeah. Gil had to push himself in a way that most people wouldn't have in order to get to where he is today. Or where he *was*. He really does get into this a bunch in the film. It's one of my favorite parts of what we did."

"I look forward to finally seeing it," Frankly said, sounding far less sarcastic than usual.

"It's part of why we made the doc," Milt said, drifting off into a reverie at the thought, supplemented by his wonder at what he was looking at on the wall. "Not only with his stuttering, but also just everything else he had to overcome. He's a fucking survivor, and I really admire that. No matter what other bullshit might go on."

They both stood there gazing at the mural on the wall before them.

"Mmm, well, you ready to go back to Gabe's?"

"Yeah," Milt said. "But this is just crazy."

"What, the mural? It's Bukowski."

"Right, but that quote..." Milt stepped back to take in the full mural of Charles Bukowski and the cursive quote beneath it emblazoned against the wall...just at it had been emblazoned across the top of Devlin's crack two nights earlier: *What matters most is how well you walk through the fire.*

"What about it?"

"I'm not kidding. It was what was scrawled across that stripper girl's ass at the club," Milt said, with a hint of whimsy in his voice. "I never heard or read it before and thought she came up with it herself. But here it is! And it's Bukowski! That's fucking nuts! It's like..." Milt raised his arms triumphantly, purposely histrionic, "...like...a gift from the universe! Look how magical it is! It's here just for us, just for me right now. What are the chances? It's miraculous!"

"Hmm, that's kinda fucking lofty for a chick grinding her bald vag up against your leg for nine-hundred and ten dollars, dontcha think?"

"Well, she was surprisingly well-read and mature for a twenty-year-old stripper," Milt reminisced fondly.

They turned around and started walking back to Gabe's.

"I don't know. All the stuff I keep worrying about—the money, Laney, the deadline on the new book, and all the bullshit with everyone and everything else...This makes me feel like it's going to be okay."

"More reason to get back to Gabe's so we can start getting all our shit together," Frankly said, totally unimpressed by Milt's epiphany. "You've got a movie premiere tomorrow afternoon, young man!"

"Don't forget we have that meeting in the morning," Milt said.

"Who's this one again?"

"That dude Gil set me up with for one of the series we've been developing together."

They passed by the homeless people who were still asleep. Their dog was licking himself. "Gil and you are doing a lot together lately, huh?"

"The other day," Milt said, "we were on a podcast interview and he referred to me as basically being his adopted son."

"Sounds like you guys have gotten really close after all this nonsense," Frankly said, eyes forward, walking around another white plastic table and red plastic vintage chairs being set up outside another coffee shop on the way back to Gabe's apartment. "Is your...*actual* dad coming tomorrow?"

"That's a good question."

"Why?"

"Because I haven't invited him yet."

CHAPTER 11

Frankly and Milt climbed up the three flights of outer stairs to Gabe Martinez's balcony, scrunched their way through the clutter of old lawn furniture and two pink plastic chairs, and opened the glass, then screen door into the apartment proper.

Milt pulled out his phone to check his emails and saw he, unsurprisingly, had one from Jessica Chen which he ignored. There was also a text message from Silverstein which he could see was so lengthy that he deleted it before reading past the first few words—

"DUDE, I KNOW I SAID I'D STOP, BUT I HAVE TO TELL YOU ABOUT...."

"Hey, man!" Gabe said, coughing up wake-and-bake smoke from one of the large glass bongs that had been strewn across the carpet otherwise covered in empty paper cups, yellowed paperback books, and other dorm-room type detritus.

Appearing as always as a kind of executive hippie with relatively well-kempt brownish beard/mustache combo and long brownish hair tied behind his head, a gray vest, khakis and, for the morning, a silken, regal-red smoking jacket that had to have come from one of the many vintage stores up the street, Gabe stood in his beige plastic sandals to his full six-foot-two from the couch, dropped the bong on the carpet as though it wasn't made of translucent purple glass or filled with scummy greenish water, and rushed over to Milt and Frankly.

Frank Zappa (or maybe it was Dweezil) was blasting out of Gabe's circa 1980s boombox, complete with cassette player, and Milt was a little worried it might be too loud for 8 a.m.-ish. Until he remembered he was in LA.

Gabe, with his characteristic massive kid-like grin, advanced on Milt like some lumbering Hispanic Jesus on his way to the office. Gabe embraced his old friend in a bear hug that Milt for a split-second thought would turn into his being lifted up off the ground.

Gabe let go and turned to Frankly, who was too small *not* to pick up from the floor in a bear hug.

"Hey, man," Frankly exhaled between strenuous Gabe squeezes. "Good...to...*unnngh*...see you."

"I can't believe how much this place looks exactly like it did when I was here last," Milt said, walking into the living room past the filthy kitchenette to his right.

"Yeah, man," Gabe said gleefully, walking behind him, Frankly in tow. "What's it been, like, three years?"

"I can't even remember the last time I was back here," Milt said. "I think it was when I was doing that author event at Book Soup for my travel guide about coffee shops."

"Oh, yeah!" Gabe said, motioning Frankly and Milt toward the other side of the apartment, opening the screen door and beckoning them to come out with him to the balcony.

Milt and Frankly followed. Once they were outside, Gabe dashed back, closing the sliding glass door and leaving the screen door open before he turned to them to say, "Sorry, but my roommate and his girlfriend are in their room, and they're still asleep. He's been really sick. I don't want us to be too loud in there. Better out here right now."

Milt turned around, wondering how Gabe expected to keep the place quiet when he was blaring Zappa, but that was just Gabe.

And there LA was, what with the majestic and verdant Hollywood Hills to his right, imperial and almost phantasmagorical. Milt could just barely see the grimy white letters of the H O L L Y W O O D sign hiding in the far rocky distance beyond the yellowish-gray morning smog.

To his left was the rest of Los Angeles, or mostly, Hollywood. The arterial streets were clogged with morning traffic, the various buildings, none too tall courtesy of earthquake safety precautions, hole-punched by innumerable glass windows. Again, veiled by a thin veneer of yellowish-gray morning smog.

"Your roommate's sick?" Milt turned back to Gabe to ask, growing concerned.

"Yeah, but he's just getting over it now, so he should be good," Gabe said, puffing on a Camel Light.

"I'm not really worried about *him*," Milt said. "I'm assholishly worried about *myself*. I'm just starting a nationwide fucking tour for my film and I don't want to get sick."

"Awww," Gabe snickered adorably, "it's all good. Like I said, he's pretty much over it, and his girlfriend didn't catch it. They pretty much just share joints and fuck all day, so even if you do *that* with him, you should be fine."

"I'll make sure not to fuck him," Milt said. "But you're telling me he's not contagious?"

Gabe laughed, buckling over and coughing up cigarette smoke. "What do I look like, a doctor?"

This was all a moot point. Milt couldn't afford to stay in a hotel, and nearly everyone else he used to know in LA had moved on years ago. The two or three aside from Gabe who had stuck it out had vanished into the mire of becoming exactly the kind of duplicitous, opportunistic jackasses that the town and industry was so well-known for sheltering.

Milt was stuck at Gabe Martinez's, and he could continue to irrationally write-off the terrible fiduciary fiasco at the strip club two nights earlier, knowing that at least he wouldn't be paying for lodging while in town (or, thanks to Frankly's good-Catholic munificence, gas and most of his food).

Frankly was himself pulling some thin, crackly plastic sheeting from off the scattered dark wood picnic benches and chairs that crowded the balcony along with far too many different kinds of (dead) plants pendulously spilling out of all manner of broken and dingy pots.

Gabe somehow plucked yet another bong from off the ground and fell back into one of the wooden chairs, taking a hit from what had apparently been a full and ready device.

Milt waved him off when Gabe offered the bong, but Frankly gladly took the invitation to smoke while sitting on the edge of one of the picnic benches.

Milt remained the only one still standing, espying the morning dew droplets moistening the furniture. He turned once more to gaze out longingly at the Hollywood Hills and H O L L Y W O O D sign, the 1950s sci-fi style Griffith Park Observatory, and anything else he could see out there that made him just a little nostalgic for his earliest days out of film school, living a few blocks from here before chucking it all for the life of a nomadic outsider in "the industry."

"You still smoke cigarettes?" Milt asked without turning back to Gabe.

"Not really," Gabe said, lighting his second of the morning. "I sort of gave that shit up."

"That's cool," Milt said. "You think I could have one?"

"Sorry, man, this is my last one," Gabe said, taking a drag off his cigarette before exhaling the smoke to the side.

"It's all good," Milt said. "I still don't really smoke either, but I'm in LA and, I dunno, I have this weird craving for it."

"I'd give you one if I had one," Gabe said. "Maybe my roommate's girlfriend has one. I'll ask when they finally get up. They're usually up around noon."

"Wait," Milt leaned forward. "Every day? Not just Saturdays?"

"Yeah, well he's a professor or something at some school in the Valley, and she's been working on and off on her PhD I think, so neither one of them really has a regular schedule."

Gabe took the bong back from Frankly and placed it on the ground in front of him, spilling some of the water, which he dabbed up with sheets of toilet paper from a roll that was for some strange reason nearby. "Aw, fuck. Whoops. Lemme grab you another one, Milt."

Gabe was about to get out of his chair when Milt shook his head. "Don't worry about it," he told Gabe, who immediately collapsed back into his seat Lebowski style. "I probably shouldn't be fucking with my throat on our tour anyway."

"Yeah, so *why* are you doing it this way?" Gabe asked, sitting up and appearing far more executive than hippie at this point. "Why aren't you hitting up the festivals? Did you apply to the North Shore Film Festival or Tribeca or anything? This sounds like something that would be *perfect* for them."

"Mmmyeaahhhh, *whhhhyyyy* not?" Frankly practically hummed, raising his head for the first time since lowering it after his large bong pull minutes earlier.

"It's funny you bring up North Shore," Milt said. "When we were traveling around during principle photography getting a lot of the stuff from Gil's early days and whatnot, there was this chick in Montana and she and her husband completely pestered us to let them do some stuff on the shoot. I don't even think they knew who Gil Gladly *was*. But they were one of those local filmmakers in the middle of fucking nowhere who hop onto any shoot that comes along."

"Oh, shit!" Gabe said, eyes completely shut by this point and a huge, sated, shit-eating grin on his face. "One of *those* people. I thought I left all them behind in Iowa!"

"Nah, those people are *everrrrrrywhere*," Frankly said, scratching his double ear before lowering his head again.

"I just said fuck it and let her husband shoot some stuff for us, but then of course *she* wanted to be an associate producer—"

"Ass pro!" Gabe laughed heartily.

"And again I said sure, why the fuck not?" Milt said. "I gave out bullshit 'associate producer' credits to a bunch of people who helped us out in some small way."

"Better than *payin'* 'em," Frankly said.

At the same time, Gabe and Milt said, "Yup."

"This chick is saying that since we gave her an associate producer credit, she'd get us into the North Shore Film Festival because she's friends with the main programmer's son or some shit."

"Okay..."

"And me and my crew all go back to our respective homes after the shoot; you know, to our regular *real* lives...."

"Right..."

"So, this chick is saying over email—when I *do* hear from her, because she's yet another one of these fucks who only talks over email, barely even text—"

"What's wrong with that?" Gabe sat up and opened his eyes finally.

"Don't ask," Frankly replied and Gabe slunk back down deeper into his chair.

"She's starting to say all this shit about how we really need to amp the sex and drugs and rock-and-roll as we keep shooting stuff and as we start getting into shaping the whole documentary and whatever."

"Awww, tell me she didn't say 'sex, drugs, and rock-and-roll!'"

"Dude, that may have been the worst part. She *DID!*"

"Ohhhhhh!" Gabe said. "Welllllll..."

"What?"

"She's kind of right, but I get where you're going with this."

"Dude, you make documentaries about how fucking dirty the ocean is and shit for YouTube Red and all that nonsense!"

"Yeah, but I'm not trying to get into North Shore or any *real* festivals, man," Gabe said, eyes shut, beaming like the Cheshire

Cat. "That's why I don't got *nooooooo* money and need a room-mate and his girl."

"The shit just got so stupid, and of course Gil kept saying the same thing he always says about this kind of thing: 'Opinions are like assholes...'"

"You never know what you're gonna get?"

This time they all laughed a little.

"No," Milt said. "Gil's kind of adorable in espousing these old cliché aphorisms like he just discovered them. Like, 'Opinions are like assholes: Everyone's got one.' And anyway he kept agreeing with me that there *are* no sex, drugs, and rock-and-roll in his story. We weren't gonna push shit in there just to get into fucking North Shore. I mean, it's not 2005 anymore."

"Do they even sell movies there anymore?" Frankly asked. "Or is it just a place for tech bloggers and shit to jizz all over themselves about the latest what-have-you, and entertainment reporters to talk about how shitty the catering was at the after-party for some new indie film starring Ryan Gosling and Keira Knightley?"

"Whoa, Frankly!" Gabe said, lighting up.

Frankly shrugged. "Meh, that's what comes out when I spend too much time with *this* fawkin' guy," he said, pointing a thumb at Milt.

"The *point*, Gabe," Milt continued, "is that scene is just not for us. It's for people who already have deals with HBO or Netflix or studios or whatever, and they have agents at CAA and want to go waterskiing and jet skiing the whole time they're there. It's for people who can *afford* to go. It's not like they pay all your expenses even when you get in. I had a friend who went to Cannes a few years ago, and she and her director had to stay at some place way out of town where they didn't even have running water. When they tried to get into one of the events their own movie was playing at, they had trouble because they didn't have the right kind of super-expensive clothes, and it was an event they were *supposed* to be at! It's crazy these days at these festivals. Besides, call me lofty or whatever, but I really do think this film is something different."

"A doc about some TV show guy from the eighties?" Gabe said, smirking. "Mmm hmm."

"Well, okay, it's not that different," Milt admitted. "Not in the way of what it's *about*. But the way we *made* it is different. You'll see. I wanted to do something different with how we got it out there. At least in the beginning. We'll probably just end up selling it to Netflix in the end like everyone else, but for now, I was hoping we could get *something* going that no one else really does anymore. Our own little hardcore punk DIY tour. Y'know? Thought it might get us some unique press, too. A few weird clickbait headlines: 'Good Golly, Gil Gladly! He's Taking His Own Stream To Netflix.' Or some shit like that. I don't know. I don't ever write for those sites anymore."

"Yeah, rrrrrright," Gabe smiled. "The people writing articles like that probably don't even know what 'DIY hardcore punk' *was*. They probably weren't even born yet."

"None of this matters anyway," Milt said. "Because even if we wanted to go to the festivals, we couldn't afford it."

"Dude," Gabe laughed, choking up. "Why do you keep saying that?"

"Come on, dude," Milt said. "You know the drill. Even before you get in and have to spend all that money on whatever they don't take care of for your expenses, the fuckin' *applications* are totally expensive too, plus the packets you have to print out and make copies of and put together and send out, which ain't cheap, especially when you have to include DVDs and press material and one-sheets half the time...."

No one said anything as Milt calmed down. Gabe and Frankly exchanged a giddily nervous look.

"But come *on*, man," Gabe tried. "You gotta go to *some* festivals. That's where the *buyers* are, dude. "

"Oh, we *gotta?* We *GOTTA?* That's exactly why we're *not*. We're doing it our own way. Fuck it. The buyers already know what they're going to pick up, anyway, and those are the ones that already have big names in them and are produced by the 'big' indies or whatever. The way we're doing it gives us our own standalone things, around the country, we get the press, hopefully, then these networks and distributors or whatever come to *us*, or it'll be easier when we have meetings with them later to say, 'See? People are already talking about our flick and they dig it.' Helps when we get bought and end up on a queue for some streaming service too. We'll already have word-of-mouth, press, and all that, so we don't get buried under the one hundred other movies that get released that week."

"Damn, man," Gabe said, and could have either been talking about what Milt was saying but also how he was saying it, so vigorously and out of breath and all. "Guess you got it figured out."

"Also," Milt added, "unless you know someone who can pay our way to one of those places, it doesn't matter anyway. Or someone who can just slide our film into the series, which is pretty much what you need to do anyway, since, guess what? You're *not* getting in unless you do. It *is* like Harvard. Elitism, man. It's a sham, and nobody out there realizes it. Because they say 'innnndddddepennndent filllllmmmm'," and with this, Milt waved his hands around like a magician, eyes wide and, well, nuts.

"Hey," Frankly sat up to say, finally engaging more formally in the conversation. "Didn't that douchebag who was working with you on this for a minute in the beginning, Tony, or whatever his name was, get his new film into North Shore?"

"Ugh, don't even remind me," Milt said. "Tony Rigatoni."

"No way."

"Yeah, dude. That's his name," Milt said. "Tony *Rigatoni*. The dude was trouble since day one, fucking up every possible thing and just continuing to lag on things we needed, treating the rest of us like idiots just because he had some doc on Hulu already like right when Hulu first started getting big. It was a good flick and all, which is why we brought him on, but he didn't have to act like that. Especially when I'd get these whiny emails from him that made it clear he can barely spell. I thought at first he might have dyslexia or something, but then I talked to some people I knew from the scene where he came up in Cleveland before he moved to LA and turns out he's just some dumbass rich kid who couldn't even graduate college—*community* college—and whose parents pay for all his shit. I'm getting so tired of that same fucking story over and over again."

"You and me both, brother." Gabe sat up, looking over his left shoulder at the Hollywood Hills brightening with the moving sun. "A *lot* of dumbass rich kids out here. And yeah, you get these texts and emails from them and it's like, 'Dude, do you even use autocorrect or spellcheck? It's not fucking hard, moron. Read a fucking book some time.' Then they get a film into Sundance every other year and it's like, 'C'mon. You don't even know how to use Google Drive. Who you kidding?'"

Gabe reached down to the ground, grabbing his bong and smoking what he could, despite almost an entire lack of ecru water by this point.

"And of course I couldn't tell Gil about this while we were dealing with Tony because then I'd look like a fuck-up for bringing him on in the first place. And Gil was already freaking out about so much anyway with the film, and money, and his medical stuff and everything...."

Gabe handed the bong over to Frankly.

"I guess if those are the kinds of people going to North Shore these days—community college dropout rich kid douche-bags and gals who think sex, drugs, and rock-and-roll should be jammed into a documentary about Gil Fuckin' Gladly," Frankly said, "I guess we just, uh...yeah...."

Frankly shook his head, trying and failing to remember what he was about to say. Then he stared at his right shoe.

"It ain't Richard Linklater or Robert Rodriguez or Mumble-core over there no mo'," Milt said, breaking into a sing-song to the tune of "Old Gray Mare." "Ol' film fests, they *ain't* what they used to be, *ain't* what they used to be...."

"Were they ever?"

"Go ask Peter Biskind," Milt said. "Or Amy Taubin. Hey, Gabe, do you have any sunglasses I could borrow? I lost mine."

"Nah, sorry, man," Gabe said. "What medical stuff, by the way? Like Gil's stuttering thing? I always heard about that, but what's the real deal with it?"

"The stuttering is a thing, yeah," Milt said. "Some of our film is about it. But not too much, because we didn't want to make it all about Gil's stuttering or mental differences or whatever."

"Mental differences?"

"Yeah, we didn't want to make it one of those typical trendy docs about social ills and shit," Milt said. "We made a doc about Gil fucking Gladly, and that's that. No sex, no drugs, no rock-and-roll, and only a bit about his stuttering thing, which just happens to be a part of his life. I meant his health stuff with some heart shit he's been going through lately."

"Ohhhh," Gabe said, "I didn't hear about that."

"Yeah, no one has," Milt said. "We get into it a little bit in the doc, but he didn't want us going into it too deeply because it might fuck up his career or whatever."

"*What* career?" Gabe laughed. "Duder's not been on TV in like ten years or more."

"Yeah, he hasn't done too much lately," Milt admitted. "But he still guest hosts on things and has done a lot of shit behind the scenes."

"Grotcha," Gabe said with a beatific, cherubic grin, not really caring one way or another about Gil Gladly's current career or lack thereof.

"I feel bad for the guy, actually," Milt said. "He has to go through this stuff with his heart, and even none of us who worked on the film really know how bad it is. He can't talk about it with anyone or deal with it in any public way because, yeah, he's worried it will fuck his chances to do other stuff."

"Yup, no one wants to hire someone who's gonna have weird heart stuff on set," Frankly said. "Insurance goes sky high."

"What's so weird about it?" Gabe asked, turning to Frankly, giggling. "Mnnnyeeahh!"

"Fuhhhh-UHHHHH-ckkkk you," Frankly said, reaching down to grab some of the wadded-up, bong water-wet toilet paper and lobbing it at Gabe's smiley face.

"Hey, don't be a douche like that Tony Spaghetti dude!" Gabe said, throwing the wet toilet paper ball back at Frankly.

"Tony *Rigatoni*," Frankly said.

"Tomato sauce, to*mah*to sauce," Gabe said.

"Dude's the fuckin' Alan Alda to my Woody Allen from *Crimes and Misdemeanors*," Milt said.

"I wouldn't say that too loud," Frankly suggested. "Or too often."

"Woody Allen's a *crrrreeeeper*, man!" Gabe ejaculated, finding it to be the funniest moment of the morning for some reason.

"All I meant," Milt continued, "is that Alda's character in *Crimes and Misdemeanors* is this super-faux, smiley jackass with no integrity whatsoever and yet got all this success for his documentaries, and Woody's character is this curmudgeonly contrarian who won't play the game and has too much integrity and ended up with jack shit."

After an awkward grace note, Frankly asked earnestly, "Wait, how can someone have too *much* integrity?"

"You guys want to go back inside and have some coffee? I can't use too much water because of the drought limitations we're 'sposed to abide by or they ticket us for use on our monthly bill, but—"

"No," said Milt at the same time Frankly said, "Yes."

On his way to the sliding glass door, Gabe asked, "Hey, but you guys have a publicist, right?"

"You think we can't afford to apply to or go to film festivals, but we can hire on some twenty-grand a week publicist to get us three interviews that *maybe* will help us sell a few more tickets and get the word out?"

Gabe stopped, confused. His smile dissipated and his brow furrowed. "Well, how *else* you gonna do it, man? You're *'sposeda* get *some* publicist. You're not gonna get *shit* without one."

"Sounds like someone's got a case of the 'sposeda's," Frankly chimed.

"Dude, we *can't afford it*," Milt said. "How do I get you to understand what that means? You have your Silicon Valley 'philanthropists' who want to change up their images or whatever dropping in money to projects about water pollution and birds dying in Africa. They're not giving money to us for something about a TV show guy from the eighties, all right?"

"I don't know," Gabe smiled again and opened the glass door. "Sean Parker'd probably be up for something like that. That dude's *nuts*, and—"

Milt's phone vibrated in his pocket, and he picked it up. "Hold on a second, it's one of my guys. I gotta take this."

Milt pressed the phone against his ear and walked to the edge of the patio, his free hand on the brown, chipped wooden barricade, looking right out into the Hollywood sign.

"He has 'guys'?" Gabe said quietly, smirking at Frankly.

"From what it sounds like, he has *many* guys," Frankly quietly said back, obscenely pounding his closed fists together over and over again.

What followed was a brief phone conversation between Milt and Ronnie, who wanted to post on their film's social media shit he was running. Gil had been getting into a fight on Twitter with some troll fucker and Ronnie wanted to post a few screenshots from it.

"Gil's such a badass muh-duh! He don't take no crap from nobody!" Ronnie reasoned, paraphrasing *Cool Runnings*.

"No," Milt said, explaining that even though Gil had a tendency to give into those people and actually fight with them on Twitter or Instagram or Facebook or whatever else, *they*—Wallace, Ronnie, Milt, and the rest of the gang—wouldn't perpetuate that shit.

They were going to keep everything positive, Milt said, reminding Ronnie that it had been Wallace's original idea to not even allow any of the frequent swearing that was such a major staple of Gil Gladly's vernacular into the film so they could keep it family-friendly and salable to a wider audience.

"Ah, boo," Ronnie said on the other end of the phone. *"But this thread is so funny! Gil is hilarious!"*

"Doesn't matter," Milt said harshly, as though talking to a toddler begging for more ice cream. "We're not going to have any of that crap on the film's socials, no matter what Gil does. I gotta run. I'll let you know how the premiere goes."

"Fine," Ronnie said. *"You're no fun. Good luck at the screening. Say hi to Gil for me. And don't fuck it up, boyyyyyyyyssss!"*

Milt chuckled. "You're not the boss a'me."

"Yeah, yeah..."

They said their goodbyes and hung up.

Milt dropped his phone back into his pocket and stepped across the large balcony to Gabe and Frankly who had been listening—not intently, considering their state of mind—and were now standing to walk toward the sliding glass door.

As Gabe opened it, letting Frankly inside, he said to Milt, "What the fuck was that all about?"

"Nothing," Milt said, making his way back inside where a Zappa (most likely Frank, Milt determined) was still blaring.

They closed the glass door behind themselves, and Gabe went to make some coffee for everyone in what looked like a junkyard of a kitchenette across the city dump of a living room.

"Dude, it really is crazy to hear you talking about someone like that who I used to watch on Balloon all the time as a kid!" Gabe called across the living room from the kitchen, barely making it over the Zappa. "Does he seriously fight with kids on Twitter?"

"Not really," Milt said, collapsing on the feculent, scratchy couch, upon which he would be unfortunately sleeping again that night before the premiere the next morning.

"He seemed pretty cool at the San Francisco Comic-Con," Frankly said, collapsing into his easy chair.

"He's just a person," Milt said. "Like anyone else. He's not a robot. He's not a cartoon character. Then he happened to end up on TV for a long time at one point, and there it is. He's got issues like anyone else."

"Sounds like a *lot* of them," Gabe called out after grinding the coffee.

"I guess that has to do with being on TV too," Frankly said.

Milt nodded. "Probably."

Gabe finished up the coffee-making, pouring what he had into three mugs that he found in the pile in the sink. "Whatever. Duder still sounds like a total butt-ass."

Gabe came in with one mug in one hand and two in the other. His hands were like bear paws, huge. But he also clearly had a great backlog of experience as a server and barista from his earliest days out of UCLA.

"That's one of the things we love about Gil Gladly," Milt said. He kind-of meant it too. "'Cause we're all butt-asses too. He's one of us!"

"We're *all* butt-asses," Frankly affirmed, reaching up for a mug.

CHAPTER 12

As more of Gabe's friends piled into the scenester dive bar in Silver Lake that evening, the verdict became unanimous. The new *Blade Runner* movie boasted *incredible* cinematography and art direction, everyone really dug the music, but the script and storyline left far too much to be desired.

The *Blade Runner* sequel, they all agreed, was *never* going to hold a candle to the original.

"Well, sure," Gabe's scruffy, gray-bearded pal in a worn-out trucker's hat that had a faded map of Tennessee on it for no good reason, black thick-rimmed glasses, and a striped vintage store track suit jacket with a 49ers logo on it agreed. "But it could have been way better. I was expecting a lot more, especially from the guy who did *Arrival.*"

"Now *that* was a fantastic flick," said another one of Gabe's buddies, who looked younger than the first, but not by much, and who Milt was pretty sure had at one time been on a series of commercials in the early 2000s that he couldn't quite put his finger on.

Everyone could agree with that too, including the bartender, Meg, who was once probably very beautiful and still had a certain Hollywood (Blvd) mien to her. What with her long, silken onyx hair, slight Sunset (Blvd) goth-lite makeup, and a ratty Mötley Crüe shirt holding tight to her forty-plus years of zaftig pudge.

"I fucking *loved Arrival*," Meg crowed, as she brought another pitcher of frothy amber ale to the boys' side of the rather small, crowded bar blaring with some early Rolling Stones song Milt only partially remembered. There was an unhealthy number of TVs with three different basketball games on, surrounding the bar from every angle.

"What did *you* think about *Arrival*, Milt?" Gabe laughed, doing his best to draw everyone's attention to his friend sitting on the stool next to him and drifting off into space.

"Uh, yeah," Milt muttered. "Laney and I saw it before I came out here. We were pretty surprised by how good it was."

"This dude fucking hates every movie that comes out!" Gabe gleefully barked even louder than before, and now it was extremely obvious that everyone was looking at Milt, who would have blushed if he were a cartoon.

"I don't hate *every* movie. I just can't stand most of the crap that comes out these days. What can I say? I also don't like McDonald's, comic book movies, and current television. I'm like Brian Wilson," Milt smirked, being knowingly snide. "I just wasn't made for these times!"

They all had a chuckle at that, two of the guys around the bar meaning it. Gabe's friend in the trucker hat poured a beer for Milt, though he declined.

"What, you don't drink beer?" the generous soul asked.

"I haven't had beer in a few years," Milt said. "I'm a whiskey man these days, and besides, I'm trying to lose some weight. Carbs, dude."

"You're *always* trying to lose some weight," Frankly said to his right.

"We're *all* trying to lose some weight now that we're old and disgusting!" Gabe said, grabbing the beer that was originally being handed over to Milt.

"No chicken wings either?" Meg asked on her way back over to the boys, two platters of large, fat, succulent, miniature drumsticks in her mannishly large mitts.

"Paleo, baby!" Milt said, helpfully taking one of the large platters of steaming meat from Meg's right hand and placing it before Gabe, Frankly, and himself. Gabe's pal in the trucker hat took the other platter and placed it in front of himself and his own trio down the bar apiece.

"You know, I have to tell you something," Meg said. "As soon as you came in here and Gabe introduced you, I could've sworn you were—"

"Don't say it!" Gabe cracked, busting up completely. Frankly looked down at the bar in front of him, shaking his head and giggling impishly.

"I need a break from the Rogen sightings," Milt said, chomping down on a wing. "Man, this *is* the best chicken wing I've ever had! I spent almost a year a while back producing short foodie videos for *Vanity Fair* online where all we did was try to find the best chicken wings in the country."

"You worked for *Vanity Fair*?" one of Gabe's friends noshing on his own chicken wing asked.

"Well, *online*," Milt said. "It's not like it paid much, but traveling around meeting buffalo wing aficionados was pretty cool. Of course, I'm married now, so one of these days I'll have to figure out how to make *real* money with this shit. But who knows?"

MATHEW KLICKSTEIN

"Ain't easy," Gabe's friend who may have been from those commercials said in earnest solidarity.

"Milt's here promoting a movie he made," Gabe chimed in, devouring a chicken wing.

"What movie?"

"Did you ever watch *KidTalk* on Balloon?" Gabe asked.

"I didn't have cable growing up," the friend who might've been in those aforementioned commercials said, taking a shot that Meg had dropped down in front of him before she fled away to the patrons at the other end in her frantic back and forth game of Pickle.

"It was this show that was on all the time on that channel," one of the other patrons overhearing said, leaning over to join the conversation. "I watched it a little in between *KidDerp* and that other show..."

"*KidLab*," Milt said.

"Yeah! Yeah, *KidLab!* I fucking loved those shows! *KidLab* and *KidDerp* were my jams back then, man! I'd watch *KidTalk* in between them. I fucking *loved* Balloon as a kid."

"Didn't you say a while back that someone was making a documentary entirely about Balloon?" Frankly asked.

"Yeah, but there's always a few people trying to do that," Milt said, not really wanting to discuss it and ordering a double Wild Turkey on the rocks from Meg when she made her way back to his side of the bar.

"There's that new one they're almost done with and they were going to interview you for it, right?" Frankly asked.

"Yeah," Milt sniffed. "I was going to be their Balloon expert, but I never heard from the dude again. Another rich kid who

170

lives with his parents, travels all over the country on their dime shooting stuff for his doc. Blah, blah, blah. Must be nice."

Meg dropped off Milt's Turkey *doubler* and he went right at it, swigging as to the manner born.

"Fucker has one of the creators of *NiñoPrograma* onboard as EP, helping him get access to everyone else he's trying to interview," Milt said, finishing off the last drops of his bourbon. "Apparently his dad went to NYU with him."

"*Which* show?"

"*NiñoPrograma,*" Milt said.

"It was this Balloon show back in the early eighties—"

The possible commercial actor took it from there. "—And they had these puppets who were supposed to be these Mexican guys, and the whole point was supposed to be that, like, they were trying to be all educational about other cultures—"

"—but when you look back on it now," Eavesdropper kept the ball in play, "it was *soooo* fuckin' racist!"

"Mmm." Milt was holding his glass of ice and looking into it like he was trying to will whiskey back into the thing. "Yeah, it got called out pretty hard about two years ago by Jezebel and a few other sites in the blogosphere."

"Wait," said Trucker Hat, "so this rich kid asshole you're talking about brought on the creator of this Mexi-hating kids show to EP his doc on Balloon?"

Milt shrugged. "First off, the show *wasn't* Mexican-hating and in fact they were *trying* to be promoting of the culture, but... ugh, never mind. Fuck it. Not my problem who he wants to work with on his doc." Milt tore into another chicken wing. "And hey, you gotta have *some* kind of celebrity EP or whatever onboard these days. Either you got the money or you need the celebrity, even if it's someone who's kind of a nobody but has access. And knows enough people who can get you your Kickstarter link or articles on AV Club and shit like that. It's all a game. Money, publishity, chelebrity...."

Milt was beginning to slur.

"Didn't Tony Rigatoni pop onto their film after you guys bounced him from yours?" Frankly asked, clearly already knowing the answer but wanting to be part of the discussion.

"Yeah," Milt said, finishing his wing and wiping his hands with a napkin. "Gil found out about it when they brought him in for an interview...courtesy of Tony hooking them up after he'd gotten to know Gil from our film. Nice, huh? Right before we kicked him to the curb, Tony bragged about how he just jumps from pop culture doc to pop culture doc, watching whatever seems to be doing well on Kickstarter and Indiegogo, then shoves his way in and basically takes over. He told us about it like this was a good thing. We didn't let him do that to us, so I guess he found another team who would. Congrats."

"They interviewed *Gil*?"

"Yeah, duder. You would *have* to interview Gil Gladly if you're doing a doc about Balloon," Gabe said.

"We talked about it when Gil got the invite to be interviewed," Milt continued, "and Gil even asked if he wanted me to have him send them a cease and desist order for potentially competing with our project. But I said he shouldn't do that. He should just wait and see what comes of the production before doing the interview." Milt drank the ice water that was left in his glass. "And then, you know, next thing we see on Gil's Twitter page is a pic from his interview with the Balloon doc folks. So, whatever. Gil does what Gil does. Force of nature. Can't stop him. Trust me."

"Man, I never would've thought that someone like Gil Gladly would be all like that," the interloper a few seats down injected. "He sounds like a real ballbuster with the whole cease and desist letter thing. I always thought he was like a Mr. Rogers type or something."

"Aw, c'mon, man," Gabe said, leaning over the bar with a clownish stretch. "Just because he was on a kids show doesn't mean he's not gonna act exactly the fuck the same as everyone else in the entertainment industry. You know?"

"I guess that makes sense," Interloper said, leaning over to Gabe to shake hands. "My name's Trevyn, by the way. You guys want some shots? Jameson? On me?"

The boys did want. Trevyn the interloper called for the shots from Meg, who went off to go retrieve them on yet another platter.

"Gil's got a lot riding on this thing," Milt said. "He paid for most of the budget himself. Then there's all this shit going on in his life right now. Plus, he's got all these insecurity issues in general and—"

"Insecurities?"

"Fuck *yeah*, insecurities," Frankly said. "Kids channel or not, Gil was a talk show host, man. You ever watch *The Larry Sanders Show* with Garry Shandling? All that stuff is real."

"Hell *yeah*," Trevyn said, nodding. "Fucking loved that show. Nah, I get it. And Shandling was all fucked-up in real life too, wasn't he?"

"He was," Milt said. "Who wouldn't be? Gil will tell me about how depressed he is and how he doesn't think anyone cares about him anymore or would even give a shit about a doc about him or whatever...then like five minutes later, he'll text me right back and tell me a whole bunch of kids saw him coming out of a restaurant in SoHo or wherever and totally swarmed him, then he's all good again. Dude's all over the place. You'd be too."

"Didn't you say before you had to basically force him to do the documentary in the first place?"

"Oh, I always gotta force everyone to do everything," Milt laughed. "You know me. I'm an asshole."

"This is true."

"Yeah, I don't know," Milt considered. "It's like...sometimes I wonder if these people really want to do any of these kinds of things. You have all these people doing documentaries about themselves and reality shows about themselves and, yeah, books about themselves. It must be really great in a lot of ways, but then really *weird* and even a bit *embarrassing* too. It's their *name*."

"Like *The Crucible!*"

Milt smiled. "Well, no, not like *The Crucible*."

"It's my *naaaaaammmme!*" Gabe, Frankly, and Trucker Hat shouted.

"Oh, man." Frankly laughed. "Did you see that awful movie they made of *The Crucible* with Demi Moore?"

"That movie did suck donkey balls, but Gary Oldman was badass in it," Gabe said.

"I just hope all this shit worksh out," Milt said, downing his complimentary shot and speaking with a more punctuated slur.

"Becaushe I don't want Gil to have done all of thish for nothing. Or me or *any* of the guys like lil' Frankly over here, who worked on thish goddamn thing for sho long. I jush...want thish shit...to work out. For *everyone*."

The other guys applauded sarcastically, including Trevyn the interloper.

"Fuhhhhhhhck you *all*," Milt said, holding in his laughter.

Frankly gave Milt a much-deserved but playful smack to the face. Milt whipped his pen out of his pocket, wielding it like a knife. The laughter now spread throughout the whole section of the bar.

"Is that supposed to scare me?" Frankly chortled.

Milt clicked the back of the pen, engaging the pointy tip. Everyone lost their mind and would've fallen over off their stools if they had been cartoon characters too.

Before they could continue the bibulous charade, Milt's phone began vibrating in his pocket, and he hopped off his stool to make his way through the crowd of standing customers drinking and watching the multiple basketball games bombarding them from every possible angle.

Out the door, there was a small group of people smoking cigarettes and laughing at whatever story the principle lady talking had just told.

One of them pointed at Milt and called out that he "looks like that guy from that movie where the guy gets the girl pregnant," and Milt kept walking, already in conversation with Louis Bradley.

"*Hey, Milt, wussup?*" Louis asked on the other end of the phone.

"In LA with a couple of my old friends out here and some of their buddies in Silver Lake," Milt said. "We're getting ready for the premiere tomorrow. Should be good. What's going on in Portland?"

"Ummmm" Louis said. *"So, I just got a call from Gil."*

"Uh huh...." *Uh oh.*

"And, like, he's all freaking out about the numbers of tickets sold for the McMenamins show."

"Okay...." *Fuck, fuck, fuck, fuck, fuck....*

"I just wanted to make sure I was handling it correctly."

"Right," Milt said, taking a breath and looking out to the constipated early evening traffic before him on the street beyond the cracked sidewalk upon which he was pacing back and forth. Each car was nearly stock-still, illuminated by red brake lights of the car in front of it and white lights of the car in back of it as though they were all in some kind of nightmarish electric parade. "So, what did you say?"

"I told him the truth," Louis said.

"Awww, man, *seriously?*"

"Yeah, but I mean...I inflated the numbers a little bit of course."

"Oh, thank god," Milt said with a heavy exhale of relief. He suddenly had a serious hankering for a cigarette and turned around, striding back to the group of smokers outside the bar, wondering if it would be worth asking them for one. They were getting more raucous and he just didn't feel like dealing with that crap.

"Yeah, I mean I get it," Louis said. *"There's no way we could possibly know how many people will actually be coming out*

*anyway, right? I'm sure there will be plenty of walk-ins, espe-
cially with all the radio and press stuff you guys are doing out
here. It's all good. I have to go through this kind of thing with
Vinnie sometimes too. I'm welllllllllll aware of the game, man."*

"Yeah, no, you did the right thing," Milt said, shuffling back
toward the bar and steadying himself to ask for a cigarette to
soothe himself.

Milt knew Louis understood the drill. They'd met six or
seven years earlier while both working some horror movie
festival in Baltimore. Louis was a few years older than Milt and
had already begun making his own documentary about his
pop culture "mentor" of a sort, schlockmeister extraordinaire
Vincent Van Groan.

Vincent Van Groan had made a name for himself pioneering
the next wave of campy, goofy, over-the-top, culty movies in the
vein of Russ Meyer and Roger Corman. In the eighties, he'd had
a string of minor underground hits, particularly with his one
truly commercially successful franchise about a woman with
demon tits. They'd made seven of the goddamn things over
the years, and there was now a Broadway musical in the works
based on the first one.

Milt had known and worked a little with Vincent Van Groan
himself and really admired the guy's passion for filmmaking,
but he also knew that, yeah, Van Groan could be somewhat
curmudgeonly and difficult at times. Heck, Van Groan had to
be—what?—in his early eighties? Amazing he was still working,
sort of, but Milt could only imagine some of the challenges
Louis had to face on his doc and other work with Van Groan.

"Gil kept hitting me up about the numbers for the different venues," Milt went on, "and I had to explain to him that we don't know yet, we don't *want* to know yet, and he should be cool about it and not worry. Part of it is because of how fucked the CineRanchero event keeps getting—"

"Oh, yeah? What's up with CineRanchero?"

"The chick they gave us to 'produce' the thing is just a total fuck-up and doesn't seem to give a shit about anything we're trying to do here."

"Typical."

"You know how this shit happens. Did you see the CineRanchero website for our event? They couldn't even spell the goddamn name of the movie right. From what Gil and I could see, they're not doing any promotion at all. Everything is just word of mouth now, and if they had bothered to tell us that months ago, we could have gotten shit going on our own like we're doing at every other fucking place, but too late now!"

"That fucking sucks, man," Louis said. *"Sorry to hear it."*

"I don't understand how people like this Sally broad can end up in charge of these things. I've been running around in this game for, like, half my life, and it still baffles me every time how these people make it through that we gotta deal with. It's like kids who never learn to read but still get passed along to graduate high school."

Knowing the drill when it came to dealing with Milt too, Louis quickly changed the subject. *"Oh, hey, by the way, you guys need to make sure you're all prepared for the heat wave out here."*

"Heat wave? It's almost winter," Milt said. "They're having snow storms destroying everything in parts of the country."

"Yeah, I know. But I think it's related to the drought down there in SoCal or something. I dunno. Crazy world these days, ain't it? Whatever it is, it's going on, and old people are passing out in the streets, little kids are slipping into comas, and it's just something you guys gotta be prepared for. Make sure there's lots of water at the event and make sure you all have A/C in your hotel rooms and shit."

"Jesus," Milt said. "2017! Woo-hoo!"

"How you doing otherwise? You holding up?"

"I guess," Milt said, stepping up to one of the fatter, older guys in the smoking group. "Hey, man, could I bum a cigarette?"

"Sure thing, Mr. Rogen!" the man said, guffawing along with the rest of the group, handing Milt a Camel Light from his battered pack.

"What was that?" Louis asked on the other end of the phone.

Milt toddled away from the rollicking coven and pulled out an orange Bic lighter he had in his back jean pocket, lit his cigarette, and took a drag, exhaling before responding. "Some people outside the bar. They all think I look like Seth Rogen. Worth it for a cig. I can't believe I'm smoking again."

"You do *look like Seth Rogen!"* Louis cracked up. *"But aside from that indignity, you're doing okay? Not jumping off any bridges or anything?"*

"Not yet."

"How's the book you're ghostwriting? It's coming along while you're doing all this other shit with the movie?"

"For now."

"Laney?"

"Still married."

"Hey, man. Then you're good. And you're gonna be fine."

"You sure about that?" Milt asked, sucking on his cigarette, exhaling his smoke, and watching someone screaming out of their car window at a motorcycle struggling to get going in front of him in the electric traffic parade a few feet away.

"Yup," Louis said. *"Money-back guarantee. You just gotta remember that this is the life, you know? This is the industry you're in, the one you chose to be a part of and work in. You gotta just deal. But it's worth it in the end, ain't it?"*

"Yeah..." Milt said, somewhat reluctantly. "Well, do what Vanilla would do and stay 'cool as ice' out there in the heat wave."

"Yeah," Louis said, *"I'm following Schwarzenegger's advice in* Batman & Robin."

At the same time, Louis and Milt said, "Chhhhillllll!"

CHAPTER 13

Milt Siegel wasn't sure *what* he wanted, though he did know he wanted sleep.

He thought of the Edgar Allen Poe quote—*"Sleep / Those little slices of Death / How I loathe them"*—that was used in not one but two *Nightmare on Elm Street* movies.

He was lying there—recalling that a *person* "lies" and a *thing* "lays" (how to remember the grammar rule? people *lie*)—on Gabe's couch, staring up at the cottage cheese ceiling. It had to have been 2:00 a.m. by now.

There was no way he was getting to sleep tonight.

He was grateful Frankly didn't snore. This was something he had learned from the two years or thereabouts he had lived with the man back in his firebrand LA days. What had it been, *ten* years ago? How did it become that long? How was that possible? Milt flashed on *Back to the Future*.

Milton Siegel was a pop culture guy. There was no getting around it. Maybe he was, deep down, a salivating fanboy. But couldn't he be an *executive* fanboy? A la how the comedian/actor Eddie Izzard had in the past referred to himself as being an *executive* transvestite? Back when you were "allowed" to say such things? It had only been, *what?* oh, ten years. Again.

As much as he wanted to divorce himself from that entire fandom scene, had he become one of them? He worried that, in analyzing and scrutinizing and observing his own Chernobyl here, he had accidentally found himself tainted by the fall-out radiation.

You can't get that close, he thought, *without becoming part of it.*

Could you?

Maybe *he* was on the autism spectrum. Maybe...maybe everyone was? Especially these days.

He turned on his side and regarded the large, beautiful TV screen, immaculately onyx, bordered by polished silver trim. How was it that Gabe could have such a shitty apartment, so vile, and yet here in the middle of the squalor was this incredible, super-expensive television? What was wrong with *that* picture?

And here was Milt lying on the scuzzy, scratchy couch. Who knew what material it had been made from...or what street Gabe had plucked it from?

It was LA, where *anything*, unfortunately, was possible. Milt cringed at the "pregnant couch" his roommates and he had had back in their off-campus three-bedroom while he was finishing film school at UCLA.

They called it the "pregnant couch" because, after dragging it in off the curb about a quarter mile up the street in an alleyway, they lugged it into their living room to discover that, though it was comfortable as all hell, it was so disgustingly squalid that even after wiping it down with every bit of cleaning product they had, they still determined that it remained so infested with grody-ness that if a girl were to lie on it naked, she'd likely get pregnant.

Milt thought of these things, clenching his bowels, wanting to take a shit worse than anything he could imagine. But he *would not*. Not in Gabe's bathroom. It was not safe. He was too coy to use the facilities here. The pregnant couch was one of his Corinthians 1:13 "childish things" that he had done away with on his way to becoming a man. *Never* again would Milt sit on something that could get a girl pregnant...or give him hives.

He knew Laney would make fun of him about it. He didn't care.

His mind raced. And it was losing.

Milt tried to recall a time in his life—it had to have been when he was a dumb kid, back in high school or maybe junior high school? *Elementary* school?—when he didn't worry like this. When he wasn't so tremblingly nervous about *everything*.

MoneygirlsLaneyloveromanceEVERYTHINGAll-ThatthestufftheshowsBalloonGilGladlyGoodGollyGil-GladlyShitsmelledSilvertseinThoseASSHOLESEVERY-ONEEVERYTHINGeverythingEVERYTHINGEverythin-gAllAtOnceTVShowsWHOCaredWHOCARESWhyAM-IDOINGTHISGODDAMNITMONEYMONEYMONEY-LaneyLaneyLaneyMarriageGettingOLDERThingsHurtA...LOTLoveRomanceMoneyThingsEVERYHINGALLATON-CEAGAINGODDAMNITPLEASEGODHELPMEDoyoureally-existatallSHOULDIPRAYTOANCESTORSWHOAREDEAD-ANDMAYBEWATCHINGOVERMEOhGodIdon'tknowifI'mly-ingaboutEVERYthing.

This was the swirling folderol of thoughts in Milt's mind that consumed him, wrapped around him like the smoky words from the Caterpillar's hookah in *Alice in Wonderland*.

Throughout it all, his stomach was begging him to *please* evacuate his bowels. He would *not*. No way. Gabe's bathroom was a travesty. Talk about Chernobyl.

Especially since Gabe's roommate had been sick, there was no way Milt would touch anything in that den of evil.

No. He could hold it in.

Staring up at the ceiling, listening to Frankly on the chair next to him not snoring and the white noise of his fan, Milt realized that he should have used the bathroom at the Thai place up the street they'd all gone to after the bar and acerbic deconstruction of *Blade Runner 2049* only a few hours earlier.

He could feel the churning, burning feeling in his stomach. The shifting around of what felt like slugs set aflame moving about freely and without care in his guts. He worried about colon cancer. He thought of a friend of a friend only a few years older than he who had died of colon cancer about two years earlier. His mutual friend had sent out a group email to everyone he knew, proclaiming, **"PLEASE, GET YOURSELF CHECKED OUT SO THIS DOESN'T HAPPEN TO YOU!"**

Oh, my God, Milt thought. *Am I dying?*

He was getting so *old*. Things *hurt*. He remembered an older friend—upon Milt's thirtieth birthday, at which he twisted his ankle dancing at a party—patting him (*hard*) on the back and guffawing, "Welcome to *thirty*, motherfucker! Now *everything* will hurt! All the time!"

Yikes and zounds.

Oh, but if he could only afford medical insurance....

What was he doing on this fucking tour? And why hadn't he taken a shit at that goddamn Thai place they'd all gone to after the bar?

The Thai place.

It was only a few blocks up from Gabe's place. It was a few hours after Meg's bar that they ended up meeting with three of Gabe's team members from his intramural beer-swilling softball league, grabbed a few more drinks at a different bar, then stopped in for a late-night snack at the aforementioned Thai restaurant by Gabe's house.

Milt didn't remember much. He had had a *lot* of Wild Turkeys by the time they'd arrived at the spicy-sweet smelling exotic eatery.

There were blurs of the very two-dimensional, pastel-colored Asian paintings framed cheaply on the walls. Sumo wrestlers, haunting wilderness nymphs, angry demons and beasts, some with feathers and some with wings. No dragons, but he got the idea without having to completely check out every single randomly-sized and randomly-shaped picture hanging on those off-white eggshell walls.

The tables had been wood. Likely wood. Maybe wood? They had been a dark cherrywood color, hadn't they? Milt couldn't quite recall in his distrait, half-asleep mezzanine state staring up at Gabe's ceiling.

Next came muddled memories of some kind of peanut butter chicken noodles. *Wasn't that what they had been?*

The Thai place had not been too large or too loud. He was fairly certain he was the only person there along with Gabe, Frankly, and Gabe's three indistinguishable hangers-on pals.

Milt was fairly certain Trucker Hat from Meg's bar had joined them too, now that he thought about it. There was definitely something they had ordered and potentially eaten that had some kind of peanut-buttery goodness to it.

There were the two girls—he remembered *them*—at the Thai place bar across from Milt's gang's table.

Milt had no recollection of the music, if there had been any at all.

But those girls at the bar. Neither of them could have been over twenty-eight. The perfect age. Young enough to be feisty and supple. Old enough to be experienced and knowledgeable. He loved twenty-eight-year-old girls.

It had been all in good fun. Especially since he'd soon learn one of the girls was a lesbian. Perhaps both. *That* he'd *never* learn.

What had happened was the two girls were there in a heated discussion with one another. It couldn't have been much earlier than 11:30 p.m. Maybe after midnight.

The girl on the right was likely younger than the one on the left. They straddled their stools like men. The left girl was darker, exotic. She had tousled brown hair, zits, and purple-rimmed glasses. She wore (pre-)ripped jeans and a silver rain slicker that seemed extremely inappropriate weather-wise for Southern California, even during the late fall. Her shirt under her slicker had the wording and logo for the show Daria watched on her eponymous cartoon, *Sick, Sad World*.

Girl on the right was taller, larger, chubbier, more doll-like, with wavy dirty-blonde hair down to her shoulders. She had impressively large azure eyes, nervous wrinkles lining her forehead, and wore what appeared to be a reddish (diamond-studded?) jumpsuit that she had to have gotten from an old relative or wildly overpriced vintage shop on Sunset. The kind of outfit that looked like it was purloined from the trash but probably cost a minimum of $700. Pre-owned.

She had, of course, dark-red Beatle boots on.

She was, overall, a dead ringer for an older, funk-influenced version of Kirsten Dunst's "Claudia" from *Interview with the Vampire.*

The two girls were fighting (perhaps?) over something Dirty Blonde had said about breaking up with her latest girlfriend. The one on the left (who may not have been a lesbian) was upset that her friend was still pining after this bitch when she knew Dirty Blonde was better than that.

They hot potato'd the conversation back and forth, and Milt, watching all along while Gabe and the guys were loudly laughing and carrying on about some kind of sporting something-or-other that Milt didn't give a shit about, couldn't help himself any longer. He had to break through the TV screen. He called out, "You girls having a good time? Because *I* almost am! But I'm surrounded by fucking *dudes*!"

The girls turned to him and said nothing. At first.

Then Dirty Blonde got into the circus act. "Oh, yeah?" she said, directing her Dunst doll eyes right at him, blinking amorously.

Gabe and the guys curtailed their loud chatter and turned to the girls at the bar who they apparently hadn't noticed until now. There were only two people working this late, likely the owner's son and his wife, and they didn't seem to care that customers were yelling across the restaurant to each other.

"What do you know about what it's like to get dumped by your girlfriend...on your *birthday*?" Dirty Blonde asked.

"You think you chicks are the only ones who know what it's like to have your heart fucked with like that?" Milt said, surprised that the words flowed out of his mouth so easily.

Gabe laughed awkwardly as he tended to do, fucking up the whole thing. "Did you just say *heart*?"

"Yeah!" Dirty Blonde and Milt had said at the same, looking at Gabe, before turning back to one another. Oh, shit, and now Dirty Blonde hopped off her stool (she was much shorter than she had appeared; maybe five-foot-two?) and advanced on Milt's communal cherrywood (?) table.

Everyone at the table was laughing loudly. Except for Milt, whose eyes were locked with Dirty Blonde's.

"You're the asshole of the group, aren't you?" Dirty Blonde said, walking right up to him. Milt would not turn his head. He would not look away. He was up for the challenge. *He would WIN, goddamn it!*

She came closer to him as he replied, "We're all assholes here, but I'm definitely the head."

"What's that?" Dirty Blonde's friend back on the stool asked. "You give good head?"

"No, no," Milt said shaking his head, smirking. "*You* guys are the requisite gays in the Hollywood late-night Thai place. Not we."

Oooooooh! It felt like they were back in elementary school, calling and responding to the girls' table from the boys' table.

"You sure about that?" Frankly asked from the side of the table where he was sitting, smug and sardonic as always.

"Well, I don't know these three guys that well," Milt said, pointing at Gabe's softball teammates who were all cracking up, "but I'd think they'd dress a bit better if—"

"Would it surprise you to know that my friend here is *not* gay?" Dirty Blonde said, pointing to her pal back at the stool.

"Congratulations?" Milt said.

Huge gales of laughter now, with Dirty Blonde's face right in Milt's. A game of Chicken now. Who would flinch first?

She gazed into his eyes with the intensity of a Steve Jobs death-stare, but Milt was unmoved. He leaned back in his chair away from her as she lunged at him, grabbing him by the shoulders. She hugged him tightly, turning to everyone else at the table and her friend back at the stool. "I love this guy," she said. "You're my favorite."

Then she pecked him on the cheek.

Reminiscing about this back on the couch in Gabe's den of iniquity, Milt couldn't help but wonder—*Sex and the City* style— if he had said something different (or at all) at this moment, if he had made some kind of move or maneuver, if he had kept the goofy bullshit going, or had maybe kissed her back on the cheek, if right now he'd be home with Dirty Blonde at her place, really proving to her and to himself that, indeed, sexuality was amorphous, that anyone could be anything they want to be, that labels really were for cans....

But no.

That's not what happened. *Thankfully*. He didn't need to do that. There were any number of ways that could have gone bad. He enjoyed flirting. He likely always would. Laney enjoyed flirting too. She also likely always would.

But, goddamn it, they were *married* now. He couldn't go flounce around with any random girl who happened to pay him some positive attention, no matter how much he craved it, particularly after a youthful existence of celibate nerdiness that led him wanting well up into his early twenties.

Was this the story of everyone? he wondered, staring up at the wall, hearing Frankly not-snore but shift around in his puffy easy chair.

Did a lot of people like Milton Siegel grow up with little or no sexual conquests to speak of, only to grow into a better, more improved person in his or her twenties, then suddenly go mad with lust once the attention started to pour in from the outside world at last?

Milt thought about looking into this idea more. It seemed trite, like some kind of rom-com plotline he'd seen far too many times before. But perhaps he could put something together. Interview various "geek icons" out there about what their child-hood was like compared to the successful adulthood they were now in, and perhaps talk with psychologists and neurologists and sexperts and....

Then he shifted to his left side, lying on his left arm, which hurt his left shoulder as it always did, and stared at a purple stain on the couch (*does anyone really drink* grape juice *anymore? Jesus* Christ, *Gabe!*) and realized if he were any real writer, he would go off and try to put together some kind of well-re-searched thinkpiece on the topic....

But who was he kidding? He wouldn't do that for any number of reasons, the least of which being he couldn't put himself through the process of researching, reaching out to people, conducting interviews, transcribing the interviews, and putting it all together in a snappy, short piece that he'd then have to pitch around and talk with friends and editors at different outlets only to find out he'd get to have it published, but for little to no money. And not for *months* in the future.

Did his *not* doing it make him *more* of a writer then, or less?

He shifted to his back, staring again up at the cottage cheese ceiling.

Milt knew he would not check his phone. He had left it off, and it would stay off. He would not look at light. He would not see what Gil Gladly was hitting him up about now, also likely still not sleeping. He would not try to pretend that he could get some work done on his ghostwriting project.

He would not even see if Laney was up too, knowing she slept the sleep of someone with no guilt and no anxiety.

He wished he could find out how she figured that particular trick out. And he wished he had used the bathroom at the Thai place before they had left. His magma-filled stomach was really going to town now. He wasn't sure how much longer he could take the searing pain.

To distract himself, he tried to piece together the events that had transpired after the Thai place.

It was a complete blur by then, of course (*should he not drink so much anymore? was he drinking more because he was on his tour, because of the stress of everything, because he was also technically at the same time sort-of/kind-of on "vacation" since he was traveling, even if it was technically for "work"? did it even count as work if he wasn't getting paid? was it Knut Hamsun who wrote, "Business is labor that is worthy of its hire"? should he really be quoting someone like Knut Hamsun to himself?*).

He remembered Gabe's friends leaving, right around the time they finished at the Thai place. He remembered getting back to Gabe's, taking one look at the bathroom, and promising himself he would *not* use it.

Then Milt remembered....

The couch was occupied when they got back. Sitting on it, stretched out in his ratty robe, professorial glasses, long wispy brown beard and hair, was Gabe's roommate Philip. Gabe's *sick* roommate Philip. Sitting on the couch, Milt's bed! Infesting the raggedy thing with his germs!

Next to the fever-sweaty and pallid Philip was Philip's tiny-tot of a girlfriend, a hippie girl with princess-braided auburn hair, vintage Gloria Steinem glasses, and a loose, sack-like nightgown that immediately in Milt's head made him think of yet another line from *The Virgin Suicides*. (So much Dunst this trip!)

Still a bit punch-drunk from the run-in with the dirty blonde lesbian at the Thai place, Milt had to watch his tongue around the delightful little girlfriend of Philip's, who reached out her hand to Milt and introduced herself as Annie.

Aside from not wanting to appear too eager to make physical contact, Milt hesitated to shake Annie's hand, at once realizing she was likely on her way toward getting sick too, and just hadn't yet been exhibiting any symptoms.

Annie was slightly on the tubby side, probably a new development, Milt felt, and it made her look more like a cherubic angel in Gloria Steinem glasses from some Renaissance

painting. Or maybe that had to do with her beatific, near-expres-
sionless Mona Lisa grin that didn't seem to go away as she
passed around a pink glass pipe and smoked pot along with
her (*sick*, goddamn it!) boyfriend, followed by Gabe and Frankly.

None of the others seemed to mind that Philip looked like
he was ready to stand in as background in one of those nineties
Outbreak-type films that were mercilessly foisted on the unassuming public one after the other.

After declining the germ-laden pipe when it was his turn
in the rotation, Milt asked Annie what it was she did. Annie
explained that she had been working at the library at the college
where Philip earned his PhD and where she had been working
on her own, off and on.

Then the combination of working on her thesis with the
library job became far too stressful for her. So stressful, in fact,
that she evidently got "sick from stress."

"My body hurt all the time," she elaborated. "I couldn't
get up in the morning most of the time." So, she had stopped
working altogether. No library job. No thesis. The fact she lived
off of Philip didn't seem to matter to either of the couple. At
some point, she had added, she'd go back to work. Maybe she'd
finish her thesis. "Some day. I just don't know when."

"What's your thesis about?" Milt recalled mumblingly
asking.

"Tracking and investigating the relationship between the
trauma of having grown up with certain scenes in movies and
TV shows that we all watched and their impact on certain issues
a lot of our generation ended up later having with anxiety,"
Annie answered without a tinge of irony.

"Oh yeah?"

"Yeah," she said. "You know, like the Swamp of Sadness scene in *NeverEnding Story* where Atreyu's horse Artax dies, or the way we never got to see what Nanny from *Muppet Babies* looked like and she was always abandoning the kids in the nursery, and also the whole sequence with the little girl who gets banished to the painting and disappears over time in the film version of Roald Dahl's *The Witches*. Though that one's a little more esoteric."

The blurry memories continued bombarding him as Milt lay there on the couch wondering what time it was and if he could sneak out and go to a bathroom up the street. There had to be a Denny's that was open *somewhere* nearby.

He remembered now too that while they were all discussing Annie's failed thesis, on the television was a new HBO documentary about Steven Spielberg. It had dawned on Milt that Gabe and Frankly were meanwhile getting ready to settle in on their own areas of the couch/lounger and continue laughing, smoking, drinking whatever booze and beer Gabe had in the kitchen or that was rolling around in bottles on the floor beneath their feet, meaning no one would be getting to sleep any time soon.

When it was Philip who had politely asked about an hour later, "Are you okay, Milt?" Milt wasn't sure how to say, "Well, to be honest, I have a super-important meeting tomorrow with a producer on a possible new project that Gil Gladly hooked me up with, followed almost immediately by the first screening of the documentary I've been working on for the better part of the past two years as part of a full fucking nationwide tour I spent the last six months putting together...."

But instead, he had said something like, "Uh, yeah. I'm just a little tired...and, uh..."

"You need to get to bed?" Gabe hazarded to guess.

"Oh," Annie said, passing the pipe to her boyfriend who was a pale, moist ghost by this point, "are we keeping you up? I sometimes forget other people have to *work*!"

They all had a chuckle about this, including Milt, who was forcing it more than the others.

Milt nodded and said, "I mean, it's your place and all. But yeah, I was hoping to get to bed soon if possible. And am I crazy or is this Spielberg documentary—"

"Uh oh, here we go!" Gabe busted-up. "You hate this too, don't you? Milt hates *everything!* You probably never even liked *E.T.* as a kid, did you?"

Annie and Philip looked over to Milt sympathetically, and the three shared a look that said the same thing. Philip then turned to Annie and they shared *their* look, before Philip turned back to Milt, asking, "Do you want to use our bed? We can just stay out here. We probably won't go to sleep until the morning. We're kind of night owls."

"Uh...shouldn't you get some rest to take care of your cold?" Milt asked, nervous he'd be forced to end up in Philip's room, breathing in all the toxic contagions of his *Outbreak* cold.

Annie's face registered the fact that Philip had clearly misread her look. She wasn't saying, *"Let's let him have our room."* She was saying, *"You know what, guys? We probably* should *hit the hay. What is it? Like 2:30 a.m. already?"*

Thank God.

There had been a jump-cut there leading Milt to where he was now, staring at the ceiling and contemplating all of this.

This long-running, loud film festival blasting him in the brain while the hours crept by so-slowly. His stomach demanding satisfaction. His worrying about how much he always worried about things, including how much he worried.

Did everyone worry like this? And why the hell would it matter if they did? Why did he always worry about whether or not "everyone" else was doing what he was doing?

Frankly shifted again, got up, coughed, belched, and toddled off to the bathroom. Milt was jealous of Frankly's bravado.

Milt finally wondered if he could operate in a few hours on two or three hours of sleep, realizing it didn't matter. He'd have no choice.

CHAPTER 14

ilt knew he shouldn't have used Gabe's bathroom. He just *knew* it.

After finally giving in and taking the massive, disgusting, chicken-wings/whiskey/Thai-food dump his stomach had been demanding, he reached behind where he sat on the bowl, found the flusher...and flushed.

He sat there momentarily, looking around the room, at the scum, grit, and grime. The color scheme ventured from faded motel mauve to a kind of sad sunflower yellow, and finally around to the shitty browns and pathetic grays revealed by numerous cracks in the walls, the Pepto-pink, cracked tile floor, and faded flowery wallpaper.

There were used towels—two brown, one kind-of white—drenched and left on the floor. Two empty bottles of what had been blue Listerine were tipped over on their side, one on the muddy sink lined with circuitous networks of black and dark brown hair, and the other on the floor not too far from Milt's feet, next to a green plastic trashcan overflowing with diseased bathroom detritus.

There were so many used, wadded-up tissues that Milt did everything he could not to breathe, particularly because of the rank smell that had been present even before he took his triumphant shit.

That was when he heard it. *Nothing.*

The water didn't go down. It hadn't flushed all the way down. He *heard* it not go all the way. That was what he heard when he had heard that dreaded bathroom noise of...*nothing.*

He lifted himself slightly off the toilet seat, which sort of fell to the side a bit.

Fresh off of hearing Annie's impractical thesis, there came here an obvious flash in his mind of the Rockbiter explaining what the *Nothing* was in *The NeverEnding Story.*

Back to reality. Milt had clogged the toilet in his friend and fellow filmmaker's absolutely abominable bathroom. At god-knows-what-hour (6:00 a.m.? -ish?). The very morning of his two-years-in-the-making feature film documentary about *Mister* Gil Gladly.

Where were *these* stories in *Variety* and the *Hollywood Reporter*?

They kind of get left out of the mythology of the whole thing, don't they? Milt thought.

Then the noise got worse...the *Nothing* grew to *something.* And that was when he felt it.

That was when Milton Siegel *knew* it.

He felt the warm trickle of water first on the back of his right ankle. Then his left ankle.

He recoiled like he'd been bitten, glad he had already wiped, because he sprung up from the toilet bowl as though it were on fire, and *Jesus Fucking CHRIST* the goddamn thing was overflowing!

There was what appeared to be brownish-yellow tea flooding out from all around the rim of the toilet bowl now, rushing like someone was willing the fucking, literal shit out all over the cracked pink tile floor. The towels there were already drenched, so they'd be of no help to sop up the lava of muck.

This was certainly not Milt's first overflowing toilet. So, the initial panic that propelled him forth quickly waned as he pondered what to do next. He was in someone else's house now, and half the people here he didn't really know. Should he go get Frankly?

Philip was still obviously so incredibly sick—*Fuck*, Milt suddenly thought, *I better not get sick being in this shithole bathroom! Don't* touch *anything else!*—and could not be bothered. Annie with her Gloria Steinem glasses was *a GIRL*, and there was *no way* he was gonna bring her into this fetid morass.

Gabe was a heavy sleeper, Milt remembered from previous visits, and would always lock the door to his room.

Frankly was the only answer. Poor, put-upon Frankly.

Milt made his way tiptoeing through the poo-and-piss water cascading across the floor, opened the door, and there was Frankly in mid-sun-salutation.

"You do yoga now?" Milt whispered loudly.

"What did you *do?*" Frankly fired off once he turned to see what was going on in the bathroom.

"Dude, we need to figure this out *right now.*"

"Where are the towels?"

"Drenched on the floor, totally no good," Milt answered.

Frankly rushed to the kitchen, turning on a few lights—one of which, an orangish vintage lamp, sparked before going out.

Milt, stunned like a deer in headlights, heard his phone vibrate and ran over to it—the soles of his feet sopping wet—and ignored the mess that was only worsening in the bathroom, to check his phone that displayed a text from Gil:

"Got a weird call last night from Entertainment Weekly. They wanted to know about my last hospital visit. I never told anyone about that. I think they're gonna do a hit piece on me about my heart!!!!"

Milt saw that it was indeed 6:13 a.m. (*had Gil slept either?*), and turned back to the bathroom, where water was rushing out now onto Gabe's carpet that thankfully sopped up the flow.

Frankly darted over from the kitchen, carrying piles of old, faded *LA Weekly's* and used them to start covering the flow from the bathroom.

Doing his best to remain calm and collected, Milt texted back to Gil:

"All good, man. I'm sure that's not the case. EW doing something on you and the film would be HUGE and there's no reason they'd do something like that about your heart. It'll be fine. Get some rest. BIG DAY TODAY!! See you in a few hours."

Christ, Milt couldn't believe that Gil was freaking out about *this* now. And putting it on *Milt*. He was just waiting for Gil to ask him to hit up the unassuming random *EW* girl and see if she could kill the story.

Milt had essentially taken on the role of Gil's publicist for the tour and elsewise. Like when he had tried to get BuzzFeed to do something about the screenings, and the one gal there they could get to even respond to their entreating emails barely seemed to care at all. Milt had written up this great proposal for her, with all the information she'd need, and an exclusive video of some stuff they'd cut out of the film that she could post along with the story.

In the end, she declined, which sort of made Milt feel the way he had in the past when he'd been rejected by girls he wasn't really that into anyway. It was BuzzFeed, after all. On one level, that would likely be of some help. On another, who gave a fuck? It was BuzzFeed.

Two days later, when he looked the girl up to see what else she had been working on, there was some random video she had posted about Olivia Wilde's dog. Milt had joked with Gil, "Looks like Olivia Wilde's dog is just a little more likely to trend than you."

Gil had laughed at the time. He knew better. He hoped. Milt hoped. Gil had a friend who had been interviewed by the same girl, revealing she lived somewhere outside of Nashville. "And that's why she'll never get out of the middle of fucking *nowhere*," Gil said, granting his most typical rebuke of someone he didn't like. For him, if you were in the entertainment or media industry and didn't live and work in NYC or LA, that alone was a clear indication of what a loser you must be, of how you'd never amount to nothin'. He'd even playfully gibed Milt about living in Boston a few times.

That Gil happened to live in New Jersey these days seemed to be lost on the man of many contradictions.

All of that notwithstanding, here they were, with Gil possibly getting ready to drop a deuce on their premiere by getting all nutty on some possible piece in *EW* that may or may not come out and that may or may not be about Gil's heart condition.

Oh, God, Gil, PLEASE don't tweet about this! was all Milt could think, not wanting to put the idea in Gil's head by telling him not to do just that.

"A little help?" Frankly called out to Milt, standing paralyzed, gripping his phone, seeing that Gil had texted back:

"You're probably right. Leave it alone for now. Don't forget about the meeting with Blake. And don't fuck that up. I've worked with him twice and want to keep working with him. You're welcome!"

Milt dropped his phone on the couch, dashing with still-wet feet and trying his best to rub off the mess on the carpet as he did to Frankly, who was on his hands and knees frantically laying out page after page of the *LA Weekly's* on the floor around the bathroom.

The door on the left of Philip's room blasted open. "Oh, shit!"

Annie rolled out of bed and, eyes still squinty from being half-asleep, stepped over in her long purplish muumuu that reminded Milt of something Mrs. Roper from *Three's Company* would wear, and cried out, "Oh my god! You finally killed the fucking bathroom!"

"I didn't do shit!" Milt yelled, not meaning to make a pun.

"Clearly ya *did*," Philip said, rather humdrum and as though he was rather used to this by now.

"Fuck, Philip!" Annie hollered. "What is this, like the fucking third time it's happened *this week*?"

"I told you I was gonna call the landlord, okay?" Philip said, surprisingly calm or maybe just waked-and-baked already. He shouted out across the way to Gabe's door, "Hey, Gabe!"

He shuffled over in his Jesus Birkenstocks to Gabe's door with an upside-down *The Dark Side of the Moon* poster haphazardly gaffer-taped to it and started pounding. "Hey, man. Gabe. Yo. Wake up, man. The toilet's all fucked again."

Milt stood there helpless, gobsmacked.

Frankly, the only one actually doing something semi-constructive, remained on the floor, running out of pages of *LA Weekly's*.

The water kept coming out. Annie was on the couch squeezing her legs under her muumuu up to her chest, putting on her glasses that had been left on the upside-down plastic trash bin next to said couch. She lit up a joint.

Gabe's door finally opened and he hobbled out, wobbling, eyes shut. For once, he was not grinning impishly. "Whhha...?"

"Dude, the toilet's overflowing," Philip said.

"*Again!*" Annie shouted from the couch, coughing after inhaling a heroic hit from the joint.

"Hey, could I get some of that please?" Frankly asked from the floor by the open bathroom door.

"You sure you want it?" Annie said. "I might be getting a little bit of what Philip has."

Frankly looked up to the bathroom, the waterfall of shit-piss water still rivering out like the toilet was projectile vomiting, and turned back to Annie. "Yeah, I think I'm gonna need something pretty soon here to take the edge off, if you don't mind. Besides, we all smoked together last night, so...*ya* know."

She shuffled over to Frankly on the floor, handing him the joint.

Gabe opened his eyes slightly. "Oh, man. I called the goddamn landlord like *two weeks ago*. I don't know what happened."

"I think *I* know what happened," Frankly said from the floor, coughing up smoke and handing the lit joint back to Annie, who shuffled back to roll herself up in a ball on the couch, mumbling to herself something like, "Awww, man, now I got water on my feet."

"Do you guys need me to do anything?" Milt asked, trying to be as proactive as he knew how in such a domestic disaster situation. Not his forte. This was the kind of thing Laney, being the man of the family, would have fixed.

"Yeah," Frankly said. "Could you please get off my finger?"

Milt hadn't seen that in moving closer to Gabe, he had stepped on Frankly's right index finger. Gabe laughed, then coughed up some morning phlegm, spitting it onto the floor.

Milt probably wouldn't have been able to do anything real to help anyway. Aside from using the plunger, he couldn't do much with overflowing toilets. Getting out of the way and letting someone else handle it was the best thing he could do in such situations. Milt was a true master of delegating responsibility.

"I'll try him again in a few hours, okay?" Gabe said.

"Well, we need to do something about this right now," Philip said. "It's still overflowing. Look."

He pointed at the toilet, which was indeed still overflowing volcano-style, and Gabe leaned forward out of his doorway slightly and saw the mess. "Whoa, that is a *lot* of shitty water."

"Is anyone else hungry?" Annie asked. "I might go for a breakfast burrito run to the taco truck down the street."

"Nah," Gabe said. "I'm going back to sleep. Hey, Philip, can you just turn off the water and, uh...we'll deal with this later or something?"

"Yeah, I'll have some chorizo in my burrito, babe," Philip said to Annie before turning to Gabe. "You got it. Water off. Oh, man. It's really wet in there."

"You want me to go with you?" Frankly asked from the floor.

"Sure, I don't give a fuck," Annie said. "Let me just find a towel somewhere and wipe off my feet. Ich."

Milt breathed in deeply and realized he had done absolutely nothing to help out the situation. He wondered if this was really his fault, though. The toilet had been apparently overflowing a lot, according to the people who actually lived here. He was only visiting. Just getting ready for what was likely going to be the biggest day of his life up to this point.

He couldn't help but worry that this right here was a bad, bad sign.

CHAPTER 15

"So, who are we meeting up with again?" Frankly asked, gripping the wheel with one hand, and leaning back in his driver's seat. Milt, on the passenger side as always, was looking out the window as they tooled through the urban landscape toward the newly renovated downtown LA gentrifying before their eyes.

"I've never met the guy, but Gil set me up to talk with him and his production partner about some idea a friend of mine and I have had for a while that Gil liked," Milt said.

"And what is the project again?" Frankly asked.

Milt was craving a morning whiskey as succor for his slight hangover from the evening before and to forget the early morning maelstrom they'd all gone through together only an hour earlier as some kind of ragtag latter-day *Goonies* team.

"Basically, my friend Shaun wants to try to summit a series of the tallest mountains in the world," Milt said, not turning away from the window, his head practically leaning on it by this point. "I think there's like six or seven main ones that are kind of like the ones you 'have to do before you die' type of thing. We think we can get enough together from that to do a limited series or a doc."

"And who are *you* again?" Frankly asked.

Milt turned to him now and saw he was looking at him as well. They had a minor staring contest, both exhausted, both slightly hungover, both trying not to think about all the brutal realities that came with the morning's earlier lamentable episode.

"Keep your eyes on the road, man," Milt said.

"You're only saying that because I'm Asian," Frankly said, shifting his weight and switching hands. Now he was only driving with his left hand.

MUCH safer, Milt thought.

Milt's phone vibrated and he plucked it out of his pocket, expecting something either from Gil, Silverstein, or perhaps Jessica Chen. He wondered if she would actually show up to the screening after threatening for so long to do so. He wondered if she would try to steal the show or pass out black-and-white glossies of her over-produced headshots.

The fact that he never watched her show when he was younger—or, rather, when he was already getting too old to watch Balloon—made him feel eerily delighted in a way that also made him feel a little guilty.

"What is it?" Frankly asked.

"My dad," Milt said, looking at his phone and yet another ridiculous animated GIF his dad had sent him.

For the past year or so, Milt's dad seemed to only communicate with him via text message this way. Like a child who had just learned his first words and couldn't stop with the recitation of them.

Milt's dad would send meme after meme, animated GIF after animated GIF, usually making fun of Trump or some other trite and unimaginative gag, regardless of the fact that neither Milt nor his father were the least bit political or had ever once had a serious conversation about politics.

"What's he say?" Frankly asked, erratically turning left down an alley to avoid the traffic.

"Nothing," Milt said, clenching his left hand on the armrest between them. "Just a picture of the presidents on Mount Rushmore all throwing up and rolling their eyes at Trump standing before them."

"Borrrriiinnng," Frankly said.

"That's my dad."

"Why didn't you invite him?"

"Well, I did send him some of the articles and things promoting the event and whatnot," Milt said. "So, it's not exactly like I was keeping it from him."

"Okaaaaaay."

"But I know he never reads that stuff. This way I can feel like I, you know, did my best but still don't have to deal with him showing up. Besides, he'd never want to come up all the way to LA anyway. This way, we're both happy."

"Why not just tell him you're here and that he should come?"

Milt thought about this, and there was quiet in the car except for some late nineties Flaming Lips playing off the car stereo that was probably from the same CD mix that Frankly had always played way back when Milt still lived in LA with him.

Good ol' reliable Frankly and his CD mixes.

"Meh, not worth the trouble."

"What the hell does *that* mean?" Frankly grumbled through nearly closed lips as though he were sucking on a matchstick.

"Mmm," Milt said, actually considering how to put it. He knew Frankly knew what he meant, and he knew Frankly knew he knew. Frankly *had* lived with Milt all that time. They had taken a *lot* of drugs together; there'd been many evenings of heartfelt confessions and revelations.

Frankly and Milt knew everything about one another.

"This one time," Milt started, "my dad had this *huge* party at his house."

"He still in the one in La Jolla?"

"Yeah," Milt said. "So, there was this party my dad had for his birthday and there were all these people over at his house..."

"Mmmm hmmmm..."

"I just remember that everyone there, all his friends and employees and neighbors were...they all gave my dad *toys* for presents. Like *kid* toys. Not shit from Sharper Image or even Spencer's or whatever. *Toys* toys."

"Remind me, what did your dad do before he retired?"

"Sales."

"Ahhh..."

"But, dude, it was my dad's sixtieth birthday and all these people were giving him *toys*. And the thing about it was, like, at first it seemed kind of funny, because one after another he'd open these presents and they'd be a box of LEGOs or a Teenage Mutant Ninja Turtle action figure, or a whole bunch of Matchbox cars bundled together. But then it was more and more clear, the people there hadn't planned it. It was just something that happened organically because everyone was—"

"Everyone knew your dad really, *really* likes toys."

"Right," Milt said. "Everyone was laughing at first. But after the sixth or seventh present, they stopped. It was like the joke wasn't funny anymore. Then it was like, *This isn't a joke.*"

Frankly swerved to the right, making his way into another wet alleyway.

Milt clenched his left hand *and* teeth. He closed his eyes for a second, trying to drone out the fear and hangover. "When I was young, like before high school, he used to take me to these DIY comic book conventions and baseball card conventions and shit like that. He was into *Magic: The Gathering* and all that crap."

"Sounds fun."

"It was...when I was like *ten*. Then I got really bored of it, especially when we would always go out and get whatever the hot new videogame was, and he would always just end up playing it himself, you know? I'd be sitting there and would eventually go to the guest room and read. Then high school hit and I got really bored with all that stuff and moved on, but my dad clearly kept going with it. Which is fine. It's his thing. It's what he does instead of watching sports or something, I guess."

Milt pushed the button to roll down his window and felt the wind rushing against his face. It smelled like hot dogs and truck exhaust. The tires of Frankly's Civic were splashing against the drainage water of the alleyway they were dangerously zooming through.

Neither said anything for a pregnant few seconds of nothing but window breeze and the light sounds of the music playing softly now off the car stereo, the tires swishing through shallow water.

"It's funny, there's this one thing I always think about with all this stuff with my dad..."

"What's that?"

"The other thing about the whole video game thing was that whenever we'd get a new game, he'd always want to read the instruction manual cover to cover."

"Okaaaaay?"

"Like, he couldn't even turn the fucking thing *on* until he knew every single control and move and whatever."

"Riiiighhhht."

"But me," Milt said, "I never wanted to read the instructions. I just wanted to play. For me, part of the game was learning how to *play* the game while I played it. It made it more fun and exciting for me. But my dad needed to know exactly what to do and how to do it and where to go and all that shit."

"Nintendo Power Magazine!"

"Right, all that nonsense. He would even call the hotline numbers for codes and tricks and shit."

"What?! That shit was a rip!"

"Yeah, seriously. But my dad was totally into it. He had to know *exactly* what to do or else he couldn't play the game. I was the total opposite. I didn't want to know shit. I just wanted to explore and play and, I don't know, like, get lost in the game. Neither way was better or worse, just different. My dad and I are just different people. In a lot of ways."

"I guess it was your way of rebelling as a kid," Frankly said.

"Yeah, it's probably why I got out of all that geek shit when I turned twelve."

"Except now you're writing about it and making movies about it."

"Well, he's still my dad." Milt sighed. "Shit's in my DNA." He glanced languidly at the side mirror beyond the window and knew. "Shit, we even look exactly the same. I can't escape him."

"Or Seth Rogen," Frankly snickered.

"Not until the grosses go down or Rogen finally says something on Twitter that pisses off enough people. It's still the same thing even today. My dad's the kind of guy who chooses which book he's going to read next based on the *New York Times* bestseller list. He figures out what movie he'll watch according to the reviews."

"Makes sense."

"But it doesn't! It's stupid to do it like that!"

"Not to your dad," Frankly said calmly with a twinge of tease. He loved goading Milt on and knew exactly how to do it.

"I do the exact opposite," Milt said. "I go exactly *against* whatever that shit tells you. I can't help myself. My dad still craves guidance like with the video game instruction manuals. If I ever got into playing video games again, I'd just throw the manuals away first thing."

"Such a rebel still, hmm?"

"I see movies based on what the reviews *don't* say."

"That must be exhausting. And pretentious."

Milt nodded, smiling. He got it. Okay, Frankly won this round.

"I'm only saying my dad and I were different when I was a kid, and we're different now. Sometimes those differences can make it difficult to be around each other for too long or at important events like this."

"So, what are you going to say back to your dad's meme?"

"Nothing," Milt said. "I'm gonna send him an animated GIF back."

"Which one?"

"Hillary falling down the stairs over and over again."

"Sounds like you're not too different."

"I love my dad. I respect him and admire him for a lot of reasons. But yeah...*not...worth...the...trouble.*"

Frankly was speeding up through the alleys now, rows of identical, white, smog-stained garage doors attached to an endless line of identical, sienna apartment buildings on either side of the car. They nearly caught some air going down and up a drainage ditch, and Milt finally said, "Easy, easy...."

Frankly slowed down, though not much, and abruptly turned right to get out of the alleyways and back on the main street lined with the Korean street signs and businesses of K-Town.

Despite the fact the breakneck turn caused the car to wobble, Frankly didn't bother putting both hands on the wheel, only shifting his weight and using his right hand once again.

"You really expect a lot out of people, don't you?" Frankly asked.

"I definitely don't want to die in this car," Milt said, trying to be as insouciant as Frankly.

"Why not?"

"My mom. It'd kill her."

"Mmm."

"You know that managing editor I told you about from the last paper I worked?"

"Yeah, the one you guys called 'Shitsmelled'?"

"He actually said to me, 'You know, Milt, you can't expect everyone else here to work as hard as you.' He actually said that to me. *Twice*. Once in front of this other kid Silverstein I worked with when we were in the little fuck's office."

"Wow," Frankly said, unaffected. "Twice."

"Twice."

"Twice," Frankly repeated zombie-like. "The horror."

"Seriously," Milt said, "it's like what I've been dealing with with this gal at CineRanchero and—"

"All right, all right, all right," Frankly cut in. "I don't need to hear *all* your complaining."

"Hey, *that's* anti-Semitic."

This got a laugh from Frankly, who also granted a little relief from the accelerator as reward for Milt's *bon mot*. "But really," Frankly inquired, "aren't you worried sometimes that you might push people you work with too hard?"

"I've actually been thinking about this a bunch the last few months. Especially with all the stuff I had to do with all these people all over the country on the doc and this fucking tour. It's come up here or there, and I've been wondering whether I'm too much of an asshole when it comes to these things."

"Or anything at all for that matter."

"You know what?" Milt said, ignoring his friend. "I realized I'd rather get yelled at for pushing people too hard than having whatever we're working on fail because I'm *not* pushing people hard enough.... Then not only do I still get yelled at by everyone—in this case, fucking *Gil Gladly*—but also *the fucking project FAILS too!*"

"Okay." Frankly nodded. "That actually makes a *little* sense." Then he turned up the next Flaming Lips song, "Moth in the Incubator," one of Milt's and his old favorites.

It was a little past noon before Milt found himself at the table with Frankly to his side and Blake Douglas across from him with his buzzed haircut, meticulously groomed five-o-clock shadow, and onyx black button-up shirt open (two buttons) at the collar to reveal his bony, perfectly tanned skin.

They were all drunk by this point. Frankly and Milt had gotten to the restaurant Blake had recommended for their meeting about twenty minutes early, thanks to Frankly's insouciant driving that minded not for most speed limits, yellow lights or, for the most part, other drivers. Blake's production partner had not deigned to attend.

Frankly and Milt had probably had something like two doubles. It was hard to remember how many Blake Douglas had had after they had taken the recommendation of a fantastically delectable scotch that the Hispanic bartender in his posh hipster gray vest, pink bowtie, and Skrillex haircut/glasses combo had made.

Milt flashed on the swanky place they were in, the low chandeliers, the tasteful white walls, black-and-white checkered floor like they were in some kind of gourmet fifties diner knockoff. It was chic and New York. Only a few years earlier, when Frankly and Milt had gone to UCLA, the entire downtown area was verbally cordoned off from the kooky college kids, left there for the dregs only. Now here they were, the whole region having been gentrified on an epic level, and the place was, well, "trendy." Meaning *expensive*.

Milt was thinking about this urban transmogrification when he realized Blake was speaking to him. Luckily, Blake, being a true-blue Hollywood guy, didn't seem to notice Milt wasn't paying attention.

Everything was already sounding to Milt as though he were under water. The NYC cocktail lounge trip-hop sounded absolutely lo-fi, as did most of whatever Blake was saying while talking nonstop about his company, his past work, and future projects he was developing. Most of which, from what little Milt did hear, sounded like the kind of things that would never go anywhere.

The scenario reminded Milt of having lived and worked in Hollywood all those early years when everyone had a business card that read "P R O D U C E R" without their ever having *produced* much, if anything, rambling on and on about their hopes and dreams like they were rock-hard investments. *Hey, we have Mark Ruffalo attached! This is gonna be GOLD!*

Frankly, crammed into the blood-red leather booth to his side, was saying nothing. How could he, when Blake was talking and chuckling loudly, nonstop? His eyes were wide and excited.

Milt was fairly certain Blake was not on coke right now; he was probably always like this.

Milt kept nodding, trying his best to sound sincere in his own laughter, regardless of whatever Blake was actually saying, and guzzling scotch after scotch that Blake kept suggesting he order every time the tiny waitress with black hair in a ponytail and big, beautiful green eyes in her own gray vest and pink bowtie came by to ask if they wanted any more.

"I'm putting it all on the card!" Blake said, triumphantly. "Don't worry. Have as many as you want! It's your big day! *Film premiere*, motherfucker!"

Milt wondered if being drunk like this made him more of a self-centered asshole, hence why that *last* part he actually heard and paid attention to.

Milt was so out of it, in fact, he had completely forgotten that this meeting was not supposed to be about Blake Douglas and *his* projects at all. Milt was supposed to be doing the talking here. Wasn't he? About *his* project he'd pitched to Gil, who in turn had pitched it to Blake, who set up this very meeting with Milt?

At least there were free drinks involved.

Blake kept talking and Milt understood what was really going on here. It had happened multiple times before at meetings exactly like this.

Conclusion: Blake was just trying to get his shit going like anyone else. Like Milt. That "producer" business card must've worked on Gil, as it did on so many others, and here now Milt was meeting with the guy, listening to him rattle off his aspirations for the future.

Frankly was guzzling down another double and had some speckles of white powder across his nose from the coke they'd done in the car before coming into the "meeting" Blake was luckily fifteen minutes late to.

Blake luckily didn't notice (or care) that the coke mustache was on Frankly's face, and Milt had to say he admired his friend's ability to stay so composed even when on multiple stimulants. Even on only a few hours of sleep. Even after an early morning of sopping up shit water with *LA Weekly* pages.

Yes, Frankly drove like a maniac, but he was fucking *good* at it. Maybe having three ears somehow helped him have more sensitivity to things.

Milt was still considering this very notion while they were parallel parking an hour later out in front of the Egyptian. They had promised to meet Blake inside after they all had made their way out of the downtown bistro and Blake had taken the check, not registering any sense of surprise or worry when the bill had come.

Milt stumbled out of Frankly's car, completely running off of scotch and adrenalin by now. They were out of coke. Thankfully. He fixed his *Simpsons* tie, buttoned up his brown vintage Mr. Rogers-esque sweater-jacket, and walked toward the theater with Frankly running after him after having paid the meter with his credit card.

They stopped briefly before the old-timey marquee hanging high as they made their way through the European style, tree-lined courtyard leading to the box office.

There it was. The name of *their* movie in bold, red, big letters: *Good Golly, Gil Gladly*.

"Want me to take a picture of you under it?" Frankly asked.

Milt was trying to understand what exactly this meant, wobbling a little from side to side, and seeing now, lined against the pink Spanish tile wall a line. *Of people*. People who had come—were in fact *waiting*—to buy a *ticket* to *Milt's* movie that *he* had made with *his* friends...about fucking *Gil Motherfucking Gladly!* The dude from *Balloon! KidTalk!*

Milt broke up laughing.

He was pretty sure Frankly asked something like, *"Wuzsofunny..."*

Milt was inside the theater. A grand, beautiful, majestic ballroom of a place. The kind of movie palace you see in documentary footage showing regal, elegant premieres from the mid-century.

He stumbled into the lobby, the wide, double glass tinted window doors being opened for him by two large black security men with walkies squawking, who were escorting Milt (right?) through the red-carpeted lobby, along with a babbling, frazzled lady of indiscernible age (twenty-three? forty-six?) with frizzy hair pulled back into a ponytail, while Milt was trying to recall if Frankly had actually come into this place with him or was left back outside with the line of plebeian ticket holders.

...Walkie talkies squawking everywhere...

The crowds were growing, their plangent sound of the sea rising, and on closer look, the carpet was filthy and fuzzy and there was an empty yellow popcorn box over there on the other...

"Milton!"

He wasn't sure if he'd already been talking with YouTube star and host for the Q&A that would follow the screening Astra Singh for long, but here she was. With her geeky, oversized pink-framed glasses and her big ol' bright agate eyes, her perfect caramel skin, and her butt-length platinum blonde hair.

He remembered reading somewhere she had it dyed that way in order to look more like what's-her-face from *Game of Thrones.*

"...so amazing! Congratulations, can't wait to see it.... Thank you for inviting me.... I'm so super-excited...and, ohmygodyouknowwhat?"

Milt's right knee had been ready to give out, but he stood tall and strong and kept trying to focus on what Astra Singh was saying, what information she was conveying, but could only think about Astra Singh as a *thing unto herself.*

How did Astra Singh make *money* being a "sexy geek girl" so to speak? She just went around to these different comic book conventions and events like this and then posted these kind of DIY videos on YouTube and elsewhere online and somehow she got paid for this stuff?

Nuh-uh.

Milt wasn't buying it.

He laughed, thinking of Gil's thing about "YouTube star" being an oxymoron.

"I know, it's *totally* funny," she said, buzzing like the detuned radio refrigerator math guy from Radiohead's "Karma Police." "It's, like, so totally amazing to be here, because, oh my god, I can't believe I get to actually *meet* and, like, *talk* to GIL GLADLY, because when I was growing up..."

Milt's mind was elsewhere, doing calculations, recalling one of his buddies who somehow had a YouTube video that went viral and got millions of hits and never saw penny-one, and that was four years ago!

"I'm really...glad you're here," Milt said, placing his hand on Astra Singh's right shoulder. "Gil and I were really happy...that you decided...to do this."

This lit Astra Singh up and she began prattling on now about how much research she had done and—

Milt was wondering where she got those glasses, and also *popcorn* box*? they still have* boxes *of popcorn in this place?*

He was feeling a *little* less woozy by the time he was face-to-face with Gil Gladly himself, who he realized *did* look like the old version of Danny Bonaduce from *The Partridge Family* and all those irritatingly sad reality shows that had followed (and hadn't he done some kind of radio show for a while too? wasn't he some kind of alcoholic?). Danny Bonaduce, *not* Gil, who didn't drink or do any drugs or smoke or do anything bad at all except eat a *lot* of crappy food, which was one of the reasons he always joked he had been run off from *in front* of the camera. ("I got t-t-t-tooo old and too f-f-f-f-f-fat.")

Gil kept his tired, slightly cerise eyes—almost like those of a bunny—locked on Milt's, which were both doing their damndest to cooperate and stay focused.

STAY FOCUSED!! THIS IS GIL GLADLY! THIS IS THE GUY!

This made Milt think for a second about the line from *Swingers,* and he explained that the meeting with Blake had gone well earlier (*hadn't it?*) and thanked Gil for having set it up. They shook hands, and Milt wondered why Gil always felt the need to stand so very close to him, and wondered too when Gil's reddish, fuzzy Danny Bonaduce hair had become so mottled with Father Time whiteness.

"You really made this all happen, Milt," Gil said, and there was a momentary look in his eyes, with a few drops of light amber sweat drizzling down the side of his right jowl covered in light orange five-o-clock-ish peach fuzz intermingled with whitish flakes of old man hair, and that momentary look was one of gratitude and pride.

Milt didn't have time to process this rare instance of direct gratitude, because he was marveling first at the fact that Gil had always seemed so short on TV, and yet whenever Milt met him in person he was always so tall, then at those burly Danny Bonaduce arms folded across his Danny Bonaduce paunch in his black outfit that made him look like he was getting ready to rob a bank or fight a ninja...gorilla.

Milt reflected back on something comic book writer Alan Moore had said about the fact that people thought he wore all black to look more like a wizard, and in fact, he did it these days because it helped him look slimmer.

He found himself being taken away by two more gigantic black security escorts with walkie talkies squawking and there he was, left alone, drunk and completely overwhelmed by the crowds and....

No, no. They're only here to help. *Remember? It's* your *event, and they're taking you through the crowds*—careful!—*to where you need to*....

Then he was at the bar inside the actual theater, no longer just in the lobby, apparently introducing himself to folks and being introduced to folks and telling everyone how glad he was that they were there (Wait. *Had he actually met Jessica Chen? Had she shown up? Had they talked?*).

Milt was conversing, more or less, with the young-ish, hipster-ish bartender behind the beautiful, elaborate old bar with a wall of glowing spirits behind him...and the bartender kept giving Milt free drinks "on the house—congratulations on the film! This is *amazing!* Look at all these people! I think I saw Gavin Hellman from *Stay After Class* come in. I think he's sitting *right over there two rows up!*"

Gabe was there now, with his roommates Philip and Annie (both of whom looked as though they had not gotten out of their rumpled, hippie-ish bed clothes or combed their hair or show-ered or anything of that sort).

Frankly was there now, and in addition to the *gratis* drinks a-comin' one after the other from the bartender, there were little bottles of airplane booze coming from a backpack that Gabe had brought—"Congratulations, man! You did it!"

"Here we are!" said Frankly, the first time in god-knew-how-long that Milt could remember Frankly actually expressing some sense of excitement or anything aside from an everlasting blasé *meh.*

Philip and Annie seemed particularly stoned and were smiling brighter than Laney ever did when she was this stoned, and Milt thought about how well Laney and Philip and Annie would get along, all being latter-day hippies, and then there was Adam-Anthony Andrews, who was on another eighties Balloon show called *KidNStuff*, which was one of Balloon's first actual sitcoms before they became *only* sitcoms with pretty actors and actresses and animated shows that all looked and sounded like everything else on Disney and Nickelodeon and PBS Kids.

But it was nice seeing Adam-Anthony again for the first time in years: "Congratulations, man!"

Adam-Anthony, who still looked not only pretty good but pretty *young* for someone now in his forties whom Milt had known a few years back when they'd become friendly after he'd interviewed Adam-Anthony for a...a thing and

"Thanks, dude," Milt said, standing a little to the side and holding himself up with one hand against the bar.

This didn't seem to affect Adam-Anthony's gleefulness, as he advanced even closer to Milt. Why did these people always get so close when they talked to you? Was this a Balloon thing or an LA thing? Because Milt remembered that there were a lot of other people he knew back in the LA days who would do the same thing and practically come nose to nose to you when they talked right into your fucking *face*.

"I have this idea I really want to talk with you about, if you're up for it," said Adam-Anthony.

"I'll sallma time or make the ferm ter," Milt said, though it very likely came out something much more cogent, because Adam-Anthony smiled brighter and said, "Great, man. I'll give you a call. Congrats again, dude. This is just *terrific*. Look at all these *people!*"

....Milt was in the bathroom of the theater, tears welling down his face, nose running, so full of absolute joy and jubilance that Laconians would call it *jouissance,* while he was laughing and crying and talking on the phone to Laney after the movie and Q&A had finished two hours later.

"We did it, baby. We did it we did it we did it we did it!"

He had been texting Wallace and Ronnie throughout the screening the same thing: **"Boyyyyyysssss, we did it we did it we did it!"** while standing in the back over by the bar while everyone else in the theater packed the 350 or so seats (fans, mostly friends and old colleagues of Gil's, a few faces and names Milt had recognized but no one *HUGE huge*, of course; this was the *Gil Gladly* documentary, after all).

Ronnie had texted something back about how excited and proud he was, and that he was texting from a Walmart where he was snowed-in due to the massive storm still raging in Denver... but this was a time for joy! So, fuck it! And they were breaking out free hot chocolate for everyone stuck inside. Bonus! (Good ol' indefatigably blissful Ronnie.)

"We did it we did it we did it!" Milt was saying to Laney over and over again on the phone, pacing around in circles on the white tile floor of the fluorescently-lit theater bathroom, with people coming and going through the door, taking a piss, washing their hands, leaving, not really noticing or caring that there was this frantic, weird guy with eyes a-watering pacing around, maddeningly crying out, "We did it we did it we did it!" into a phone clenched far too tightly to his ear like he was trying to push the whole goddamn thing into his head.

"That's great, baby!" Laney's staticky voice said. *"Did you have fun?"*

"I still am!" Milt bleated. "It's *so much fun!* I wish you were here!"

"I'll be at some of the other ones," Laney said. *"One day we'll be able to afford to go to all of them together!"* (Classic Laney.)

"It was absolutely amazing in every fuckin' way, Laney. They *got it*. They *really got it*. It's all been worth it. Everything we've done. It was all worth it. If nothing else happens, we did *this* and it all *happened* and it was fuckin' *perfect!* This will be the best moment of my life."

"Until we start having kids!" Laney said, stonedly giggling.

"We'll see!"

People were coming and going faster and more frequently now, and Milt was starting to feel self-conscious. "Well, I'm in the goddamn *bathroom* at the theater right now walking around in circles like a madman, and people are coming and going. I probably look really weird, so I better get off. I just wanted to tell you that *WE FUCKIN' DID IT! RONNIE AND WALLACE AND GIL AND EVERYONE ELSE AND ME—WE DID IT! AND IT WORKED! I LOVE YOU AND CAN'T WAIT TO SHARE THIS WITH YOU AND I THINK EVERYTHING'S GOING TO BE FINE!"*

"Me too, baby," Laney said, sounding serious in the best possible of ways. *"I really love you, I'm so proud of you, and I know everything's going to be fine."*

They hung up and Milt was out the bathroom door, passing by some people, a few of whom actually knew who Milt was and shook his hand and congratulated him, including an older film professor, who hugged Milt tight and said, "I'm so very proud of you, son."

Milt could only hug him as tight back and whisper into his ear, because he felt like he had to tell *someone* and this guy was probably the closest thing he had to that right person, "I didn't invite my dad here."

The professor pulled away, looked at Milt, and slowly nodded, understanding. He hugged Milt again and said they should get breakfast some morning before Milt went back home. Milt said they'd do that but knew they probably wouldn't for any number of reasons including logistics, time, money, and lack of transportation.

But it was nice of the professor to have suggested it and it was nice that Milt could tell *someone*, someone of his stature and age and wisdom and guidance back when Milt was first getting into all this malarkey that he hadn't invited his dad to this thing. (Milt's mom and her new boyfriend had already left for New York for a wedding of one of Milt's cousins and would meet Milt and Laney at the upcoming Manhattan screening.)

Milt only had Gabe, Frankly, and Annie and Philip here, because he had no other family on the West Coast aside from his mom and dad, and because all his friends in LA when he had gone to film school were either gone or simply were no longer people Milt had stayed in touch with.

There had been some friend of Milt's from high school who apparently now lived in LA and had heard about the event who came to check it out, and congratulated Milt with a tap on the shoulder. Milt couldn't remember who the guy was, but he did remember the dude had said, "It's funny you're writing about and making movies about TV now. Because you never seemed that into it when we were younger. Probably because TV competed with you when we'd all be hanging out at someone's house or something."

The screening itself had been one thing, hence the tears, the texts, and the call to Laney in the bathroom. The Q&A after had been something altogether outstanding, with the audience really *being* there with Gil up on stage talking and answering questions asked by Astra Singh sitting next to him beaming like she was interviewing the one and only motherfucking Santa Claus.

There was Gil back onstage where he belonged, talking to the crowd and revealing all these different crazy, amazing, funny, sad, heartwarming, courageous, silly things from his very long life in TV, in front of the camera and behind it.

Having observed it all from the back of the theater by the bar, Milt had been astounded by the sheer power of Gil up there, like he was radiated by some kind of mystical light that all 350 people in this theater could see and *feel*. They had laughed at everything he said without any kind of patronizing quality to their laughter, even when what Gil said hadn't been very funny.

They were *with* him, and standing in the back by the bar, Milt could witness it all happening. The genuine affection was *palpable, electric*. Milt's neck hairs had been standing up the entire time.

Gil had pointed out a few of the semi-celebrities who were in the audience, and everyone applauded at each name, even though none of them were exactly Robert DeNiro. If Jessica Chen *had* been there, Gil hadn't pointed her out. Milt was sure of that.

Milt had seen it on the faces of each audience member, whether they were a fan or not, someone who had known Gil Gladly, personally or not, young or old, regardless of how they looked or who they were. They were all spellbound, captured, *captivated* by Gil up there onstage who did not stutter once. Not once.

Gil Gladly had victoriously led the audience in chants of his signature catch-phrase, the namesake of the documentary: "Good Golly!", before pointing the microphone in his hand toward them:

Audience: "Gil Gladly!"

Gil: *"GOOD GOLLY!"*

Audience: *"GIL GLADLY!"*

This right here was why Milt Siegel had made *Good Golly, Gil Gladly.* It was there in the faces of each audience member, and he knew it would be there in the faces of all of those at home who would soon be watching the film on Netflix or whatever once they sold the damn thing.

Gil was a very real part of all of these people's lives. He was there—almost *watching*, if you will (not to get *too* creepy)— as they grew up. He was not "just a guy on TV" to them. He was *real*.

It didn't matter that some in the audience were not kids. In fact, almost *none* of the audience were kids, Milt realized all at once. Looking around, all the white and grayish hair, the glasses and beer guts and Cosby sweaters.... He surmised that the average age here was probably forty. There they were, these thirty-somethings, these forty-year-olds, these fifty-and sixty-year-olds all chanting along with Gil's call-and-response as though they were children again watching his show or earlier precursors like Captain Kangaroo, Bozo the Clown, and Howdy Doody.

All of this went through Milt's head as he had been watching the audience members, old and young alike, so transfixed on Gil Gladly up there on stage making them laugh...and occasionally making Milt cringe a bit from some of the more revealing and vulgar things Gil could never help himself from saying, including badmouthing the new administration of the Balloon network and lamenting that "the people there running the place into the ground" were "too stupid to realize they should reboot *KidTalk*, but, oh well...life goes on."

And you know what? These were all fucking adults here. So, Gil Gladly *could* be vulgar and raw and *real. Fuck it*, as Gil himself would say. He came up in the late seventies Jersey comedy club scene. What would someone expect from a guy like that? He was practically reared in his early days as a merchant marine...well, a "merchant marine" of the entertainment world.

This was who Gil Gladly really was, and the audience here could take it.

Milt had felt lucky and even grateful he could see it for himself, there with Gil glowing up onstage, radiating this amazing energy that had at one time captured the entire nation, maybe the world...for five to ten years of successful ubiquitous television appearances.

Here and now, this energy was simply less diluted. It was the *real* Gil, not the TV-friendly Gil. And that was fine. Even if some of what he said *was* a little....

Then there'd been that moment at the end of the proceedings, before Gil got off the stage. That very last moment when Milt really felt the connection between himself and Gil Gladly, the *real* Gil Gladly, the true human beneath it all—as imperfect as that human may have been—and knew that, yes, Gil was the genuine article.

It all made sense, it made it all worthwhile, all the panic and worry, stress and struggle, and doubts and sacrifices. Milt was glad he knew Gil Gladly. He was glad he had made a film about Gil Gladly. He looked across the audience up to Gil on the stage and locked eyes with the man himself. Milt smiled at Gil Gladly, nodding. *We did it, Gil!*

Gil may have responded by nodding back. Or he might not have.

....and Milt was in the lobby, smiling so bright and being interviewed by different people using their phones as though they were actual TV cameras and hugging people and crying and laughing and smiling, enjoying the shit out of every fucking second of this moment that lasted for two hours.

CHAPTER 16

There Milt was, sitting at an outdoor café in Malibu, walking distance from the most magnificent stretch of beach he could possibly remember from his film school days.

It was the day after the screening, and Milt still felt, well, not hungover, but *tired*. Then again, he was *always* tired. Truth was, Milt hardly ever felt hungover, just as he'd never had a bad psychedelic trip. He learned a few years back that his mom was the same way, making him feel this was some kind of genetic superpower she'd passed down to him. He'd never asked his dad about *his* drug experiences, but that was for another day.

At least now Milt had a valid reason for being so exhausted. He had just premiered his two-years-plus-in-the-making documentary about Gil Gladly to an audience of nearly four hundred people. And they had *loved*...every...second...of it. Probably.

He *had* been pretty fucking drunk. He'd been drinking almost the entire day, starting with that unproductive Blake Douglas meeting in the morning.

Had he missed out on one of, if not *the* prime experiences of his life? *Again?* Milt did have a tendency of doing that. He would drink...then drink and drink and drink...then he'd miss out on these spectacular events he was a part of, and it would be fun and all, as the screening had been, but...*man.*

He had been there, and yet...*had he missed it?*

Milt was sitting across a large white table under a grand, extra-large, gold-colored, and sparkling umbrella blocking out the wondrous, warm sun. The surprisingly warm but welcomed misty breeze from the nearby ocean spritzed his face. To his right, the towering palm trees that had always looked so fake to him (and more or less *were*) were out beyond the table in the near-empty parking lot. It *was* Monday, and most people had *actual* jobs. Although, then again, this was *Malibu*, so maybe not.

Across that table was the skinny and stunning-at-sixty-some-thing Jayne Manning, with perfectly hemmed shoulder-length silky platinum hair, large turtle shell glasses that made her look particularly like Anna Wintour, and a shimmering diamond necklace around her perfect but noticeably pulled-back-through-more-than-one-surgery, tanned neck.

Jayne Manning had been a longtime girlfriend of Gil Glad-ly's back in the "early days," when Gil had first made his way out from Jersey to LA to perform at what would become the world-famous Comedy Claque. The same Comedy Claque stage that would rear such *enfant terribles* as Robin Williams, George Carlin, Pryor, Seinfeld, and the rest of the gang in the late seventies, early eighties.

Though Gil wasn't anywhere near their league (and he had conceded this more than once in multiple interviews and in Milt's documentary), his tenure at the Claque did help him find his way to the talent scouts at Balloon, still in its infancy at the time, and the rest was pop culture history.

Jayne Manning was one of the handful of people that Gil had connected Milt to over the years. Gil had thought Jayne and Milt would get along, especially since Jayne was very interested in old television history, a specialty of Milt's. Milt didn't much care for anything after the late nineties, but he *loved* talking with people about *Mr. Ed* and *The Beverly Hillbillies,* Milton Berle, Jack Benny, Bob Hope, George Burns, and the pinnacle of it all, *The Twilight Zone.*

Milt had at one time written an entire series for the now defunct Grantland about the meta-comedy of *Green Acres.* He was paid for his time in Groupon Bucks, which he never learned how to use.

It made sense that Jayne Manning would have a preternatural love and understanding of television history, as over the years she had become one of the preeminent *producers* of television. In fact, she specialized in creating series that were more or less knockoffs of these older programs she so admired, and could mine for good ideas no one else remembered.

Alas, she was an old maid by this point. Ageism being as strong as it was in the industry, Jayne Manning hadn't had a new show in fifteen years. As she had told Milt more than once over the phone, she hadn't exactly been trying that hard. She had made her name, her reputation, and—most importantly, as she had put it—her *money.* She didn't need much more than that.

This get-together at the Malibu outdoor café would make for the first face-to-face between Milt and Jayne, despite their having conversed on and off for the better part of the last three years via phone and email.

Jayne had been at the premiere the day before and Milt pretended to remember meeting her after she claimed to have come up to him after the screening when everyone was hugging and slapping him on the shoulder and shaking hands with him, telling Milt what a great job he'd done.

The fact that Jayne Manning *had* claimed to have come up to him after the screening, something he had blacked-out on, made Milt once again ponder over whether or not he'd met up with Jessica Chen at the screening...if *she* had been there at all.

It didn't matter, though. He was here, having let Frankly sleep it off back at Gabe's. Milt had taken a Lyft, and it hadn't been cheap. But there was no way he was going to miss meeting up with the one and only Jayne Manning, has-been at this point or no, particularly after all of the good will he'd created over the years of correspondence.

Sure, one would have thought that someone with the kind of money Jayne was always bragging about could deign to come to *him*, but as with most Malibu and Calabasas folkle, she wasn't about to leave her ultraglamorous, ultra-glorious, ultra-gorgeous fortress of solitude, and certainly not for someone like Milton Siegel. She may have been a has-been, but he was a not-yet at best and a never-was at worst.

Jayne was talking about how much she understood why Milt had left LA. The traffic, the terrible people, the traffic. She herself had been a New York gal for so long and *never* thought she'd move out to and live in "HelLA." At some point, though, this was where the work was and she *had* to come out here. She did, about ten years ago, when her career was already more or less finished.

She leaned back in her chair, breathed in deeply, and exhaled deeper still somehow, stretching out her arms as though to hug the sky and the air and the bright-bright golden sun above in the spellbindingly perfect cloudless, turquoise sky. "I mean, what's so bad about *this*?" she asked, beaming radiantly.

Milt was still preoccupied with the money he had spent on the Lyft coming out here (and the money he would have to spend getting back to Gabe's place, nearly forty-five fucking minutes away). He justified it in his mind as something he *had* to do, a meeting he *had* to take with a powerful woman who could maybe in some small way make his life slightly better.

And he was preoccupied with *just how drunk* he had been the day before at the *fucking screening!*

He had earlier in the morning hit up a few people who he *knew* had been there to see how bad he had been, find out if he had said anything strange in any of the video interviews and shit he had taken a part in. Typical press people were one thing, not that there had been more than one or two there, but he was genuinely nervous about the amateur YouTuber types who were always haunting these kinds of geek events and shoving their phones in your face, recording you *TMZ*-style without any kind of fact checkers or editors, accountability or sense of responsibility, aside from getting what they could to go viral. Why would they bother getting you to sign a release to use the footage? It was for "online" and so all responsibility went pfffffttttt!

Everyone he called said he was fine. They didn't really notice anything, they'd said. Which worried Milt *a little*, because this response seemed somewhat placating. He had obviously been pretty damn tipsy at the thing, so they should have noticed *something*. But it *was* LA, and this was one of life's many clichés that existed because they were true. No one in LA/Hollywood really noticed anything about *anyone* else. It was the capital of self-obsession.

Which in this case had been a good thing.

Milt had gotten a text message back from Adam-Anthony Andrews saying that, yeah, people could tell Milt had "had a few," but they were cool with it because it was just as clear Milt was "having a good time" and "enjoying the success of the screening" and "deserved to be a little 'giddy.'"

Meanwhile, Jayne Manning prattled on and on across from him, talking about what she thought of the movie, and how it was good but still needed a few tweaks, and how she and all of their old friends always found it so funny the way Gil Gladly had been the one person alive to "make a career out of having a severe stutter."

And how she continued to get such a kick out of watching Gil, after *KidTalk* and his other smaller programs and such, making such a big deal out of said stutter in order to get more press for himself and to keep himself seeming relevant whenever he couldn't land any "real" work.

And how she remembered in particular that one *Inside Edition* segment on Gil in the late nineties when he was talking about what a "challenge" it was to have his stutter. "I just can't stop thinking about him gazing out the window in his house, looking past the curtains and, I guess, contemplating his life and his *stutter*, I suppose...." Then Jayne burst out laughing, falling forward onto the table and pounding the table with her long, perfectly manicured fingers in a fist, her two loose diamond bracelets jangling.

Being "not hungover" but still preoccupied by money woes and how he had been the day before at the screening, and whom he had met and not met, and if there was anything weird with him online now during any interviews he had done while so completely fucking stupidly sickeningly blotto, he felt slightly uncomfortable that Jayne Manning was relentlessly unburdening herself about all these emotions she had about her former boyfriend, who also happened to be the whole reason the two of them were meeting here right at this moment.

Gil's marriage came up. Gil had married his wife Mandy only a few years after he had left the East Coast and he and Jayne had broken up.

Again, Milt was flabbergasted that Jayne could be so forthright not only about her conflicted feelings about this but also the fact that she felt so confident saying, "Mandy must be one of the strongest people in the world to put up with all of Gil's stuff," and, "If it hadn't been for Mandy, Gil never would have made it this far," and, "He needed *someone* there to hold his hand and keep him going through all of this. Some of that even came up in your documentary during your interviews with her!"

It made Milt feel weird to hear it so bluntly from someone who was supposed to be a close, longtime friend of Gil's, but she was right. Mandy *had* talked in the film, and more so in the full interview Milt had conducted with her, about how she was the one who had to keep Gil on track during his tougher periods and still kept him understanding that everything would be okay and that the world wasn't "out to get him" and wasn't all laughing behind his back about his stutter or his lack of on-camera work over the past few years or whatever it was.

Gil Gladly *was* very lucky to have Mandy as his wife. And yet why bring it up like this at the table now? And in a way that seemed less informative than defensive? Or maybe even *aggressive*?

Then the conversation *really* took an uncomfortable turn when Jayne brought up Gil Gladly's infamous kid.

"I understand why *he* wouldn't have wanted you to bring it up in the doc," Jayne said with a yawn that she covered with her jangling, braceleted hand. "But if you're going to show the full story of the man, you as the director *must* figure out some way to work it in."

Milt hadn't thought it was really his or anyone else's business what had happened with Gil Gladly's son. It was similar to how they had only barely scratched the surface about Gil's worsening heart condition in the doc. There were some things that clearly belonged in there, and some stuff that clearly did not, that were more private affairs. In the end, yet again, Gil basically paid for the goddamn thing, so he was in charge. Milt didn't want to argue with that or rock the boat. He felt lucky just to be there.

Yes, there *was* a series of revolving rumors about Gil Gladly's son, who had mysteriously died under strange circumstances no one really knew about back in the late nineties, back when things like that could more easily get swept under the rug and forgotten before 2007 arrived and brought with it the electronic panopticon of social media and blog dominance of the private lives of famous and even semi-famous people like Gil Gladly.

The whole world is watching!

Gil hadn't wanted anything about his son in the doc, he didn't want to talk about it during any of the interviews Milt conducted with him, and that was that, Mattress Man.

Yet, here was Jayne Manning, ready to spill some beans, with Milt wanting to hear none of it...when he was saved by the vibration once more. Milt pulled out his phone, checked who it was, and immediately shot up out of his chair.

"Sorry, Jayne, one sec," Milt said. "I hate when people do this kind of thing, but I gotta take this real quick. We're doing this huge event in Chicago and the people who have been helping us put it on are, uh, not very helpful."

Jayne nodded and got right onto her own phone, starting to text away like she was giving in to her own phone jonesing, and Milt took this as a cue he was excused to step away and answer the "important" call.

"Hey, Sally," he said into the phone, stepping toward the nearly-empty parking lot. "Good to hear from you!" He knew it had to be serious if she was actually bothering to *call* him for once rather than sending a lengthy, poorly spelled monologue of an email punctuated by far too many gleeful explanation points.

"Hey, Milton. How did the screening go yesterday?"

"Really, really well," Milt answered, shuddering, pacing around in a circle next to a large, imperial, black Bentley.

"Great, great," Sally Miranda said. *"Really good to hear."*

There was a strange pause, and Milt didn't know what to do next. His mind was now on his money, on the continuation of the tour, his possibly bad behavior at the screening the day before, and now also Jayne Manning looking all like Anna

Wintour back at the table waiting for him to finish his call so she could unload even more dirt about her ex-boyfriend.

"Well, I don't want to upset you any more," Sally faked a convivial laugh, *"but I wanted to see if you saw the news."*

Milt stopped pacing. "What news?"

There came a wave of brief silence from the other end of the phone.

"Uh...you don't check on CineRanchero on social media or anything?"

"No, I'm not really into that kind of thing," Milt said. "Besides, I've been a little busy with the tour and finishing up some work on a ghostwriting project I have a deadline on."

"Right, right, right," Sally said. *"So, you don't know about what's going on with CineRanchero right now?"*

"No, not really," Milt said, getting worried and turning around to look back on Jayne Manning at their table where she looked to be intensely playing some kind of game on her phone. "I kind of assholishly just look up stuff about how you guys are promoting our film. Or, I guess I should point out, how you're *not* really promoting our event, that is coming up in, like, a few days?"

Milt felt good about getting that last jab in. It needed to be said, and if this bitch was never going to talk to him on the phone unless it was something that *she* needed or that *she* wanted to bring up, he would get in every punch he could. These fuckers were fucking up *bad*, and he wasn't going to let them totally get away with it without saying *something* for himself, the film, all the filmmakers, Gil, and the Chicago fans who were all waiting to see this goddamn movie.

"*Right, well...one of the reasons we really haven't been putting anything out there about it—*"

"What you *have* put out there has been *wrong* more than once," Milt pointed out.

"*Ha, right....*" Sally said. "*Well, one of the reasons is that we've been under a little lockdown because of a sexual harassment allegation that has cropped up.*"

"WHAT?!"

"*Yeah...you can look it up on Google or whatever,*" Sally said, not seeming to care one way or the other about it. Her M.O., Milt was starting to understand. A gig was just a gig to Sally Miranda. "*Yeah, so we kind of knew this might happen, because there were a lot of people hitting up our media department wanting to set up some interviews and whatnot and, well, the end result is we're—yeah—basically in social media and promotion lockdown right now and can't really talk too much if at all about any of our upcoming events.*"

"WHY NOT?!"

"*Well, we're worried that if we bring stuff up like your Gil Gladly screening and live after-event, people will be all over us on Twitter and whatever. 'Hey, why don't you talk about how your communications director is under investigation for sexual harassment?'*"

"YOUR COMMUNICATIONS DIRECTOR?!"

"*Yeah. Rolly drinks a lot and sometimes says and does stuff he regrets later, and sometimes says and does stuff he doesn't remember, and I guess he did something or a few somethings a little while back that's coming back up now that all this stuff is going on with Weinstein and everything and—*"

"Wait, so you guys *knew* this might happen, and you didn't tell us and started working with us to put all this together, knowing we were basing our *entire fucking tour* around this largest event we were doing with you and plugging it all ourselves and promoting not only us but *you guys too*...and you didn't think to say anything?"

"Well...." Silence. *"We were...very busy. You know how busy I get over here. I don't even really have time to talk with you on the phone!"*

A silver Porsche pulled up right next to Milt, with a honk that made him jump. He turned and saw the uber-tanned sophisticate hipster in black shades and perfectly coifed blonde hair *American Psycho* style was looking at him with a taut mouth that said, "Outta the way, jerk," despite the fact that Milt had been walking around in what was still almost an entirely empty parking lot where this fucking guy could have chosen *any other* spot that didn't happen to have someone on a frantic phone call right next to it.

Milt stepped away from the Porsche, and the driver opened and slammed his door *hard* before walking away from Milt toward the café.

"So, what are you saying, Sally? That you guys are just not gonna do any real promotion about our event at all? It's too late for us to cancel! You're already nearly sold-out on tickets!"

"Yeah, well that's just it," Sally said with her sustained annoying calm. *"Since we're already almost sold-out, and since you guys are so cool with plugging the screenings and every-thing yourselves, we thought—"*

"Great. You thought we'd keep doing *all* the work, huh?"

"What...what does that mean, Milt?"

Milt shook his head and kind of wished she could see him do it. He sighed a long breath. What was the point? It was too late. He was in this. He had gotten Gil and everyone else into this. First that fucking asshole Latham at what was supposed to be the original premiere venue, Latheatre, and now this. Was Milt cursed?

This wasn't about ticket sales or profit at all. Shit, Milt and Gil and their team wouldn't be seeing a penny from the show. That was the deal they had made with CineRanchero in the beginning. No fee for renting the space or staff, and CineRanchero could keep the door.

But what Milt knew Sally Miranda knew—because he had told her about four fucking times in the past—was that the whole reason they were doing the show, the whole reason they were doing the tour, was to get as much word out about Gil and the film as possible.

They had wanted to use CineRanchero's robust social and publicity network to promote what they were doing. The film, the tour.... That's why it was going to be the big extravaganza they had been working so hard to put together. That's why the whole rest of the tour was based around the CineRanchero show. It wasn't about the money they'd never get anyway; it was about the *free publicity*. The event would be a loss leader for them. But now no one would know about it except for the few hundred people buying tickets for the one night.

Now Sally was just giving up? CineRanchero was giving up? Tickets are almost sold-out, so who cares? They had a communications director who allegedly acted inappropriately, and they knew this, and didn't bother to give Milt a chance to find another organization with which to partner up in advance so they could get the promotion they actually *needed?*

"You know what, Sally?" Milt said. "I'm at a meeting right now and we're just gonna keep doing what we're doing to—"

"Great. Just great!" Sally said, sounding upbeat enough that it was as though she hadn't just said everything she'd said. *"That's what we were hoping for. And I'm really sorry about this,"* she said with the tone of an anonymous customer service representative apologizing for "your inconvenience."

Milt shook his head uselessly.

"You know, the folks here at CineRanchero are really overwhelmed with so much stuff all the time and not exactly the most organized staff," Sally was whispering now. *"They expanded too fast, and all this stuff was always going on and... they really need to do better. It's kind of a shit show here, if you want to know the honest truth."*

"Right," Milt said, rolling his eyes and again wishing Sally Miranda could be there with him to see it so she might have some sense of what a big deal this was for Milt, the reputation of his film and film crew, and of course the already super-anxiety-trammeled Gil Gladly.

"Well, thanks for calling, and, uh, guess I'll see you at the show in Chicago."

"Oh, no. Actually, change of plans. I'm not going to be there at all now. I have some family business I need to attend to. But Kaley and Kiley are two amazing interns CineRanchero found to work specifically for this event, and they've been briefed on

everything and will be able to do anything you need for the show, okay?"

"I'm sorry to hear that, Sally," Milt said, sincerely. "Is your family okay from the freak tornadoes out there? Is that what this is about?"

"Huh?" Sally huffed. "Oh, yeah. Right. Nope, we're fine. Actually, it's pretty funny, because almost everyone else in our neighborhood got hit hard by the tornadoes, but we're fine. One of our neighbors lost their entire house, and ours didn't even get touched!"

Milt couldn't believe he had to say it, but he just couldn't help himself. "Wait, what's funny about that?"

"Look, Milt," Sally said, sounding like she was ready to wrap things up and move on to ruining her next event. "I'm on a LOT of medication, okay?"

"Ah."

What Milt had wanted to say was something along the lines of, Wait, so I had to set up everyone's fucking travel schedules, get them their flights, compensating for the osbtinate weather sweeping through everyone's towns right now, and make sure their hotels were all handled, including the one for Gil, who had me change his accommodations five fucking times until he felt totally comfortable with the choice...AND I got all of the schedule and production of the show in order over the past four months, including dealing with Dillon Rogers' live musical set while needing to find a way to fly his broke-ass out after he didn't get the early emails, all for this thing I don't even get paid for or credit for as producer...and YOU, THE ONE WHO

DOES GET PAID AND "PRODUCER" CREDIT, YOU'RE NOT EVEN GOING TO BE THERE?

Needing to be professional, needing to represent the film, the rest of his crew and, most importantly, Gil Gladly as best as he could, what Milt actually said over the phone to Sally right then was a far more diplomatic, "Mmm...."

"Okay! Well, have a productive rest of your trip in LA, and don't forget to have fun!"

"You too. Bye."

She hung up, Milt clicked off the call, and dropped his phone back into his pocket.

His sign-off may not have made any sense, but neither did anything else about the call, or Milt's nearly six months of dealings with Sally Miranda and CineRanchero. He was too tired to care and was feeling slightly feverish. His throat was hurting, but he may have been dehydrated.

He hoped that was all it was. This was *no* time to get sick.

Milt went back to the table with Jayne, who didn't bother to look up to Milt sitting back down until she was done with the level she was finishing.

"Just a second, hon...." Then she turned off the game, slipped her phone into her large brown-and-white Louis Vuitton purse that had been on the table next to her Arnold Palmer that she'd barely touched. "How did it go?"

"Fine," Milt said. "It is what it is. The usual."

"That's good, then."

"Sure, I guess," Milt said, resigned to his private fate. "It's so strange, though. I've been having nothing but trouble with this chick, then she also talks all this shit on her own company and some of the other people she works with. It makes me wonder what she says about me or Gil or whatever."

"Yeah," Jayne said soberly. "It's a tough industry to be in, that's for sure. Especially for women. Especially these days. A lot going on."

"Mmm...."

"No, really," Jayne said, leaning forward. "I've always said the most important thing is personality. Let's be honest, Milton. *Anyone* can do what we do. Producing? Come on. You just work. You just do it. You get it done. Right? So, the trick then is to make sure you've got the kind of personality that people want to be around, and that you hire and work with people whose personalities you can work with too. Right?"

"I guess," Milt said, wondering just how much money it would cost to Lyft back to Gabe's and how he would get to the airport tomorrow without having to pay for a one-hundred-dollar cab, since Frankly needed to go back home that night so he could go back to work the next morning like a *real* person. Which led to Milt pondering the concept of doing a limited docuseries about the "real" life of Lyft drivers, then onto ruing the fact he didn't have the family financial support and resources needed to make such a project like Tony Rigatoni and his new buddies making that damned Balloon documentary, which led to....

"It's not about guessing, Milt," Jayne said, leaning back again in her chair. "This is how it is. You can't work with people whose personalities you clash with and vice versa. I've seen people lose jobs over it. Good, qualified, experienced, hard-working people. If you're a jerk or you can't communicate with other people, you're out."

"Yeah?" Milt said, not able to help himself. "Then how do you explain people like this Sally Miranda chick? Or most of those 'terrible people' you were talking about earlier who run Hollywood?"

Jayne smiled. She nodded in understanding. "I suppose you have me there."

"It's the William Goldman thing. 'Nobody knows anything.'"

They both laughed, and Jayne placed her bony, surprisingly frigid, taut, and leathery tanned hand on his. Milt was glad she suggested they move on before she revealed more about what she knew about what had happened so many years ago to Gil's son or anything else. At this point in the game, Milt simply didn't need to know anything more about the darker aspects of Gil Gladly's life.

Before they stood up to leave, Milt saw something on the thick white paper menu scrawled in what appeared to be gold ink that sparked a quick *bon mot* in his head and farted it out of his mouth. "*Vegan* tacos? Aren't they worried about cultural appropriation?"

Jayne guffawed—a word Milt used too often in descriptions in his writing but in this case was the only one that was suitable—and squeezed his hand even tighter in a very uncomfortable way that if he had used Twitter, he might have referred to as "inappropriate," reminding him further of one of the many reasons he'd left LA for good so many years before, of an older woman "producer" who had tried to—

"You wanna know the truth about your hero Gil Gladly there, sweetie?" Jayne Manning asked.

Milt said nothing. He didn't need to. She didn't strike Milt as the type to need permission.

"The *truth* is that Gil Gladly always wanted to be Steve Allen, and he never made it happen."

Milt almost continued his silence, but there was one part of this boring cliché that didn't make sense to him, and after everything over the past few days and this long, drawn-out conversation with this lady, he had to ask, "But didn't *everyone* from his generation want to be Steve Allen? What's weird about that?"

Jayne smiled that smile that made Milt understand that she was much, *much* older than he. That she had had much, *much* more experience than he. It was like what he always joked with younger people about when they tried to put him in his place and he'd say, "There's still one thing I can do that you never will be able to do. *Be ten years older.*"

And here it came.

"Gil was different, sweetie," Jayne said. "He *really* wanted to be Steve Allen. It just seemed particularly tough on him when people he knew on his way up—Jay, Letterman, Conan—got a whole lot closer, and all Gil ever got was *KidTalk*."

"That show was pretty important to *my* generation," Milt said meekly, not sure why he was bothering. "And his other shows weren't so bad."

"Kid, come on," Jayne said, baring her teeth like she was the wolf about to eat Little Red Riding Hood. An expression, Milt quickly ascertained, she probably had honed over the years and used in such conversations when she was deliberating over millions of dollars for projects here and there. "You've *written* about this. How many times? Balloon, even in its heyday, was never NBC, ABC, or CBS. It was never HBO or Showtime. It wasn't even Fox. Never. Nickelodeon at least had *SpongeBob* for a few years. What did Balloon ever *really* have?"

Milt flashed on all the times people he told about his documentary on Gil Gladly had said simply, "Oh, I didn't have cable growing up. Wasn't he the dad on that show with Mayim Bialik?"

"Even later on, when Gil found his way into a few other cable shows, it was never network TV," Jayne continued. "And as we all know, he never will. It's over. No third act. The best you can say about him for TV now is he's not bald. He's a pudgy, old, gray-haired, straight white *male*. It's over for people like that, and it's over for Gil Gladly. He did *KidTalk* and his two or three other shows over the years that came and went, and that's the end of his story. Except every now and then when kids like you pop up and do some article about him for BuzzFeed or Huffington Post, or make some video about him for Mashel or whatever it's called. I can't even keep up with all these fucking things."

"He still has meetings all the time."

"Gil's *great* at meetings," Jayne Manning said, shaking her head. "People love to meet him. All these people who are your age. Younger maybe. They got their comfy little positions and offices because of who their parents are or because they fucked the right guy or gal at Fire Island a few years back when Fire Island was still what it was. You ever heard of the Velvet Mafia? Don't answer that. It doesn't matter. What matters is no one watching TV wants to hear from Gil Gladly again."

Milt wasn't even sure he meant it, but somehow it crawled out of his mouth. "*We* do."

"Yeah, well, *you're* not the ones making the decisions. Those fucking snot-nosed *kids* at NBC or CBS or Netflix or wherever Gil goes blowing all his retirement money on flights and hotels to have meetings to make himself feel like a big man are just meeting with him to tell their friends that night, 'Hey, you remember Gil Gladly? That fucking guy from *KidTalk*? The one who *stutters*? Back in nineteen-eighty-who-gives-a-shit? I met him today! He was *awesome*!' Who cares. They're not gonna give him a show. They couldn't even if they wanted to. Gil is *ob-SOH-leet*. We all are, honey."

Jayne looked down at the table. She seemed as though she was about to pass out from the exhaustion. "We all are."

She leaned back in her chair and seemed completely deflated, as though denigrating her old boyfriend had taken it out of her.

Milt felt as though she had been wanting to say all of this for far too long and instead of saying it to a mutual friend of hers and Gil's, or to a therapist, or a priest or something, she had said it to him, to Milt Siegel, some schmuck who was stupid enough to blow two years of his life and all of his career karma and friends' favors around the country on some goddamn documentary about the guy who had apparently broken Jayne's heart so many years ago despite still being friends with the guy, more or less.

Why was Jayne Manning saying all of this about Gil? Didn't she worry about Milt going off and tweeting about all of this or going to *TMZ* or something? She wasn't a recognized name, but the work she'd put out had been zeitgeist-ish. Milt could make two- or four-thousand bucks selling all this shit somewhere. But somehow, Jayne knew that he wouldn't do that. It wasn't part of his makeup. Like Jerry Maguire, he wasn't built that way.

What a terrible movie.

Heck, wasn't she at all worried Milt would go straight to Gil himself with this information? The fact his ex-girlfriend was going around talking about him like this?

But no. She knew Milt wouldn't do it. He'd be too scared. Scared she'd deny. Scared she'd somehow turn it around on Milt. She had power here. He had none. The same way she clutched his hand and could likely get away with a lot more than that if she wanted. She knew Milt was weak and had nothing on her. *This* was how Hollywood really worked. This was not the kind of "privilege" twenty-something Brooklynites whined about on Instagram. This was the *real thing*.

Milt crinkled his face. He was uncomfortable. He wanted to scratch his buttcrack for some reason, but knew, as intimate and strange as things had gotten between Jayne and he, he'd better not.

Jayne sprang up. Whatever cocktail of meds she was very clearly operating under had waned, and she went on with her eruptive, circa 1980 Mount St. Helens rant. "Gil's also very good at burning bridges. One of the best. And *that,* my friend, my sweetheart, is why he will continue to be, pardon my French, *fucked.* We all love him as much as you and your entire hopeless, moneygrubbing, gimmegimme generation. Yes, he can be at times unbelievably funny, smart as a whip, incredibly generous to those he deems his friends, and used to be *devastatingly* handsome, especially with that copper-red shock of hair. Why *wouldn't* we all love Gil Gladly? But, my dear, sometimes it's not easy. Sometimes...sometimes it's not worth the trouble."

Milt thought of all those rants and raves in interviews about Balloon and other people Gil had worked with. That old Vice video that had gone viral; the Twitter fights with no-name idiot trolls; Gil's temper; his ego; his lack of decorum; his tendency to twist facts, whether intentionally or not.

Milt also thought briefly of his father, then let that one go.

These kinds of things were part of an element of Gil's personality that Milt always worked the hardest at ignoring. He didn't want to think he was doing all of this for a guy who might not have been as good a guy as he seemed, imperfect as that "good guy" might be.

Selfishly, he also worried that if it was so easy for Gil to throw so-called friends and colleagues under the bus as Milt had watched him do either verbally or directly more than once, it would be just as easy for him to one day do the same to Milt.

No. There was no way Gil Gladly would ever do that. Milt was sure of it.

Gil certainly could be intimidating. In fact, most recently, Milt had more than once told himself, "If I can just get through this tour, we can sell the film and move on, and I can move on from Gil too."

It was a strange feeling to have about a former kids show TV star that Milt had grown up having on the TV throughout so much of his youth. It would have been like finding out that Mr. Rogers had been engaged in a series of bloody underground brutal fight clubs the entire time he was welcoming three different generations of kids to his haimish neighborhood.

Jayne Manning mercifully let go of Milt's hand and stood, preparing to leave. "You're wondering why I told you all of this," she said, while rifling around in her bag for her car keys.

"I think I know," Milt said, getting up. "I gotta get back."

"One of these days you're going to have to stop being scared of LA and move back here if you want to really make it, Milt. You're going to need to look *inside*."

"Mmm, thanks," Milt said, shaking her hand before turning to leave. "See ya."

Jayne Manning snickered as he walked away.

This was how people in LA, people in "the industry" talked about one another. Jayne Manning was Gil Gladly's *friend*. Someone who had and likely still loved him dearly, and this was how she talked about Gil. *This* was why Milt was glad he had left LA when he did, had traveled the country, spent a good chunk of time in New York where at least people stab you in the *front* and let you know quite directly if they think you're a scumbag, and why he was especially glad he had spent the last few years traveling *outside* those hallowed realms of LA and NYC, and had eventually made it to Boston to write for the paper there.

Shitsmelled was a son of a bitch of a boss, and a son of a bitch of a person, but he was nothing compared to the vileness Milt had experienced while he had tried to make his career go in LA. Experiences like the one he was having right now with Jayne Manning.

Milt turned to walk away from Jayne Manning, wanting to wander the beachside, listen to the waves, and feel the warm spritz for a bit before Lyfting his fifty-dollar way back to Gabe's before getting ready to leave for the airport in the morning.

"Good luck on the rest of the tour!" Jayne Manning called out after him. "Send my love to your wife! And tell Gil I said hi!"

CHAPTER 17

Milt had gotten himself to the airport with plenty of time to spare.

Actually, that wasn't necessarily true.

First, there was his not having Frankly to do his bidding any longer. Frankly had already gone home to get back to his actual life as a dutiful son, older brother, and manager of a Barnes & Noble.

Gabe had suggested he could give Milt a ride to LAX, but when it was time to go, he was still passed out in his room with the door locked, the alarm blaring, with no sign of his getting up any time soon.

As the minutes ticked by, Milt had done the only thing he could do at this point, which was to take Philip and Annie's offer for them to drive him, since they had an errand to run not too far from the airport anyway.

Granted, Philip still appeared deathly ill. Pale and sweaty and a mess. But Annie seemed fine, and she hadn't been apart from Philip, including in the bedroom where Philip stayed almost Milt's entire visit except when he came out to smoke pot and watch bathetic TV shows in the living room/Milt and Frankly's temporary boudoir.

Thus, Milt assumed he'd be fine too, even though his forehead still felt a bit warm from the day before when he'd met up with Jayne Manning. His throat continued feeling slightly tingly too, but he decided to ignore it. His mother had always taught him not to put negative energy out into the world, and that's what he was going to keep thinking about right now. Even though his throat *did* itch a little, and his forehead *was* a little warm. Oh well. He could laugh (inside) at the notion that LA had made him physically ill this time. *Annie Hall* syndrome.

He needed a ride to the airport so he could get home, see Laney, have "the talk" he'd been dreading ever since he'd left Boston, then jet out a few days later for the next stop on this hayride. This time *with* his wife Laney.

The cheerful hippie Muppets Philip and Annie had dropped him off, telling Milt as he got out of their late eighties beige SUV of some indiscernible kind that he was welcome to stay over any time. Actually, Philip had said it. (Well, had coughed it out.)

But the sentiment was certainly there, and again both Annie and he waved and smiled as Milt watched, wondering how the hell Philip could drive at LAX without watching where he was going.

The brusque, burly lady at the luggage scan had asked if Milt wanted to take his laptop out of its carrying case, and he'd answered, "Well, I don't *want* to, but I will."

He thought he was being cute.

She thought…. Well, he didn't know what she thought, but he thought it better to leave well enough alone.

Milt grabbed all his stuff from the other side of the scanner, got his shoes that he'd also obediently taken off, and made his way to the terminal with a half-hour to spare.

This was another reason he was proud of his heritage. *Jews are just like Boy Scouts!* he mused. *We're always prepared!*

He sat down and overheard an older couple arguing. Really, it was more the wife yelling at the uxorious nebbish of her husband.

"Well, I certainly don't want to travel with *that* person!" the harridan shrieked at him, expecting the threat to alter his grumbly personality at the moment. *"That* person" being *he*, the old man who was clearly in a mood she didn't find acceptable. He hoped Laney would never yell at him in public like this, and in third person, no less.

It reminded Milt of the kind of treatment he'd received from all those angry, middle-aged women who performed in the role of "teacher" in his elementary school days. And junior high. And high school. And most of college.

Although, in all fairness, in college, they weren't middle-aged. A few seemed only slightly older than he, but, boy, had they all been angry.

He was glad he hadn't become a teacher.

He was definitely glad he wasn't still a student, either. How could people, aside from doctors, lawyers, and maybe engineers, put themselves through four or eight more years of college to get a PhD? He was glad he hadn't had the money, time, agoraphobia, or monomaniacal desire required for grad school. He'd been too busy working.

Where would he have been if he hadn't jumped right into the media and entertainment industries straight out of school? If he *had* become one of those miserable, socially awkward people hiding in a classroom for four to six more tedious years?

But wait...was *he* miserable?

Then he became depressed thinking of what a mess his life seemed at that moment. But was it *really* a mess? Or was it all relative, like everything else? *Was* everything *really* relative? Relative to whom? To what?

Shut up shut shut upppppp!!

Milt watched the older couple bickering as they faded off and away into the deluge of the airport crowd, and thought once again of the funny juxtaposition of his life right here at this time. Having just come from the childish, innocent, fancy-free epicenter of youthful nostalgia to being here now, alone in an airport, watching an old couple fighting in an embarrassing, public display.

From there to here and here to there.

Sitting there with his beige canvas backpack and his black laptop carrying case, he also wondered if he should text Laney. He hadn't heard from her for a day or two and hadn't reached out to her. He had been worrying he'd been too clingy before and that maybe he needed to keep giving her her space. Or something. Oy, wives needed to come with an instruction manual. Like the ones his dad had always used before getting started on a video game.

There was something ironic about this thought, Milt knew, but he couldn't quite put his finger on what exactly. He felt feverish and disoriented, somewhat dizzy.

He pulled his phone out of his pocket, saw that he had an email from Jessica Chen, who apologized that they hadn't had a chance to meet at the screening—*Ah, so she* had *been there! Thank goodness he hadn't met up with her in his bibulous state.*

Or what if they had *met up, but she felt so weird about however he might have acted that she pretended like they* hadn't? *She* was *an actress, after all. Or* had *been. Nah, not possible. Why would she lie like that?*

She once again included a series of headshots he didn't download onto his phone and a link to her EPK that he didn't click on. He swiped left with his thumb to archive the message and was just about to text Laney when the phone vibrated and he saw it was Melody calling him.

He picked up.

"Yo," Milt said into the phone, widening his legs, leaning back, and relaxing as much as one could relax into his airport terminal chair. There were no other passengers around, so he felt comfortable talking at a normal volume, which for him was rather resonant.

"Hey, what's up?" Melody said in her sing-songy voice that was slightly low for someone as petite as she and, as always, connoted a certain indifference, as though she was calling out of obligation.

He could also tell that Melody was multitasking. Meaning she was on the phone with him and looking at YouTube videos on her laptop on her bed. She was also more than likely playing with her fat gray kitty Minnie Mouse.

Since Melody was about five years younger than he, she had that ADD'd millennial quality about her he always teased her over.

"Oh, just getting it done," Milt answered, exhaling hard.

"You sound stressed."

"When am I *not* stressed, Melody?"

"Yeahhhhhh...."

He sneezed, pulling the phone away from the spritz, then put the phone back to his ear and mouth. "I'm at LAX. My flight leaves in about a half-hour. They'll be boarding in ten minutes, I think. It's weird. There's really no one else here."

"That's cool."

Although she didn't sound like she really cared, Milt always appreciated that she called him regularly and that she always picked up whenever he called her. It was nice being buddies with Melody, even if she tended to be in her own world most of the time when they talked. Cheaper than therapy. For them both.

"Heading back home," he said.

"Yeah? You excited to see Laney?"

"She's coming with me to the next few screenings, actually," Milt said, subtly shifting the conversation.

"Oh, that's great, Milt! I'm so happy for you and all this stuff going on with your documentary, and your new book you're working on. I can't believe how much you're able to do all the time. I feel like so many things are happening in your life right now."

"Maybe," Milt said, exhaling again and leaning back further in his chair, sliding down lower. "Sometimes it feels like I'm in a hamster wheel."

"Yeahhhh...."

"Even in physics, Work equals Force times Distance. If I don't move what I'm putting Force against, then Distance is zero. Thus, no matter how much Force I apply, I end up generating zero units of Work. Hence why pushing a wall with all your might does not mean you've done any Work if the wall doesn't move."

"That's a damn good analogy."

"I know. I use it a lot. It's just...with the kind of stuff I do for 'work,' it's not like I get an A for effort, you know? I can't exactly tell my landlord or, heaven forbid, the doctor or car payment company or whatever that I'm quote-unquote 'working on a lot of great projects!' exclamation-mark. They just want the check at the end of the month. Until the IRS knows I made this Gil Gladly doc, it doesn't matter."

"True."

"It's not *Calvin and Hobbes*. It's not about building character."

"But you're doing all right," Melody said. *"Right?"*

"I have some money in the bank, yeah," Milt answered, not *exactly* lying. "And it's not like we're not gonna sell the doc at some point. Just *when* is the thing. I don't know. I get like this a lot, even when I *am* doing a lot all at once. I think a lot of this comes from my dad. If I'm not immediately getting a big check or some kind of prestigious award, he doesn't really care. If I wanna be a writer, I have to be Stephen King. If I wanna be a filmmaker, I have to be Steven Spielberg. Otherwise, he doesn't understand why I'm doing what I'm doing."

"That's not true," Melody said. *"Come on. I know your dad doesn't really feel that way. It always sounds like he's really proud of you when you talk about him."*

"Yeah, I guess. But...not always."

"Well, I never met him."

"Look, some of this is also a Jewish thing."

"No, it's not!"

"Yeah, it is. You wouldn't understand because you're goy."

"What's a goy?"

"It means you're not Jewish, and so you wouldn't get this whole extra thing that Jewish people—especially Jewish sons and fathers—have. *Especially* in the creative fields. We all talk about it all the time. Why do you think *The Jazz Singer* has been remade so many times?"

"Because of the whole blackface thing?"

Milt laughed, shifted in his seat, and stretched his neck, which popped when he cracked it hard to the right. "Never mind. So, you still up to come and see me when I'm in Portland?"

There was a brief pause. *"I don't know, Milt. I don't really have any extra money right now, and it's like a four-hour drive. That's a lot of gas money there and back. Plus, I'd have to take off the next day, which would mean I'd lose more money because I don't get sick days yet, since I just started."*

"Well, I could pay for your gas money or something...if you want," Milt said, feeling a needling pang of guilt on at least two different levels.

"Nah. That would make me feel weird, and besides, I just started, so it's not like I can be missing days already, whether they're paying me or not."

Okay, Milt thought, *back to reality.*

Melody was obviously not going to come out and see him when he was in Portland and that was *definitely* for the best. No muss, no fuss. He needed to turn off his constant drive toward self-sabotage.

Married married married.

"So, how's it going over there, anyway?" he asked, sitting up straight now, as the seats around him began filling up.

"Oh, you know," Melody said, trying to sound chipper. *"It's a job. It's work."*

"Do you like it?"

"It's better than my last job, that's for sure. But that's not hard to beat. That place was terrible. One thing I don't like is they get real uppity about me looking like I'm busy, which is really annoying. We have a lot of downtime, so I was bringing in my knitting and working quietly on a pink scarf for my sister in my cubicle, and one of the managers came by and pulled me aside into a conference room to tell me that if I kept doing that, I'd be fired."

"Aw, man, that sucks," Milt said.

"Yeah, and it's like, I can't even read a book or something at my desk. I swear, Milt, I've only been there like three weeks, but there are some days where I haven't done anything, so why can't I read? Why does anyone care? It gets me so pissed off!"

"'Pissed off' like Rachel Maddow pissed off, or 'pissed off' like Rose McGowan pissed off?"

"Oh, shut up, Milt," Melody said in a friendly huff. *"This is serious. It's my work. It's my life. And it's fucking annoying."*

"Jason Schwartzman annoying, or Dane Cook annoying?"

"SHUT UP, MILT!"

"You know, I was thinking about this the other day," Milt said, slightly quieter now that other people were crowding in next to him. "I was at a restaurant with Laney a few nights before I left for LA, and I saw this young girl working the hostess stand up front and she was totally lost in her phone. No one said anything or cared, not the customers coming up to get a table, not the managers milling around checking to make sure everything was okay. It's like being on your phone is totally acceptable, but if she were reading a *book*, she would get reprimanded."

"Oh, I know!" Melody squeaked. *"That's exactly how it is at my new job! You know what my manager said after she scolded me for knitting in my cubicle? She said that if I don't have any work to do, I should just surf the internet. She actually said that! She said that way it would look like I'm doing something productive. But I don't want to do that all day! I'm on the fucking computer long enough already, staring at the screen when I* am *working. I don't want to have to do it when I'm not!"*

"God, it's so scary the way that works. It's like they're pushing you into this thing that is already so addictive. And they're making you do it, like, *all day!"*

"I know! I hate it!

"So," Milt cycled back around, "you're not gonna come see me when I'm in town, then?"

"Oh, Milt," Melody droned. *"I...don't knowwwww."*

The disembodied boarding announcement trumpeted around him, and the Pavlovian effect stood him up out of his chair at attention.

"Hey, they're gonna be boarding, so I gotta go. Look, it's cool if you can't come out. But just let me know if you can. It's our last show, I'll be driving out all the way from Boston, and—"

"You're driving? Why?"

"I dunno." He grabbed his stuff and walked toward the line beginning to grow out of the terminal. "Laney can't come to that one because she can't take off that much work and, let's be honest, there's only so many times she can watch this fucking film before she loses it. So, I just thought it would be a good way for me to end the tour and have some time to myself and, I don't know, do some thinking and stuff. I miss going on those solo road trips. It was the one nice thing about living in LA. I haven't had a chance to do something like this since I got a car again. It's been almost ten years since I've had one, and I never had any time to take a trip on my own while I was in Boston since I was so fucking busy."

"Yup, trying to push that wall."

"Exactly," Milt said, smiling. He liked when Melody appeared to actually be listening. And he liked when he could actually pay attention to what she was saying.

"Well, have a safe flight," she chimed.

"Thanks," Milt said. "Oh, hey, how you holding up with the heat wave, by the way? One of our guys out there helping with the screening told me about it."

"Ugggh," Melody exhaled hard. *"Yeah, it sucks. The worst part is my bosses at work are cheap assholes, so they only turn on the A/C a certain amount of times during the day."*

"USA!"

"Yeah, yeah," Melody said, resigned. *"It's not fun. I get all sweaty and tired, then my pussy starts to stink real bad."*

"All right, all right," Milt said. "I got it. You don't have to *keep* doing the Lena Dunham self-revelation stuff. I get it—you're so *brrrrrraaave."*

Melody granted a peal of her mellifluous giggles, and Milt smiled.

They said their goodbyes, a less than heartfelt "I love you/I love you too," and then Milt did what he thought he should do before getting on a plane. He texted Wallace and Ronnie that he was so grateful for both of them and all their hard work and that he would see them soon at the CineRanchero event in Chicago. He sent a text to Silverstein saying to hang in there, a text to Frankly saying thanks for all of his help and worst experience at a strip club in his life, and left a voicemail for his mom saying he was getting on a plane, loved her very much, and looked forward to seeing her at the screening in New York.

Melody texted him before he turned off his phone: **"And say hi to Laney for me. I hope to meet her someday."**

"I'll tell her," he lied.

CHAPTER 18

"How's the job been going?" Milt asked Laney as they lay naked in bed at home in their cramped four-hundred square-foot, age-inappropriate studio apartment in Boston.

It was rare that they were naked together like this, but they had apparently had much to drink late last night when they'd gone out to "be bad" as they liked to say, what with Milt home from the LA trip and their pretending like it would be a good idea to have some kind of celebratory homecoming.

Wasn't that what typical, regular married couples did? Besides, they loved any excuse to go out and be bad anyway. And Laney had some ground-up pink Adderall in a tiny (reused, as was her wont as an environmentalist) Ziplock bag she'd acquired for the occasion from a co-worker.

They'd indeed been quite bad the night before, after Laney had picked him up from the airport at 7:16 p.m. They spent a *lot* of money at two different restaurants and three different bars. Maybe four, but Milt couldn't remember and Laney always blacked-out after bar number two whenever they'd go out on one of their nocturnal adventures over the two years they'd been a couple.

Here they were, naked now, early morning. All forgotten and, presumably, all forgiven.

Milt was never too surprised that they both had such dura-
bility and bounced back so hard and quick after a night of such
decadent debauchery. If only they could say the same about
their waistlines. And bank accounts. Particularly since Milt was
practically tapped for the time being and still needed to save the
piddling fumes he did have for the rest of the tour, at least until
receiving the next payment on his ghostwriting project, which
he knew he needed to work on a little later in the day.

Ugggh....

Normally he was up first. But Laney, who was taking the day
off from work (something she *hated* doing for various reasons,
including lack of money on those days since she was still technically a "temp," meaning she did all the work everyone else did
except she received five dollars less an hour and no benefits like
paid vacation or sick days), had woken Milt up by her telltale
coughing jag, which meant she was not only up in the darkness
of the four-hundred square-foot Boston studio apartment, but
was already smoking her vape pen filled with her favorite strain
(Gorilla Glue) in the corner on the other side of the "couch" in
their "den."

There had also been that peculiar, not especially nice,
sweet redolence of vanilla in the air from said pen, while Laney
coughed and coughed, making Milt wonder (again) how the
hell someone who had been such a lifelong, all-day-every-day
stoner like his wife could still cough like that, especially while
inhaling from a fucking *vape pen*.

If the shoe had been on the other foot, and Milt was the one
silly enough to smoke from a vape pen like that first thing in
the morning, hacking up a storm, Laney would undoubtedly be

laughing at him for being a "pussy" right about now. But he kept his comments to himself.

Laney made her way back to him. Milt and she barely touched in the bed that filled nearly half their studio. Their light-blue bed sheets were strewn about the mattress and floor surrounding them, and the cream-colored down comforter was nowhere to be found, likely thrown aside at some point during their debaucherous evening/early morning.

They were both at slight angles in the bed, looking up at the ceiling, and both kept their hands locked behind their heads on their white pillows. Their elbows did not touch. They were both thoughtful. Laney was stoned.

There were a few light-pink, dried spots of blood by Laney's foot, but neither Milt nor she saw that for the time being, their eyes both affixed on the ceiling above as though they were engaged in trying to see one of those 3D shapes from those early nineties "magic eye/4D posters" prominently featured in Kevin Smith's *Mallrats*.

Milt felt that sickly tingle in his throat, but ignored it for now, waiting for Laney to finally answer.

"Work's been fine," Laney said.

"Still boring?"

"Always boring. *Everything's* borrrrrrinnnnng."

Laney performed some kind of research tests all day long at a lab for a company whose name had recently changed and that Milt couldn't remember now. It was something like YordCorp or YardTech or something like that. He could never properly explain what it was Laney did when they were out having dinner with new friends, and so it was easier to say she did scientific research, to which Laney would pipe in to proclaim, "I've finally found a use for my biology degree after blowing my twenties working for pennies at music festivals. They always had good acid, though."

No one would ever laugh when she would say this, but Laney would still smile away, the puckish creature she was, like she was always on some kind of mystifying high, away from everyone else and just waiting for the evening to be finished so that she could go home, get in her PJs, vape, and get into bed to read *Game of Thrones* or watch *Sex and the City* with Milt on their crappy laptop whose battery had died far too many months ago, requiring its constantly being plugged in, taped-up broken cord flowing all over their damn bed.

"There's this new lady there, though," Laney blurted out, like she had been waiting for *just* the right moment to reveal the intel.

"Another chick?"

"Yup, I'm no longer the lab's only girl anymore," Laney said. "It's really fucking annoying too, because she's a little older and was brought it in to do some marketing BS for—"

"Why does a research facility need a marketing person?" Milt asked, interrupting his wife as always.

"So that we can get better clients and more clients and start expanding and all that. Still a company. Still trying to make money over there. That's why they can bring on indentured servants like me to do all that work without getting paid right or benefits like sick days. Muh-member?"

"Yeah." Milt took a deep breath and let it out. He didn't know why.

"Anyway, so this chick is there now, and on one of the first days she started, we were all at lunch in the commissary and she came over to where I'm always eating with Ralph and Christopher and Lionel—"

"Who are they again?"

"Ralph and Christopher are my direct superiors, the really geeky older guys, and Lionel is one of the other techs who comes over and eats with us sometimes because I don't think he has any friends at the company. *Anyway*, this bitch comes over and she puts her hands on my shoulders and for no reason at all just says, 'We girls gotta stick together, huh, Laney?'"

Laney let that hang out there for about four seconds before she rolled over to the side of the bed, reached down, grabbed her vape pen, took a hit, coughed three times, and dropped the vape pen—which Milt heard roll away—onto to the floor. "I mean, I can't believe she fucking did that. I just wanted to be like, 'Lady, I'm one of the *guys! FUCK YOU!*'"

"Did you say that?"

"Yeah, I said that. Out loud. To the new marketing director. So now I'm fired. Sorry, I forgot to tell you," Laney huffed. "But seriously, I really hate that kind of shit. I mean, here I am at this company for six months, working my ass off and becoming friends with all the guys there, happy as a clam in shit that I'm the only chick there, because you know how much I prefer working with dudes because they're less catty and when they get mad at each other they just punch a wall or each other or something and then move on, whereas chicks can't let it go and just let it fester and fester until it makes everyone feel shitty like a cancer...."

"Riiiiggghhhtt," Milt said, this time maybe more appropriately interrupting to move the story along. At least in his mind. *He* wasn't stoned.

"So, *anyway*," Laney said, "I just wish she hadn't done that. I like being the only girl there, and of course that's going to happen in a STEM place like where I'm working because—I mean, I'm sorry, but women just tend to not work in the hard sciences. It's just the way it is."

"Mmm hmmm...." Milt sneezed.

"Cover your mouth, please. Gross. Why don't you ever cover your mouth? Why did your mom do *such* a terrible job raising you? Arrggghh!"

"You *love* my mom."

"I do, I do. I love her. But I hate what a lousy job she did raising you."

"Nah, you love me too." With that, Milt rolled over to Laney's side of the bed and poked at the flab on her right hip, then pinched it.

Laney squealed, "Ouch-uh!" slapping his hand away playfully. "I just don't want to feel different from the other guys. My dad was a college football coach. I have two older brothers."

"You're a dude."

"Yeah, I'm a dude, and you're therefore *gaaaaaay*, and *I* don't want to feel like I'm some kind of outsider just because I also happen to have tits and a vag*iiiiiiii*na."

Milt took another deep breath and respired slow. His throat was feeling dry and scratchy, and he wanted water but didn't get up because it was nice lying there in bed with Laney, even if they weren't touching.

Laney farted. Neither made a joke about it.

"Then yesterday, before I went to pick you up at the airport..."

"Yeah?"

"She sends this email out to everyone telling us all about some goddamn who-gives-a-shit dinner she wants us all to go to for Sam's birthday at this pub up the street from our office where we go for lunch sometimes."

"Who's Sam?"

"Some other tech who works in the office across from ours," Laney said indolently, trying to get to the point. "And this marketing chick telling us all about this thing I'm obviously not going to, writes at the end of it, 'And, Laney, I really hope you go, *so that I'm not the only girl there!*' I mean, obviously she was kidding, sort of. But...*Oohhgghh!*" Laney gritted her teeth. "I shake *both* brushes at her!"

Laney had this thing where when she was much younger, instead of getting vocally or noticeably mad at her much older brothers when they did something to irk her—like, say, tricking her into stapling her own hand—she would go upstairs to her room, politely close (not slam) her door, and shake her hairbrush at them through the door. For some reason, it seemed to help get her frustrations out, without also irking them into, say, locking her in the closet or shoving her against a wall.

So now, these many years later, when she got mad at someone—particularly Milt—she would say, "I'm shaking my brush at you so hard right now!" To say, "I'm shaking *both* brushes," well, ma'am, *watch out!*

Milt flashed on the scene from Baz Luhrmann's *Romeo + Juliet* when Jamie Kennedy says he will "bite [his] tongue at them." (*Sirrrr*). Then Milt flashed on making out with the gal he saw the film with in the theater after the movie was over.

Ahh, his first "real" date.

Milt and Laney both knew she bottled up her rage (and most other emotions) until they erupted from her in this way, often inappropriately, sometimes publicly. But it was something that occurred so infrequently, maybe once or twice a year, that it never ceased to be incredibly disarming for Milt to witness it.

He rolled to her side and placed his hand on her cold, sweaty (her skin was always so cold and sweaty), alabaster skin, caressing it sloppily and steadily with the reluctance of a person who's not really sure he's supposed to be doing what he's doing.

"Anyway, how's the MC Phliphlop book coming along?" Laney fumed, blowing the words out of her clenched teeth.

"Uh, it's all right," Milt said. "I obviously didn't have much time to work on it in LA, but I did get some work done on the plane. More than I would've thought, actually. Both on the way there and on the way back, so that was a few hours. I picked at some of my notes here or there, and was able to talk with someone I met up with out there who made for a good interview."

"Cool," Laney said, not really caring one way or the other, shooting daggers at the invisible woman from work in her head, there on the ceiling. Shaking her brushes so hard in her mind.

"The one thing that sucks is that I got a call from my editor," Milt said, still rubbing Laney's arm, but slowing down almost to the point of stopping, realizing it wasn't helping and that this was one of those times where leaving her alone would probably be the best salve.

"Uh huh...."

Milt rolled back to his side of the bed. "Turns out they want to push the deadline back. Of course, they didn't say I *have* to turn it in earlier, but if I *can* turn it in three months earlier, that would really help the promotional strategy because of some of the recent publicity around Phliphlop and all that crap."

"Uh huh." Laney was unmoved.

"So...." Milt sat up in the bed, back against their cold white wall in the near darkness, "I told them I'd give it a shot. Because what I need now is *more* pressure with all the fucking shit I'm working on right now."

"Cool," Laney said.

"No, *not* cool," Milt said, knowing this was one of those times when Laney wasn't hearing him talk but rather just heard that *wah-wah-wah* sound the adults made in the Charlie Brown cartoons he never really liked much when they were on at friends' houses as a kid. (Those end credit sequences were *weird*, man!)

"Work's work," Laney said.

"Yeah, I just wish I got *paid* for things like, you know, hurrying *way* the fuck up with an entire goddamn book I've been killing myself to finish up while also dealing with this Gladly doc and tour nonsense—"

"I'm sorry, I'm listening, babe, but *guhhhhhdddd!*" Laney fulminated. "For that marketing bitch to say something like that *again* after she must have seen how uncomfortable I was when she said the other thing a few days earlier.... I mean, she's only been there barely a week and already she's making me realize yet again why I'm so glad I work in a field with only men and why I'm *never* going to call myself a fucking *feminist*. Where's my vape pen?"

She reached over the side of the bed to grab at it and take a few hits. Coughing.

"Don't worry," Milt said, rolling over again to kiss Laney on the cheek, an act of affection that she didn't respond to. Not even a flinch. Her eyes were locked with rage on the ceiling above. "I won't tweet that out to anyone."

"Go ahead. Do whatever you want with your imaginary Twitter page you don't even have," Laney fumed more at the lady in her mind and less at Milt. "I don't fucking care. I fucking *hate* that lady and all those bitches out there who think and talk the same way. Don't bring *me* into all that BS. I just want to work and make money, and, for some weird reason I still don't understand, have kids with you and then move the hell out of this country to some farm in Europe where I can grow things in a garden and tend to our animals and take care of the kids and not have cell phones and smoke pot and stare at the wall and *die.*"

"Wanna have sex?" Milt asked.

This got a visceral reaction out of Laney, broke her from her spell—part of Milt's impulsive ploy here—and she turned to him to look him in the eyes. "Can you wait a few days? I'm still on my period and it's kinda chunky."

"Yuck."

"Well, *you're* the one who wants to do it."

"I think we must have last night at some point, chunky or not," Milt said, pointing at the faded speckles of blood by their feet he now noticed.

"Yeah, but that was with *Drunk* Laney, and she'll fuck anyone, any time, for any reason."

Milt rolled back to his back and looked up at the ceiling. He could tell that Laney was staying put on her side, looking at him. Or maybe not looking at him, but still on her side.

Drunk Laney. He *hated* Drunk Laney. Sure, she could be a hell of a lot of fun while out and about, and she was a demon in bed. She didn't care nearly as much about blowing money on *buenos tiempos* as traditional garden-variety Laney, who would balk at the idea of going out for a good meal more than once a month for the cost.

But Laney was right. *Drunk* Laney had no reservations. About *anything*. She could be cruel. She could be hateful. She could be destructive and hurtful. She could go out on a Friday night to a local bar while Milt was away traveling for work, traipsing around the country and shooting the bulk of the material he needed for the Gil Gladly doc so many months earlier, and she could find herself dancing to the music, pulling off her white silk scarf (where had Drunk Laney gotten *that*? *Regular* Laney *never* wore that kind of gaudy, silly thing; did she even have one in her closet, hidden away with all her dirty baseball caps, boots, and yoga crap?).

And so it was that on that particular night, with Milt away shooting the Gil Gladly doc, when Drunk Laney was dancing with one of the particular denizens of the gay bar down the street, whether the fellow was indeed gay himself...or maybe bisexual or curious or non-binary or god-knows-what it might be these days—Drunk Laney had taken that adage of "it doesn't count" to another level, had gone home with the fellow in question and hadn't brought it up—as Drunk Laney—until quite some time later: "I wanted to wait to tell you until after you were done with all the movie stuff. I know how stressed out it's been making you and I didn't want to add this to that," even though it *had* come out, with Milt responding he too had strayed while out on the shoot...

And now here they were some months later (six? eight? *o, the torpid blur of the last year for Milton Siegel!*) in their studio apartment in the earliest morning, hungover and going over just what it meant to be in their mid-thirties and married in 'Merica, 2017.

When Milt took a deep, pensive breath and slowly exhaled it this time, he knew why. "Do we want to talk about...the *thing* now, or....?"

Laney rolled back on her back, hands behind her head, elbows out to the point that they nearly touched Milt's. "We don't have to. I think we'll be okay."

"What does that mean?"

"It means that, you know, after the tour, I'm going to totally stop drinking. I've done it before. I can do it again. I can't get another DUI. I'm already practically fucked, and that ten-thousand dollars wasn't fun to pay off. We can't afford that again."

"We?"

"Yeah, you know how we're all *married* now and all that? We. When *we* do the taxes this year—or when *I* do them for us, since you're totally incapable of doing anything except making movies and writing books and articles and somehow knowing everything about books and movies and music and pop culture, which is one of the weird reasons I fell in love with you sort of in the first place because of how smart you are even though you're a total fucking moron—"

"Gee, tell me what you *really* think."

"Well," Laney laughed, "when I do our taxes, I'll be combining everything since it's our first year filing as a married couple, which means that I'm here for the long haul, Milt. I've signed the contract and I'm in. It's one of the things I realized while you were gone."

Milt almost thought he was going to cry but knew that it would only make Laney feel strange even though they'd be tears of joy, something Laney never liked seeing or experiencing herself (non-demonstrative Midwest girl vs. his overly tactile and affectionate Jewish upbringing). His eyes were also a little dry and crusty from dehydration courtesy of the drinking and salt intake the night before and whatever his cold was turning into.

It was funny how Laney could be so indifferent and adverse to any tactile experience, and yet whenever a dog on the street would come bounding up to her, she'd bend down and instantly devolve into some kind of blubbery child or overprotective mommy, petting the mangy thing, rubbing its belly and talking in repulsive baby talk, all the things Milt would never expect someone with as rock-hard a constitution as Laney to do.

It was a lot like Melody, actually. Melody could at times seem so aloof, and yet she was also at the same time the consummate "dog mommy," with two little doggies at home who would tear the place up and nip at her ankles and cause all sorts of harm and malfeasance to her and to her house and to anyone (like

Milt, *hint hint*) who would visit. Yet she loved those doggies like they were her babies which, in many regards, they were.

Or how about the slew of other cold-hearted ex-girlfriends who always seemed to hate everyone, and yet every time had a cat they adored to no end. Typically black, with very creative names. Milt thought about this for a moment. Had he always been drawn to witches? Actual fucking witches with their fucking familiars like some kind of eighties Disney movie?

Oy. *Let it go, Milt. Let it go. Stay in the conversation here now with your wife. Your* wife.

"I've actually signed *three* contracts," Laney said. He only looked at her through the corner of his crusty left eye. "We own a car together now, we have the lease on this shitty studio apartment together that we can't get out of for another six months, and we have our shared cell phone bill."

Milt turned away from her, laughing hard. Laney asked what that was all about and Milt said that he thought she meant before that she had "signed the contract" *metaphorically* but what she really had meant was she had signed *literal* contracts, and this actually made Milt feel a lot better. Because he knew how money-obsessed Laney was, especially after she had gone through the devastating trauma of her parents going bankrupt when she was eleven.

"Well, you got me now, Milt," Laney said. "I'm not going to run away. Not anymore. I'm in this, you're in this, and *we're* in this. We have to see this thing through, even if we've misstepped in the past and aren't exactly jumping each other's bones."

"Unless you're drunk," Milt added.

"Well, like I said, that part of my life—of *our* life—will be ending soon. We *will* grow up, *guhdddd-dem-it!*"

"But not yet."

"Oh *hell* no," Laney said. "If I have to go to Garbagetown, New York with you for your screening there, I'm going to be *drrrrrr-UNK*, son!"

With that, as though triggering something in her already besotted brain, Laney got up and out of bed. Oh yes, she was indeed totally naked, Milt could see, even in the near darkness, the slowly rising sun outside peeking its rays meekly through the slats of large plastic white blinds in their one window. She shuffled over to where her vape had rolled over, bending over to grab it.

Milt glanced over to his wife standing there, bending over, nude. He admired her legs for the first time since they met.

He also had enjoyed Laney's legs that first night when they had met at the Lincoln, Nebraska, bar and Laney, on acid and Molly, had stumbily introduced herself to him sitting there reading Norman Lear's autobiography. He enjoyed reading books at the bar, and it had the added bonus of, more than once, attracting a girl. ("Who's that weird dude over there *reading a BOOK* at a *bar*? That's sooooo...weeeeeeeird. Gosh, who *is* he? Maybe I should talk to him. What are you reading?" Etc. etc. etc. etc.)

Laney's black leather knee-high fuck-me boots had caught his attention in particular. And even though he had thought her ears stuck out, her hair wasn't exactly how he liked it (lazily up), and she didn't possess those all-important large doll eyes he so craved when it came to the kinds of girls he had pined for in the past, those legs *did* pull him in...along with that goddamn infectious smile of hers, that smile that went all the way across her whole face and made her light up like some kind of happy-go-lucky cartoon character, a mischievous imp that knew you were looking and kind of liked the effect she had over you while you were doing it. Yes, there she was. There Laney had been standing, his future wife in all her imperfect, magnificent glory.

She certainly wasn't watching him look at her now, bending over to grab her vape pen, naked in their Boston apartment. Over the past few weeks her legs had become so much fitter and defined.

He felt himself lusting after her. Partly. He also felt a certain kind of irrational envy about it.

Milt could work his ass off trying to lose weight, doing everything possible—exercise, diet, portion control, the works—and he'd be lucky to lose five pounds in a month. Laney would lose five pounds in a few *days* even when she *wasn't* starving herself to look good for the leg of the screening tour she'd be joining him on in the short days ahead.

Milt was perplexed—watching Laney stand back up and take a few hits from her vape pen, facing away from him with her nearly flawless ass and her slightly more defined legs—with how he really felt here. Was he envious that she could lose weight and look so much better faster and easier than he? Or was he upset that now she could go out and get another guy much easier and quicker than before? Some imaginary guy who would steal away his wife and get to enjoy physical pleasures with her due to her better body and legs and ass that Milt hadn't really gotten to enjoy because it would be too late? Was he just "future tripping" here, as his mom, the therapist, would put it? Totally fabricating a future scenario and then worrying about it so ridiculously?

"Milt, are you all right?"

Milt looked up and realized he had been lost in a daze before Laney had finished vaping and came back to the bed looking down at him from where she was standing. "You okay, babe?"

Milt nodded slowly.

"Look," she said, sitting on the edge of the bed and placing her hand on his shoulder, "you know I'm not the kind to say, 'Oh, Milt. I *do* love you *soooo* much.' I'm not built that way, and that's not how my family ever is. We're not like you and your family."

"Jewish."

"Well, yeah, but being Jewish isn't totally what I mean here. You can't use it as a reason for why you're maybe too clingy sometimes or get on my nerves or whatever else. You can't always use that as a card to get out of things when I'm annoyed by you. You don't get special treatment like that. Being Jewish isn't a disability."

She smiled at that, and Milt nodded, smiling too. He really did love her.

"It's funny you're saying all this and doing all this, Laney." He placed his own hand on hers on his shoulder. "Because I *totally* wasn't expecting you to say anything like, 'Oh, I love you so much,' or any of that crap. You know I don't fully trust anyone. Not even my mom. *That* might be a Jewish thing, but I'm not sure."

"I'm still learning."

"Right." Milt smiled brighter and sat up, Laney's hand falling to her side. "But just the fact you said all of that at all means something. It does mean you care even more, even if you think you don't. And that's nice. I appreciate it. I trust you as much as I can trust someone because of the contract thing you said earlier."

"I forgot one, actually," Laney said. "There's one other contract I signed. *We* signed. Our marriage license."

"Oh yeah, I forgot about that one."

"Me too. Hashtag me too," Laney chortled. "God, do you have any idea the paperwork and time and legal fees and all that bullshit we'd have to go through to cancel out, or whatever it's called, our marriage license? No way. We're stuck together."

CHAPTER 19

M ilt's phone began vibrating. "Annulled."

"Huh?" Laney said, lost in her own stony world again.

"It's called annulled," Milt said, reaching for his phone.

"Okay, I guess back to your phone. Your own addiction!"

"It's probably Gil, and I gotta make sure everything's okay. Our Manhattan screening's only...." Milt checked the phone. "Yup, it's Gil."

He answered the call while Laney bent down to peck him on the cheek and get ready for her shower before going to the gym, a behavior Milt always found odd. Who showered *before* going to the gym?

Gil was screaming loudly. What *time* was it, for chrissakes?

"M-m-m-milt, I n-n-n-n-need you to r-r-r-r-r-remove that video now!" Gil hollered as though holding Milt's ear with his hands through the phone speaker.

Milt looked to Laney, who could clearly hear Gil's remonstrations, rolled her eyes, and went into the tiny, cramped bathroom to start taking her oddly ritualistic pre-gym shower.

"Uh, Gil?"

"What?!"

"Umm, I don't know what video you mean. What video do you need me to take down? One of the trailers for the film we posted? I don't understa—"

"Goddamn it, no!" Gil shouted. *"The v-v-v-v-video some dumbf-f-f-f-fuck kid posted without my exp-p-p-p-press p-p-p-p-p-permission of the Q&A at our LA scr-scr-scr-s-creening. You h-h-h-a-ven't seen it yet?"*

"Hold on a sec, Gil." Milt pulled the phone away from his ear and looked up "Gil Gladly documentary screening LA" on YouTube on his phone, while Gil could be heard shouting, *"Wh-wh-wh-what?!"*

Milt scanned through some of the clip, which, not surprisingly, had all of about twelve views in the four days since having been uploaded, with no comments and one thumbs-up and no thumbs-down, posted by someone named Dweebeee431 who had a whopping four other videos posted, two of which were of himself—some super-skinny, salt-and-pepper-haired geek kid with crossed eyes and big ol' glasses—talking about the new *Batman* movies versus the old *Batman* movies and one of him with another Balloon star for a three-minute-and-twenty-nine second "interview" whose screencap was blurry.

"I'm looking at the video now, Milt, and I don't know what you—"

"Don't fuck with me. Just d-d-d-d-do what I s-s-s-s-s-say. That kid p-p-p-p-osted the v-v-v-v-v-video without asking m-m-m-m-me, and it h-h-h-h-as me talking about one of my f-f-f-f-f-former pr-pr-pr-pr-producers at B-b-b-b-b-b-balloon getting a b-b-b-b-blow j-j-j-ob in the drrr-drrr-drrressing room from one of h-h-h-h-his in-in-in-interns. My l-l-l-l-lawyer said the producer could s-s-s-s-s-sue, so I n-n-n-n-n-need you to tell that kid he n-n-n-n-n-needs to t-t-t-take it down now or I'll be the one t-t-t-to s-s-s-s-sue."

The shower door opened with a plume of steam and a bright lemon-curd light, the sound of rushing water, and Laney, her hair up in that messy way Milt didn't particularly care for and a peach-colored towel around her mid-section, asking, "Jesus, I can hear him from in here. Even with the water running! What the fuck does he want? It's six in the morning!"

Milt muted the phone for a second as Gil continued raving, and—instinctually—still held his hand over the mouthpiece. He told Laney, "One of those autistic YouTube geek kids was at our screening in LA and recorded Gil talking during the Q&A and posted some of it, and part of it has Gil talking about some producer at Balloon he used to work with who got a fucking blowjob from an intern backstage, I guess."

"What? What does that have to do with you?"

"Gil wants me to take it down."

"Why *you?*"

"I guess because I'm not only his documentarian but also his de facto assistant sometimes? Who else is he gonna get to do it?"

"How much is he paying you for all of this, again? To fix all his own goddamn messes?"

"Nothing," Milt said, taking his hand off the phone mouthpiece, realizing how inane that was. "Not until we sell the film. I just gotta stay on until we do that, get my percentage, then we can all move on with our lives."

"Great," Laney huffed. "Well, go track down that Aspergersy YouTube nerd—"

"Asperger's doesn't exist as a clinical classification anymore, Laney," Milt corrected. "And he's not a nerd, he's a *geek.*"

"Oh my god, you are so fucking *Jewish!* Who *carrrrres?* Just call *whatever* this moron 'fanboy' is and tell him to take the video down like a good little doggy. Good luck." She haughtily popped her lips into a kiss, closed the door, and could be heard stepping back into the shower.

When the hell had Gil brought up *blowjobs* at the Q&A? Milt didn't remember a moment of that. Then again, he remembered little to nothing of the screening. He did remember that feeling of cringing when Gil had said certain things onstage with Astra Singh moderating. Maybe that was one of those moments.

Although there was still the question of, *how does Gil Gladly at a screening of his own documentary about his career, in front of a bunch of his fans in LA end up talking about a goddamn Balloon producer from back in the day getting a blowjob, anyway?*

"Have you been listening to me at a-a-a-a-all?" Gil was shouting through the phone.

Milt took himself off mute and shoved the phone back to his ear so quick it hurt. "Uh, sorry, Gil, I was just checking on who this kid is. He's got like *no* subscribers and this video barely has any hits at all. Do you know what the Streisand Effect is? It really might be better to just leave this alone, and—"

"I f-f-f-f-f-fucking hate fucking Barbra St-st-st-streisand. She's a cunt. You're lucky you've n-n-n-n-n-never h-h-h-h-h-had to s-s-s-s-ssit through a dinner with her," Gil stuttered, much to Milt's chagrin. Milt momentarily thought of how surprised he was when, three years back, he had finally given her directorial efforts a shot and realized what an incredible filmmaker she was; but now was not the time to quibble over film tastes and, sure,

maybe she *was* a cunt in real life; who knew? *"Y-y-y-y-ou tell him to t-t-t-t-t-take it off, or I'll s-s-s-s-s-sue his ADHD ass st-st-st-straight into the n-n-n-n-n-n-nuthouse."*

"Gil, dude, you gotta calm down, man," Milt tried. "Your heart condition—"

"D-d-d-don't y-y-you w-w-w-orry about th-th-that r-r-r-right now, M-m-m-milt," Gil barked. *"And you better not be talking about any of that shit with anyone during any interviews."*

With that, Gil hung up.

Milt had wanted to ask what ADHD had to do with anything, but it wasn't worth the call back.

He was also confused by Gil's progressive paranoia about anyone talking about his heart condition, especially Milt. Didn't Gil know he could *trust* Milt? After all of this? Plus, hey, Milt wasn't *doing* any interviews. He hadn't even been up on stage during the premiere. The only show he'd be a part of on stage at all would be the CineRanchero one, if it didn't *totally* collapse.

He hadn't really considered it before, but when he would send around the few interviews with Gil and articles about the film to some of his friends, there were questions they had about why the hell Milt was never interviewed. He *was* the director. It *was* his film. Many of the articles didn't mention him at all.

Milt was a latecomer to the whole "personal branding" B.S., and frankly wanted to keep the focus on Gil Gladly. There were more and more filmmakers who were doing the whole Michael Moore thing of putting themselves in the damn film and making the whole thing more about their own experience dealing with the subject at hand.

That was a Tony Rigatoni move, not a Milt Siegel move. Milt wanted to keep it that way. Even if the marketing and, yes, production trend was going the other way.

Milt *had* made the film, but it was *about* Gil and *Gil Gladly* was the one who got people buying tickets to the shows and talking about it. *Right?*

So, what the *hell* was Gil talking about?

Milt looked to the closed bathroom door and saw more steam rilling through the bottom and side slats, heard the rushing water, and wished he could be in the shower right then with Laney. Unfortunately, it was too small, and Laney and he, unlike a few of his girlfriends in the past who *loved* doing so, never took showers together.

He went over to his desk in the corner, in the "office" to start up his laptop on his small black "wooden" IKEA desk that had been shoddily put together but worked for now—sort of, if not a bit slanty—and sat in his similarly shoddily put-together IKEA roller chair with the net-like backing that kind of worked but kind of was annoying, one of many reasons Milt tended to take the stupidly expensive option of doing his work at one of the three coffee shops up the street.

As a "digital immigrant" as opposed to "digital native" (he was not *quite* a millennial, thank god, he always said to himself), this would be a job for the computer and not his phone. He needed to make sure he was concise but firm in his email to the YouTube geek posting that video of Gil. This needed to be handled just right.

He knew it could be a tightrope to contact this guy. He didn't want whatever it was he was about to do to "escalate the situation," as was the phrase clickbaiters loved using along with "slammed" and "backlash." Right now, no one gave a good goddamn about the video except for Gil, who was always looking his name up like any other celeb or pseudo-celeb and somehow found the video that no one else was looking at and would just ignore if left alone.

Just then, Milt—naked on his wonky IKEA chair—heard the vibration of his cell phone over by the bed, and got up to go check to see what Gil Gladly's emergency was *this* time. As he crossed the small room, he could feel the steam emanating from the door of the bathroom where Laney was taking her long, relaxing shower. She had probably gotten lost in the comforting warmth of the water and the stoniness in her head, but that was fine, because Milt had work to do.

He huffed, picked up the cell, and placed the phone to his ear. "Hey, Dabney. How you doing?"

"Fine, just fine, m'boy!" Dabney Malloy (not his real name; his "stage name," despite having an almost non-existent IMDb page). *"How was the screening in LA? I was reading up about it yesterday and it sounds like it went really well! Some nice press there, and some great pictures by people on Twitter and Instagram."*

"Yup, it went pretty well," Milt said, exhaling hard and walking back over to his chair where he sat his naked ass down. "The rest of the shows will go pretty fast, then hopefully we'll keep getting some more good press, sell the thing, and that'll be that, Mattress Man."

"Righty-o!"

Dabney Malloy was always saying things like that. Milt had never actually met him, but Dabney had been recommended to him through a colleague of an acquaintance of a friend of someone Milt had called months ago when he needed some consultation on how to clear licensing rights and deal with Fair Use and all that stuff Milt (and, as he learned over time, *everyone*) didn't really understand about how to use clips from TV shows, movies, radio spots, etc., that were needed in brief for the documentary.

"I look forward to being there at that one glorious meeting when I sell this film for you guys!" Dabney said in that faux-radio-show-host-from-the-1980s voice that Milt always found slightly irritating but also slightly admirable. Clearly, at one time, Dabney had the voice for TV or film and he knew how to use it well. However, in cases like this, Milt wanted to talk to a person and not a character.

After months of back and forth with Dabney over the phone, email, and text, it was clear Dabney was also slightly delusional, slightly bipolar, and the kind of slick, double-talking, I'll-do-whatever-I-have-to-do type of guy who would go from failing in film and TV in the eighties and nineties to somehow figuring out how to help people with licensing rights on their movies and TV shows—all five or six of them in the past (but, hey, because of this he was also *cheap*, Milt kept reminding himself)—that made for a challenging experience.

Dabney also had this way of always talking about his recently deceased two cats who had died in a fire that hit the shed in the back of Dabney's house before he had been forced to move to some outback hellhole he was always complaining about as though Milt and he were best buddies instead of the actual dynamic of being pseudo-compatriots, with Milt only needing a few pieces of advice from Dabney on how to handle the legal logistics before they could screen the doc.

"Did you see the latest video I posted about Mitsy and Flitsy?" Dabney asked seriously, in that same mock-game-show-host-from-the-1980s way.

It made Milt pull away from the phone to laugh before placing the phone back to his ear. "No, Dabney, I've been kind of busy with the tour and the new book and—"

"That's right!" Dabney exclaimed, shifting gears. Milt could *hear* the desperation in Dabney's voice. *"You still think at some point you could hook me up with your agent? I'd love to get her my book. The one about Mitsy and Flitsy? Once I'm done with it. The story of a young man, forty-eight years young, of course, ha ha ha! Haw! And how he arose through the ashes like the Phoenix to find himself pitted against the elements...."*

Milt pulled the phone away from his face again and rubbed his closed eyes with his other hand. He needed a respite from Dabney Malloy. If only he had the *cajones* to lay down the law and say what needed to be so obviously said: "Dabney, you helped us with some of the licensing stuff. We paid you...*way* more than anyone else on the film, because that's what you had demanded, and now we're done with you. Go away, please. We have work to do." Milt couldn't bring himself to do it.

He guessed for the same reason he couldn't oust Tony Riga-toni until they were nearly done with the film because he just didn't have it in him to say, "Tony, you are a selfish, untalented, moronic, mentally-deficient rich kid asshole who doesn't do his work and doesn't care about anyone else or this film that we only brought you on because you had made one other film four years ago that was pretty good and that we thought would mean you knew what you were doing. We were wrong. About a *lot* of things. Now get...the *fuck*...out."

Milt would need to learn how to fire people or cut away from people at some point. He couldn't even do it with asshole friends or with evil, vicious girlfriends. It was why he still remained closely connected with so many people around the country throughout all the travels and work he'd done. He was like a human Facebook.

Milt heard the rushing water in the bathroom stop and Laney stepping out of the shower to wash up and do her "girl stuff" with her face and whatnot in the sink whose faucet he could hear shooting on.

"...and had the most adorable little kitten face you've ever seen before, Milton. I'm telling you, it's just heartbreaking every time I think of her, and I can't wait until I finish my book and you help me sign with your agent so we can publish it and I can help others cope with the loss of their cats."

"Okay," Milt said. "So, everything is going all right?"

"Right as right can be! Now, there is *one small, teensy thing, though, Milton."*

"Okay...."

"You remember all those things I was saying about my psychotic landlord at the new place?"

How could Dabney even ask that? Aside from his stupid dead cats, it was the only thing Dabney constantly railed on and on about it, hence the whole "slightly bipolar" thing. Dabney

295

would suddenly go from sweet and gentle middle-aged man vying to be best buddies with Milt, to this maniacal and evil beast who would go on and on about the most diabolical and brutal schemes he had as means to do away with his "crazy" landlord who was always making noises outside Dabney's small cabin window in his bumfuck woodland area. You know, like, mowing the lawn and hedging bushes and trimming trees and all that "insane" stuff.

"Mmm hmm," Milt said, not liking where this was going, especially not at this time of morning. Why couldn't Dabney have been up this early when Milt needed him to actually do the job they had been paying him for?

"If you can believe it, the bastard is raising my rent," Dabney spat indignantly. *"Again! Can you beat that? Can you believe it? Can you, Milton? Can you believe he'd do that? To me right now, when I'm barely able to get by as is and am trying to finish this book about my kittens and help you guys out with the film and deal with chasing down the two other clients I had this year who still haven't paid me?"*

That had been bothering Milt too. Why hadn't Dabney's other clients—if they even existed—paid him? What had he done to them? For the little he was supposed to do for the film, Dabney had caused a ton of problems for Milt, Ronnie, and Wallace in their dealings with him. But they still were fine paying him, even when he had asked for a bump in his compensation. Despite not deserving it or having brought it up until after he had finished connecting them to the right people and numbers and organizations to get their licensing handled.

"What can I do for you then, Dabney?" Milt said, getting to the point and feeling the vibration that an email had come through.

"Well, here's the thing, Milton," Dabney began the pitch. *"We're friends here, right? Right. Considering everything I've done for you guys, considering the discount I gave you on my services—which was pretty respectable, and which I was happy to give you because of the respect I have for Gil and for what you guys are doing with this beautiful documentary—I was hoping, I'm really needing one more payment if you could get Gil to give it to me to help me pay rent this month. Then I can get through the month, handle my asshole landlord, chase down my other two clients, and get paid, so I'll be back in the black. Can you do that for me, good buddy?"*

Milt just *loved* how Dabney would call him "good buddy" and act as though Milt was Dabney's only real friend when he needed something but would hang up on him or not get back to him at all when Milt had needed something from him. Milt loved it almost as much as he loved Dabney constantly bringing up the notion, as though they had always agreed upon it, that Milt would hook Dabney up with his agent for his asinine book or, more importantly, the notion Dabney would somehow be involved in the sale of the film, as though being a failed actor, a failed memoirist, and a halfway decent licensing consultant weren't enough.

They had already given Dabney two checks, three credits (including "producer"), and all the venting therapy he'd asked for. What more did Dabney Malloy want from Milt and the film crew that they hadn't already given him just to get him to shut up and do his one simple job?

Milt breathed out hard, put the phone on speaker, and checked his email to see—*surprise*—a vitriolic, misspelled, frantic email from Gil Gladly. He didn't stutter when he wrote, and two of my industry friends saw the fiilm at the screening and they both agred that I NEED MY MONEY BACK FROM THE GUYS YOU HAD DO POST-PRODUCTION WORK ON SOUND AND COLOR!!!!!!!! IT LOOKS AND SOUNDS TERRIBLE!!!!!!! I WNAT MY MONEY BACK! tell those ideaiots now. call me.

Milt rolled his eyes. Didn't Gil ever sleep? Take a nap?

Milt pulled the phone away from his face again, looked at the closed bathroom door, and listened to Laney go about her business in the sink. He closed his eyes, fantasized for a flash about a porn he really enjoyed involving a redheaded, pigtailed Pippi-Longstocking-type girl, riding some anonymous dude reverse cowgirl style in her pink 1950s letterman's sweater and black-and-white Mary Janes, and got back on the phone with Dabney, who yet again didn't seem to notice Milt hadn't been saying anything and was likely not listening to his rambling screed.

"So, what do you think, Milton, good buddy?"

"Yeah, I get it, Dabney," Milt said. "But, first off, we already paid you. Twice. You've probably gotten more money from this project than anyone else involved, to be honest."

Brief silence.

"Well...I did give you guys a pretty good discount."

"And we really appreciate it, we do," Milt said, conciliatorily. "But, man, come on...you made some calls. You hooked us up with some other people to help out. Ronnie and I did a lot of the actual work as far as finding out who owned what license and cataloguing everything for you, frame by frame from the film—"

"Hey, I told you, that Ronnie kid you had help me out didn't do shit. I had to have my assistant go over everything he did. Okay?"

Oh, yeah.

Milton kept forgetting that even though Ronnie—who had done a fantastic job, in fact, cataloguing everything because Milt was the one going over his work when Dabney was too busy fighting with his landlord that week to do it himself—was the one who had done so much to get the work done, Dabney had *still* employed some "assistant"—which was where some of the second check needed to go to, he claimed—to help him even further.

"Mmm hmm," Milt said. "Right, but, look, we did help you out a bunch with what you did, we did pay you twice, you did get pretty much more than anyone else on the crew, including me actually, and…. Hey, Dabney, I gotta call Gil, man. He was just emailing me and we're having some other problem with the post-production—"

"I saw that! Part of what I love about the film when you sent me the private Vimeo link. Your guys did a terrific job," Dabney said. *"I was very impressed, especially with how fast you got that done. How much did you say they did it for?"*

"I'm not sure right now, but it was a really good deal because I got some friends of mine at their post-production house in Austin to do it who are big fans of Gil, and…." Milt checked the email again. "Look, I really gotta call Gil."

"Can you ask him about getting me just a little more payment. Good buddy? Can you do that for me? For ol' Dabney Malloy here?"

Yes, Dabney did talk about himself in third person.

"I'll do what I can," Milt said, knowing Dabney would be calling Gil as soon as they got off the phone and would get the money from Gil the same way *he* had added the symbolic "producer" credit to the film's IMDb page and everyone had just let it go because, along with Milt, no one on their team was very good with confrontation.

"All right, Dabney, well, I *really* gotta call Gil now...."

"Sure thing, Milton. Oh, one more thing. In addition to you asking Gil for more money for me, maybe one-thousand and five-hundred dollars more, I wanted to tell you about the funniest thing I saw when I was working at my desk yesterday looking out the window to some squirrels fighting in the woods...."

"Mm hmm," Milt said. "Dabney, I really gotta go."

"Righty-o, right right. But the squirrels looked exactly like Abbot and Costello. Do you know who they were? I know you're young, but—"

"I know who Abbot and Costello were," Milt said. "I gotta go. Thanks for everything, Dabney."

As Milt was placing his finger to the red call-end button on his screen, he could still hear Dabney yammering on about the squirrels.

Milt hated hanging up on people, and had probably only done it three times in his life, if that. But he needed to call Gil, and he knew Dabney would get his money, regardless of if he should or not, because Gil, well....

"Hey, Gil," Milt said as the bathroom door opened. Laney's face displayed her shock that her husband was back on the phone *yet again,* with Gil Gladly.

Milt shook his head rapidly as though to say, *"Shut up, don't say anything at all. WORK'S WORK."*

"I'm not doing anything at the screening in Manhattan, and I don't want to hear anything more about it!" Gil shouted through the phone, so enraged by now, he had stopped stuttering.

"What? Gil, come on, we already nearly sold-out the tickets, and it's been advertised for weeks that you were going to do Q&A with the audience and a mock-up of *KidTalk* with Dillon Rogers, who you'd sing a quick song—"

"I d-d-d-dd-d-don't care! I'm n-n-n-n-n-not a d-d-d-d-dancing monkey! I kn-kn-kn-knew you'd say all this, and I don't care. I've been th-th-th-th-thinking about it, and I j-j-j-j-j-just want to be in the theater with my w-w-w-w-w-ife and the cr-cr-cr-crowd watching the movie together and they can eat their p-p-p-p-p-p-popcorn and g-g-g-g-g-go home."

"Gil, you agreed to do the stuff with Dillon months ago! We're lucky he's still in New York so he doesn't have to fly anywhere. Plus, we need this show as a rehearsal for the large event in Chicago. Do you have any idea how hard it was getting everything arranged for Dillon for Chicago? He didn't get the emails I had been sending and—"

"I d-d-d-don't c-c-c-care about D-d-d-dillon R-r-r-ogers! It's n-n-n-n-ot his film! What m-m-m-ade you th-th-th-think

I'd go up on st-st-st-stage and dance around like a fucking m-m-m-m-m-m-monkey?"

"Gil," Milt practically cried, "you agreed to this months ago. We advertised it this way. We charged twice as much as a regular movie because it's gonna be this special thing! We'll get crucified on Twitter and in the geek blogs if you don't do it now last minute like this. It will ruin the whole tour! The rep of the film!"

"D-d-d-d-did you t-t-t-t-t-tell them about my h-h-h-h-heart condition? D-d-d-d-d-don't they kn-kn-kn-know I'm n-n-n-n-n-not well? What d-d-d-d-d-do they w-w-w-w-w-wwant from me?"

"You want me to tell the Manhattan theater about your heart?"

"NO! DON'T YOU DARE! DON'T TELL ANY-ANY-ANY-ANYONE! IT'S N-N-N-N-NOT THEIR B-B-B-BUSINESS!"

There it was again. The complex human being that was Gil Gladly. Did he want Milt to tell the Manhattan people running the show about his heart or not? Milt was getting so exhausted by Gil's damned-if-you-do-damned-if-you-don't injunctions.

And it was still—*what?*—barely 7:00 a.m.

Laney stepped toward Milt, drying her hair with the towel, and gave him a loving peck on the cheek. Her lips felt warm. Milt smiled at her and they locked eyes briefly. She nodded. *It will be okay. Just a little longer.*

She went toward the dresser on the other side of the room by the shitty desk and shitty office chair and began going through her clothes to get dressed for the day. She took a hit from her vape pen, coughing.

"Gil, please," Milton pleaded somberly and almost in a whisper. He had so little left, and it was so early in the morning, he was still somewhat hungover and depleted from the LA trip. Probably sick. His throat hurt. His eyes were dried out.

Couldn't Gil just do this one thing?

"I'm n-n-n-n-not doing it. No. I n-n-n-n-eed to go to SLEEP."

"Look, Gil," Milt said, going through it all as quickly as possible in his parboiled, burnt-out mind, "people *love* you. Okay? I know you're scared. I know this is so difficult for you. This whole tour and everything for the film. Revealing yourself like this. Putting yourself out there like this. I know you're worried not enough people will come or like it. But we're practically sold-out at Manhattan, and most of the other shows are nearly sold-out too. These are your people! They're your friends and family and fans. People who grew up watching your show. They are there to show you love. It's like in *42nd Street* when she calms the new girl down before she goes out on stage and reminds her, 'They're here to enjoy you. They're here to like you.' No one will make fun of you, Gil. No one will heckle or boo you. This is your church. These are your congregants. You won't be a dancing monkey. You will be a god. Go out there and give them everything. Just a few more times, we sell the film, and everyone's happy. People loved the film and they loved you in LA. That will keep happening. It *will*. Don't worry about your two 'industry' friends who said the post work didn't look and sound so great. People know it's a sneak preview and it's good enough for the regular viewer. We'll fix it later when we sell the thing and have more money for it. It's a good movie, Gil. You are *great* up on stage. Even now in your sixties, you are. Can you do that?"

Silence.

Milt looked at Laney and she was smiling that inimitable full-face smile that had tricked him into falling in love with her, eventually making her his wife.

She was proud of him. This pride gave him strength.

"Gil?" Milt asked. "Will you do it?"

"You're good," Gil said with an avuncular haw. *"All right, look. J-j-j-just m-m-m-m-m-make sure n-n-n-nothing else g-g-g-gets f-f-f-fucked up. Not for a few days, okay? And I'll do wh-wh-wh-whatever you n-n-n-n-need me to do. It's j-j-j-j-just... everyone w-w-w-w-wants a p-p-p-p-p-iece of me."*

"Well, you're so damn delicious, is the thing," Milt said, reaching too far for a laugh that never came. "So, you're cool, then?"

"Y-y-y-yeah. Y-y-y-y-y-you kn-kn-kn-know me. I get all m-m-m-m-m-mad at f-f-f-f-first then c-c-c-c-calm down. I g-g-g-g-g-gotta w-w-w-w-w-work on that."

"You're an old man, Gil," Milt chuckled. "I think it's too late for you!"

"Ha!" Gil said, adding cheerfully, *"And fuck you too, junior!"* Then he hung up without his goodbye, as always, and Milt dropped his phone on the coffee table.

"I think I did my mitzvah for the day," he said.

"What is that, some kind of Jewish Boy Scout thing?"

Milt's phone vibrated and he checked to see Gil had texted him: **"By the way, People said yes."**

"Which people?" Milt texted back.

"PEOPLE. MAGAZINE. They're going to do a large feature on us. In PRINT. Coming soon to a grocery store checkout aisle near you!"

"NICE!" Milt texted back. "That's great press. Woo-hoo!"

"Also, I think you got me sick."

"We gotta stop making out so often."

"You wish."

Milt smiled and shook his head.

"What?" Laney asked.

"Kinda cool," Milt said. "We're gonna have a piece in *People Magazine* about the tour and the doc."

"Yay! That's so great, baby! I toldja it would start happening!"

Milt went over to Laney by the dresser. She stood there, eyes on him. They were both naked, Laney holding clothes in both hands. Milt put his body against hers and hugged her tight with her arms at her sides. She didn't hug him back, but she did permit him to do this.

"Why do you let him do all this to you?"

"Babe," Milt began, "it's my *job*. We made a movie about the dichotomy between the confident and polished character Gil Gladly is onscreen and the real person he is off. What do you expect?"

Laney pulled away from Milt, kissed him on the lips. "When I was in the shower I was thinking about it. I want you to know that I really *do* love you. I do. A lot. I don't even know why."

"Me too," Milt said.

"Me too!" Laney squeaked happily. "Hashtag me too! It's like, I don't understand why I want to be with you, but I do. Bad. For a very long time. I don't know why. It's some weird thing and

I want to have babies with you and travel with you, and I just don't get it. Errrggh!" She kissed him again.

"I think that's why what we have is weirdly special, you know?"

"Gay."

"Aw, c'mon," Milt said, pulling away and beaming.

She laughed. "Don't worry. I told you. Contracts. I'm here. I'm not going anywhere. You won. You won me. You're my husband, and we're getting older and I'm glad I'm doing it with you. It's an adventure! Always! So much more to come! The rest of the tour is gonna be *great!*"

"So, you're still my good girl, then?"

"I'm your *fairly decent* girl, yes," Laney said, kissing him one more time before going back to the dresser to get her clothes on and grab some neon-blue socks.

"Why did you say all of that to me just then?" Milt asked, almost as though something were wrong. "You never talk like that."

"Because," Laney turned back to him to show off the goods with that winning smile of hers, "you made me feel special."

"Man," Milt said, watching her and shaking his head, "it is *exhausting* keeping you smiling. But it's worth it."

"So much of this is just about patience," Laney said, putting her socks on. "Like everything else in your life right now. I just hope I can learn how to punch some patience into you someday soon." She laughed at this and finished dressing, throwing on an Anal Cunt t-shirt and some dark jeans.

"Ugh, what's wrong with me that you saying violent things like that to me just makes me love you more?" Milt said, smiling as he walked to where he had put his phone and saw he had a text from Silverstein saying he'd quit and gotten a new job running a campaign for one of the politicos he'd interviewed often in the past.

"Shitsmelled is shitting bricks about it! I can't WAIT to rub it right in his face as much as possible!"

"That's great, man," Milt texted back, snorting. **"Very proud of you and enjoy it. PS: Forget about Shitsmelled. Go do your job."**

"It's what marriage is all about, I guess," Laney proposed. "I love you, babe, but sometimes I want to fucking kill you."

Milt snorted again, smiling at this and immediately erased Melody Winston as a contact. He turned off his phone and threw it onto the small couch.

Milton breathed in deeply and exhaled. "As long as you don't mind how long it's gonna take for me to lose all this weight, stop smoking cigarettes, stop drinking as much as I do..." he said over his shoulder.

"Don't worry," Laney said, tying up her neon-pink running shoes. "We have the rest of our lives to make ourselves perfect."

"Where do you want to go for breakfast? I'll handle Gil's video snafu when we get back. I'm hunnnnn-gray. And by the time we get back, he'll probably have forgotten about it anyway."

"Oooooh," Laney purred. "I want a *big, big* meal. Our last one for a while, okay?"

"Sure thing," Milt said, smiling back.

"Do we still have enough left on the Discover Card?"

"Uhhh..." Milt blanched. "Let's talk about it over breakfast. Waffles?"

[STUDIO AUDIENCE APPLAUSE; ROLL CREDITS.]

THE END

ACKNOWLEDGMENTS

Mathew would like to take this opportunity to thank the fantastic team at Post Hill Press and Permuted Press for their full support, helpful recommendations, meticulous hard work, and crucial consultation on this project. Particularly: Anthony Ziccardi, Michael L. Wilson, Heather King, Rachel Hoge, Devon Brown, and pinch hitter Felicia A. Sullivan.

Special thanks are also due to Jim McBride for initially connecting Mathew with the Post Hill group, as well as fellow author and Post Hiller Ellis Henican for his recommendation in working with the team on putting out this novel.

If Mathew were to have dedicated this book to an *actual* person, he would have done so to the memory of novelist and columnist Jay Cronley (1943-2017)—a man Mathew never had the chance to meet but whose hilarious and honest books were a tremendous source of inspiration in the creation of *Selling Nostalgia: A Neurotic Novel*.

Mathew finally thanks his family, friends, and colleagues around the country who continue to bolster him throughout his constant juggling of far too many projects in far too many realms. Luckily, that wife of his keeps Mathew somewhat sane and in line, capable of focusing and getting the work turned in on time...or as is too often the case, a little early. She typically keeps the brush-shaking to a minimum.

ABOUT THE AUTHOR

MATHEW KLICKSTEIN is a longtime author, journalist, filmmaker, playwright, and arts therapist.

His previous books include: *SLIMED! An Oral History of Nickelodeon's Golden Age*; *Springfield Confidential: Jokes, Secrets, and Outright Lies from a Lifetime Writing for The Simpsons* (with Mike Reiss); and *Being Mr. Skin: 20 Years of Nip Slips, Cheek Peeks, and Fast-Forwarding to the Good Parts* (with Jim "Mr. Skin" McBride). His writings have appeared in such publications as: *Wired*, *NY Daily News*, Vulture, and *The New Yorker*.

Mathew's film work includes the documentaries *Act Your Age: The Kids of Widney High Story* and *On Your Marc*, and the screenplay for Sony Pictures' *Against the Dark*. He was a casting producer for Food Network's *Restaurant: Impossible* and co-creator of National Lampoon's weekly television series *Collegetown, USA*. He is also the writer of the comic book series *You Are Obsolete*.

Mathew received his BFA from the screenwriting program at the University of Southern California and, in addition to other creative endeavors, is the host and co-producer of the nerd/geek culture podcast *NERTZ*, based on his book *Nerding Out: How Pop Culture Ruined the Misfit*.

He lives in Boulder, Colorado, with his wife Becky. More on his past, current, and future shenanigans can be found at: www. MathewKlickstein.com.

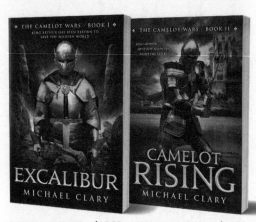

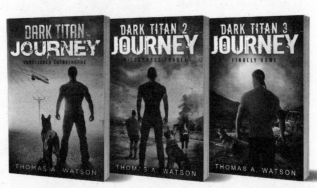

THE MORNINGSTAR STRAIN HAS BEEN LET LOOSE—IS THERE ANY WAY TO STOP IT?

An industrial accident unleashes some of the Morningstar Strain. The

EAN 9781618686497 $16.00

doctor who discovered the strain and her assistant will have to fight their way through Sprinters and Shamblers to save themselves, the vaccine, and the base. Then they discover that it wasn't an accident at all—somebody inside the facility did it on purpose. The war with the RSA and the infected is far from over.

This is the fourth book in Z.A. Recht's The Morningstar Strain series, written by Brad Munson.

PERMUTED PRESS